Fiancé by Friday

Also by Catherine Bybee

Contemporary Romance
Weekday Bride Series
Wife by Wednesday
Married by Monday
Fiancé by Friday

Not Quite Series
Not Quite Dating
Not Quite Mine

Paranormal Romance
MacCoinnich Time Travels
Binding Vows
Silent Vows
Redeeming Vows
Highland Shifter

The Ritter Werewolves Series
Before the Moon Rises
Embracing the Wolf

Novellas
Soul Mate
Possessive

Erotica
Kilt Worthy
Kilt-A-Licious

CATHERINE BYBEE

Fiancé by Friday

BOOK THREE IN THE WEEKDAY BRIDES SERIES

The characters and events portrayed in this book are fictitious. Any similarity to real persons, living or dead, is coincidental and not intended by the author.

Published by Montlake Romance
PO Box 400818
Las Vegas, NV 89140

ISBN-13: 9781611099522
ISBN-10: 1611099528
Library of Congress Control Number: 2012953732

To Crystal

I'm so incredibly blessed to have you as my friend

Chapter One

The flash of the cameras made her stand straighter, turn toward the heckling paparazzi, and smile. Lady Gwen Harrison knew the photographers weren't entirely sure who she was. Here in the States the media didn't follow her around. The photographers saw an elegant woman who looked as if she might be a movie star, but in fact was nothing more than a daughter of a deceased duke. That wouldn't stop the paparazzi from cross-referencing her image and coming up with her name. Her brother, Blake Harrison, the current Duke of Albany, was quite popular in this country. And because of him, and his group of friends, Gwen's own image had made many a paper.

Gwen took one more glance over the heads of the photographers, smiled, and turned to walk away. She had work to do.

The Wilson Charity Ball was exactly the event Gwen was born to work. Having grown up in an estate outside of London with a very proper mother and a father who rarely acknowledged her presence unless she was standing in front of him, Gwen was the poster child of a socialite. She wasn't threatening to anyone here. Most of the guests were actors, activists, political figures, or the significant others of the aforementioned people. Gwen was none of them. Her sole purpose for attending the ball was to find potential clients for Alliance.

A waiter approached her as she stepped into the room and offered her a glass of champagne. She accepted it with a smile and moved into the room.

She recognized a few faces, mainly people Eliza, a friend and former employee of Alliance, had introduced her to in the past.

"Lady Harrison." A voice called her attention to a small gathering of people a few feet away.

Marilyn Cohen, petite, stunning, and probably the most famous woman in the room, waved her over.

Marilyn kissed each of Gwen's cheeks in greeting. "It's lovely to see you again," Gwen said. "How long has it been?"

"The governor's ball, I believe," Marilyn reminded her. "How are Carter and Eliza?"

"Settling into their new roles." Carter had won the governor's seat the previous election, and the two of them had moved to Sacramento once he took office. Carter was Blake's best friend and Eliza was the sister Gwen never had.

Gwen glanced around Marilyn, expecting to see her husband. "Are you solo tonight?"

"Tom's on location in Greenland. Why the studios can't recreate that awful place on a set is beyond me. What about you, are you alone?"

Gwen offered a smile. "It's hard to be alone in a room filled with people." And it was filled. Women were dressed in floor-length evening gowns, men wore tuxes…and not the rented kind.

Marilyn slipped her hand into Gwen's arm and pulled her along. "Well, let's see what trouble we can cause, shall we?" She waved at a group of actors and moved in their direction. "Are you scouting tonight?" Marilyn whispered.

Marilyn knew enough about Alliance to warrant the question. "I'm always searching for clients."

Her companion flashed her million-dollar smile. "Let's see who we can hook up tonight then."

Alliance was founded by Samantha, or Sam as most of her friends called her. Who just happened to be married to Gwen's brother. Samantha had the brilliant idea of forming an agency that aligned couples. It wasn't a dating service. No, it was a *life planning* service. Their clients consisted of men and women who needed to marry the perfect person for reasons other than love. Politicians who needed to fit the "family profile" in order to get elected into office. Dukes who needed to marry to fulfill their awful father's will in order to inherit millions. Or perhaps an actor, or actress, who wanted a scandal to keep their name in the paper.

Gwen recruited the paying client at events like this. And on occasion she'd find a suitable match for the men already in her database.

Not everyone married for love and forever. Her clients married for their own reasons, and the matches Alliance set up paid them handsomely for it.

Marilyn introduced Gwen to everyone who was anyone. Once in a while Marilyn would nod toward a prospective client to whom Gwen would ask a few discrete questions. Alliance was a very private company and not something that was advertised on a business card.

As the evening grew late, Gwen thought perhaps it would end up a bust.

Over her shoulder someone said her name.

She turned toward the deep voice and offered a polite smile. The owner of the voice stood over her by several inches, his broad shoulders and easy demeanor told her he was very comfortable approaching strangers. "I'm sorry, do I know you?"

He chuckled as if she'd said a joke. "We haven't met." He extended a hand. "Michael Wolfe."

Gwen accepted his hand, which he quickly let fall. "Did I say something funny, Mr. Wolfe?"

He leaned against the table and smiled at a couple as they passed. "You really don't know who I am?"

She shook her head. "Sorry."

"I'm an actor."

"How wonderful for you. I still have no idea."

He was laughing full on now, delighted with himself. "Oh, how rich is that? I'd ask to buy you a drink but they're giving them away tonight."

These words from anyone else would feel like a pick-up line. Not from this man.

His eyes traveled beyond her again, this time to a group of men standing far away.

Hmmmm?

"So, Lady Harrison. How is your brother's *marriage* going?"

Gwen kept her expression neutral. "Do you know my brother?"

Michael Wolfe shook his head. "I haven't had the pleasure. We share a few acquaintances."

Which meant that Michael Wolfe wasn't asking about Blake and Sam, but rather their marriage. And that meant that Mr. Wolfe was asking about Alliance.

"How about another glass of champagne, Mr. Wolfe?"

———

"I think I found you the perfect husband." Gwen bent her knee and slid her Louboutins from her feet before tossing them to the floor. *You would think shoes that cost nearly a thousand dollars would be exempt from hurting your feet.* Sadly, that wasn't the case.

"You think you found what?" Karen turned down the volume on the television and twisted around on the sofa.

"A husband for you."

Gwen's words sparked Karen's full attention. The TV went dark and Karen patted the sofa beside her. "Come sit! Tell."

After placing her handbag on the hall table, Gwen turned the lock on the door and set the house alarm. "Let me get out of this dress first. The beading has rubbed my skin raw all night." She turned her back to Karen with a silent plea to unzip the evening gown.

Karen loosened the clasp and lowered the zipper, and then proceeded to follow Gwen up the stairs. "You can't drop the 'H' word and leave the room, Gwen. That's just mean."

Holding the front of the dress up with one hand, and lifting the hem with the other, Gwen managed the stairs without tripping.

"The Wilson Charity Ball was filled with people. Lots of couples and plenty of those actor types running about." She stepped into her closet and let the gown slide from her shoulders. After hanging the dress, she grabbed a nightgown from her chest and walked back into her bedroom. "You know, Samantha said I would tire of these dinners, but I'm enjoying them. I've met so many interesting people since I moved here." Gwen had moved to the States nearly a year ago. At thirty-one years old, she had lived a sheltered life on her family estate outside of London. She'd traveled the world, but always with a bodyguard or her mother.

Now that her brother was the duke in the family, the estate belonged to him. Not that Gwen couldn't live there, but his marriage to Samantha had presented the opportunity for Gwen to move forward with her life. Especially when Samantha had explained her business to Gwen.

With Samantha taking on the duties of full-time wife, mother, and duchess, she didn't have time to run her business. Gwen stepped in to help run Alliance, even though she didn't have a business skill to name as her own. However, living a titled life, she did understand how to brush elbows with the rich and famous, the very clients Alliance sought. Where Gwen was lacking, Karen excelled. Karen's clerical skills and ability to keep all the records were better than any high-paid lawyer's secretary. Together they ran the business flawlessly.

"Getting back to the perfect husband…"

"He's a very handsome, tall…lovely man." Gwen sat on the edge of her bed and unclasped her garters one at a time.

"You do know that no one wears those anymore." Karen pointed to her lingerie.

"If that were true, finding a place to buy garters and stockings would be impossible."

"Yeah, but you need to go to those sexy bra stores in order to find them," Karen teased.

"Men love frilly underwear."

"Lotta good that's doing you. Seems I'm the only one who sees it."

Gwen laughed and continued with her news. "His name is Wolfe…Michael Wolfe. You might have heard of him."

"The actor?" Karen asked.

"So you have heard of him."

Karen shook her head. "There is no way Michael Wolfe's looking for a temporary wife through an agency. He's like the hottest thing on the big screen right now."

"So he told me."

"He told you? You mean you didn't know?"

Gwen shrugged, removed her bra, and pulled her nightgown over her head. "When have you seen me go to the cinema? I'd enjoy a good book before watching a movie."

"But Michael Wolfe. He's a big name, Gwen." Karen followed her into the bathroom where she ran hot water in the sink and proceeded to remove her makeup.

"I don't know who he is. Perhaps if he played in a Bond film I'd know him."

Karen leaned against the frame of the door, and watched Gwen through the mirror. "You're serious. Michael Wolfe?"

"Lovely man. Very funny."

"And sexy, and single, and rich…women fall all over him."

And that, Gwen thought, was the problem.

Gwen turned toward the commode and flushed it to fill the room with noise. While the noise of the toilet filled the room, she leaned into Karen and whispered. "I think he likes men."

Karen's eyes rounded. "Seriously?"

Gwen shushed her. The Tarzana home had undergone an extensive security system installation, including twenty-four-hour audio and video monitoring. Eliza had lived in the house before she married Carter, who had insisted on the security measures for multiple reasons. Once Carter won the gubernatorial race, and they both moved to Sacramento, the security system stayed in place at the insistence of Gwen's brother.

And Neil.

"You think he's gay?"

Gwen hushed her again and pointed toward the hall. There weren't any cameras in the bedrooms or bathrooms, but Gwen knew for a fact the hall was monitored. "Our clients deserve all the privacy they can get."

Karen rolled her eyes. "Good Lord, Gwen, we parade around here half naked and you're worried about our *clients'* privacy? You know Neil; he wouldn't allow just anyone to listen to what goes on around here."

Just hearing Neil's name brought warmth to the pit of Gwen's stomach. The man was a force of nature with the ability to stand shoulder to shoulder with sixteenth-century Highland warriors. His hard lines and broad physique might threaten others, but for Gwen, all they'd ever done was invite her in.

Too bad Neil never opened the door.

"Privacy is paramount to our clients. Best we keep some details as hidden as possible, don't you agree?"

Karen rolled her eyes and they both descended the stairs.

"So if Michael is…*you know*, why is he talking with you? How did you approach him, anyway?"

Gwen made herself comfortable on the couch, and settled in for a long talk. "He came to me. Seems the *Alliance* name has found its way into a few celebrity circles."

"That's good to know. Lotta deep pockets in Hollywood."

"Actors make the perfect clients. Especially if they want temporary." Alliance helped the elite and rich find life matches. Many of whom wanted a temporary bride or groom and were willing to pay heavily for it. Beautiful women like Karen had no problem finding men, but some women weren't looking for love.

For reasons Gwen had yet to discover, Karen wanted a temporary match to set her up financially for years to come. When two people came together with the understanding that their relationship would end on an assigned date, everyone was happy.

"Michael has no problem convincing the world he's in love with every heroine he works with," Karen said. "What makes you think he's…?"

"He didn't come right out and say it. Not yet anyway. He introduced himself and was completely taken aback that I didn't know who he was."

"He's über famous, Gwen."

"That may be. Anyway, he asked me how my brother's marriage was going. Strange question. I asked him if he knew Blake to which he promptly said he did not. Michael went on to tell me that he and Blake shared a few acquaintances."

"His subtle way of saying he knew about Alliance."

"That's what I assumed. I asked him if he'd like to meet some of my friends. He winked, said he'd love to, and then handed me his card."

Karen lifted both hands facing up. "So what makes you think g—"

"Ahh, just how he presented himself. Sometimes you just know these things." Michael had flirted with the women in the room and appreciated the men. Oh, he'd been subtle but if there was one skill Gwen had perfected in the past few months, it was reading men and their intentions.

A man searching for someone…anyone…had a certain energy about him. Eliza had schooled Gwen for months about how to approach these men to help them learn about Alliance. There had been social events in which no contacts had been met. And others where Gwen was able to recruit men, and women, into their database.

"Michael Wolfe?" Karen tapped a finger to her chin.

"If he's looking for temporary, I think you'd be the perfect match."

"Oh, why?"

"First, you're both beautiful people. The cameras would eat you up. Second, Michael's high profile would prove difficult for many women to maneuver without cracking, and you, my dear, never crack."

"What do you mean, I never crack?"

"You have your eye on the entire picture and would never lose sight of that under pressure." Gwen waved three fingers in the air. "Third, you have no illusions that a temporary marriage might mold into a loving relationship."

"All of our clients say that."

"Yet some keep. If Michael is, *you know*, then that won't be possible."

Karen shrugged and pushed off the couch. "I think I'll turn in early, see if any of his flicks are on pay-per-view."

Gwen wished Karen a good night and made her way into their kitchen. She placed a kettle on the stove and boiled water for tea. She took in the small space with its cozy cottage feel and sighed. When the day came that Alliance did find a groom for Karen, she'd move away and Gwen would be living alone.

———

Neil MacBain paused the audio feed, shook his head, rewound the damn thing, and listened to it again.

"You do know that no one wears those anymore."

"If that were true, finding a place to buy garters and stockings would be impossible."

"Yeah, but you need to go to those sexy bra stores in order to find them."

"Men love frilly underwear."

Neil slapped his hand on the mouse and turned off the sound before he tortured himself anymore.

Fuck! I need to get laid!

Listening to Gwen's polished accent mentioning garters and stockings shot his brain straight to his cock.

The desire to click on the video monitor made his right eye twitch, but he refrained and forced himself away from his surveillance room.

Blake Samantha, their son Eddie, and even Samantha's sister Jordan were in Europe with plans to stay for at least a month. Their absence meant fewer people to watch over and plenty of time to think.

He hated thinking.

Doing was such a better pastime.

Doing meant standing in the shadows of tall buildings and watching over the only Harrison stateside he could.

Not that watching Gwen was a chore. Tonight she wore a floor-length, gold beaded number that sparkled in the light given off by the flash of photographers' cameras by the red carpet. Though she wasn't the focus of their lenses, she was the center of his. She offered one look, and one smile, to the paparazzi before walking inside the venue. Her lithe frame moved with the sort of grace and elegance that most of the people around her tried to buy but never quite achieved.

Gwen had played center stage to many of his fantasies.

Fantasies that would never become reality.

Neil shrugged out of his black leather jacket and tossed it on the side of his sofa. He unhooked his holster that carried the Beretta M9 he never left home without and set it on top of his jacket.

The two-bedroom guesthouse that sat on Blake and Samantha's Malibu estate had been his refuge for five years. After five years, he finally felt some degree of comfort...of belonging. Other than the housekeeper and cook, Neil had no one on site he needed to watch over during the night.

He double-checked the system in Tarzana, and confirmed that someone there had set the internal alarms that shouldn't go off unless breached. Gwen and Karen set the alarms when they left or when they turned in for the night.

Neil flicked on the local news, more for background noise than for company. He poured himself a drink and stretched out on the couch.

This was the life he wanted...low stress, even lower profile. He could guard a duke and his family in his sleep. No, make that in his sleep with a hangover...the kind you woke up from with the room still spinning. The people he'd known in the past would say he was wasting his time.

But it was his time to waste.

He brushed away memories of those *past people*, tilted his head back, and closed his eyes. His consciousness slid into sleep, his body relaxing with it.

The high-pitched scream of a security breach shot him to his feet and he was fully awake in half a breath.

Neil ran to his security room, hit a master switch, and a dozen monitors sprang to life. He scanned them quickly and found the breach in question in Tarzana. The monitor flashed red and displayed video feeds from inside and outside the house. Neil hit speed dial with one hand and placed the Tarzana feed onto his big screen.

The hall was clear, the motion detector hadn't tripped the outside lights…the front door was closed. But the back door wasn't secure.

"Gwen?" Neil overheard Karen calling from inside the Tarzana house, the audio feed now relaying every word clearly. The alarm sounded inside the house, probably loud enough to wake the neighbors. He heard the phone ringing both in his ear and in the house.

He flipped the feed, searching for her…his heart skipped several beats before Gwen appeared on screen.

She ran to the control panel, opened it, and started hitting numbers. Seeing her unharmed, Neil kept scanning the feeds. "Answer the fucking phone," he said through clenched teeth.

"I forgot…" Gwen's voice rose above the alarm.

"Turn the noise off," Karen said.

Both Gwen and Karen were standing at the control panel. Once the numbers were pressed in, the alarm went silent.

Gwen moved from the panel to the phone. "Hello?"

"What happened?" Neil's hand hovered over the mouse on the master controls, the one that would alert the local police to respond.

"Hello, Neil."

This wasn't a fucking social call. "Gwen?" His tone was strained.

"I opened the back door. Forgot to cancel the alarm first."

Karen was walking back up the stairs seemingly unaffected by the drama.

Gwen moved through one room to another. The nightgown she wore hardly covered her ass.

"Why?"

"Why what?"

"The back door, why is it open?" The backyard feed was dark, no sign of problems.

"It's a nice night. I thought I'd let some fresh air in. Everything is fine, Neil. I'm sorry I woke you."

She was leaning against the door she'd opened and talking on the phone to him.

"I wasn't asleep."

"Of course you weren't. You never sleep, do you?"

"I sleep." *Just not in a bed. And not for extended periods of time.*

"And what does Neil dream of when he sleeps?" For some reason only known to Gwen, she taunted him by talking about him in third person.

Neil turned off his alarms and sat in the tall back leather chair in the center of the room.

"Well?"

What was the question? Oh, right…what does he dream of? Platinum blondes with British accents wearing garters and stockings…and nothing else.

"I don't dream."

"Everyone dreams."

Guns, explosions…burning bodies.

"I don't."

"I've heard that a lack of dreams is a sign of poor health." She twirled a lock of hair and stared out the back door. The door that should be closed, locked, and alarmed.

"There's nothing wrong with my health. How long are you keeping that door open?"

Gwen stopped playing with her hair and looked around the room. "Are you watching me?"

Neil swallowed...hard.

"Neil?"

"You need to lock the door and reset the alarm."

Gwen turned to a kitchen chair and lifted her foot on top of it. The short nightgown rode higher on her thigh as she played at scratching her leg, which he knew wasn't by accident. She knew he was watching her. Gwen had been flirting with him for a very long time.

"Lock the door, Gwen."

"I like the breeze. It's warmer here than in Malibu."

"Turn on the air conditioner." *And put your leg down.*

"You're worried for nothing, Neil. No one is out to harm Karen or myself."

"Lock the door."

"I'm hanging up now, Neil. Try and get some sleep."

He knew she wasn't going to close the door, let alone lock it. "Gwen!"

"Sweet dreams."

"Damn it, Gwen!"

She hung up, ignoring his request. There was only one person who refused to take his direction and it was Gwen Harrison...no, Lady Gwen Harrison.

Lady Gwen finished her tea in the breeze before locking the screen door the neighborhood cat could breach. And then, she turned off the kitchen light and left the room.

Leaving the back door wide open.

I didn't want to sleep tonight anyway.

Chapter Two

Gwen moved the blinds a fraction of an inch and peered outside. Across the street, Neil reclined in the front seat of his dark sedan, his head bobbing every so often as he fought sleep.

A tiny bit of guilt laced her thoughts when she'd peeked through an hour earlier and realized that Neil had driven over sometime in the night to keep an eye on her. She'd kept the back door open to prod him, but she hadn't thought he'd actually come over and do anything about it.

She'd been wrong.

The remorse she felt was cloaked by something else…exhilaration.

The man cared. Oh, he tried hard not to, but Gwen knew that somewhere in that hard shell of a man was a huge heart.

He kept his distance from her every chance he could. Physically anyway. He'd not once taken her up on her not so subtle hints about her attraction to him. He was as movable as a brick wall at times. Yet last night, all it took was one open door and he was there.

Hmmm, she'd have to think about that.

In the kitchen, the coffeemaker pinged to tell her it was finished brewing. Although she preferred tea, she made a pot of coffee, intending to apologize for her actions by giving Neil something for his trouble.

Not the something she truly wanted to give him, but something he'd actually accept.

Gwen poured a cup, considered cream and sugar, and then shook her head.

He'll take it black. Anything else simply wouldn't fit his personality. Strong, robust…

He'll take it black.

Gwen tightened the belt on her soft, pink bathrobe and slid her feet into matching slippers. With a cup of coffee in hand, she stepped into the early morning dew.

The quiet Tarzana neighborhood had yet to wake and the street was void of any activity.

Peering into the tinted window of the car Gwen spotted a laptop computer and a tablet, both of which streamed video feeds of her home. Neil's head listed to the side and his massive chest rose and fell in even breaths.

He does sleep.

Her earlier excitement shifted back to guilt.

She took a deep, fortifying breath and laid her knuckles to the window. She tapped lightly, hoping she wouldn't jar Neil awake.

Her plan didn't work.

Neil's explosive response, complete with a gun coming from nowhere and pointed directly at her, resulted in her screaming and the coffee cup crashing to the ground.

Her heart lodged somewhere in her throat and her leg blistered in pain from hot coffee and shards of glass.

Recognition washed over Neil's face. His gun disappeared and he pushed himself out of his car.

"What the hell are you doing? Trying to get yourself killed?"

Unable to form any words, she stood there shaking.

Neil moved toward her, his foot crushing the remainder of the coffee cup on the ground. He glanced down and swore under his breath.

He kicked his car door shut and lifted her in his arms before she found her voice.

"Put me down."

He marched across the street, ignoring her request.

He plowed through the front door of her home like a linebacker who took down three-hundred-pound men.

"Put me down, Neil."

Storming through the house, he placed her on the kitchen counter and brought her aching leg over to the sink. He turned on the water, nearly ripping the faucet from the sink. With a gentleness she hadn't expected, he removed her soaked slipper and splashed cool water over her leg.

"What's all the noise?" Karen shrugged into a robe as she walked into the room. "Neil?" she asked, obviously surprised to see him there.

Gwen winced as Neil brushed over the glass lodged in the cut on her leg. "I-I dropped a coffee cup."

Karen moved from one side of Neil to the other, attempting to get a look at Gwen's leg.

"Ouch!" Gwen squealed.

"Hold still." Neil's large fingers passed over the embedded glass again, working it free.

"That hurts."

Neil huffed and continued probing her skin.

Karen moved away. "I think you'll live," she said as she found a cup and filled it with coffee. "What are you doing here anyway?"

Gwen met Neil's hazel eyes, which changed color with his mood. As usual, Neil didn't offer an explanation for his appearance.

He focused on her leg again. The cut was superficial but the hot coffee left an angry shade of red in its wake.

"Always nice talking to you, Neil," Karen said with a laugh. "Gwen?"

"I..." She cleared her throat. "I left the back door open. Neil was checking on us."

Karen sipped her coffee. "Oh." With her comment, Karen left the room huddled over her cup of coffee.

After turning off the water, Neil cradled Gwen's calf in his big hand and gently blotted her skin dry with a paper towel.

"You'll need medicated cream on this," he told her.

"We have some upstairs."

He stopped touching her injury but kept his hand on her ankle. Without looking at her face, he said, "Don't sneak up on me."

Gwen would swear his voice trembled, but that would show some sign of weakness, and Neil was never weak.

"You don't have to tell me twice. Lesson learned." She wouldn't soon forget the hard expression on his face as he drew his gun.

He hesitated when he let her go and turned toward the back door. He closed and locked it with a loud click.

Without any other words, he left the room and the house through the front door, leaving Gwen to stare after him.

———

Neil waited until he was around the corner from her home to stop on a side street.

He gripped the wheel until his knuckles were white. His heart hadn't stopped racing since her knock on the car door. The absolute look of horror and fear that raced over Gwen's face when he turned his gun on her would live with him forever. His finger had been poised over the trigger. One squeeze and he would have...He shook his head, banished the thought.

How the fuck had he fallen asleep? Not seen her approach?

He was getting soft and when that happened people got hurt. Killed.

If something happened to Gwen on his watch…and it was always his watch…he'd never be able to live with it.

With one press of a button, he had one of his men, the ones he called on when he needed backup, on the phone. "I'm going dark for a couple of hours," he told Dillon when he answered the phone. "I need your eyes on Tarzana and Malibu."

"You got it, Boss."

Neil hung up and turned off the video feeds. He needed to regroup. The only way to achieve that was hard, physical work.

He ran on the treadmill for a solid hour instead of his usual thirty minutes. He doubled his repetitions with his weights, added twenty more pounds, and pushed his muscles past their limits. After a shower, he stretched out naked on his bed…the one he seldom slept in…and closed his eyes.

And he dreamed.

Oh, he dreamed…

———

Dressed down, at least as much as Gwen knew how to, she sat at an outside café in Santa Monica sipping iced tea. She'd arrived early to assure the table she occupied was not one where others could spy upon her and her client.

She wore a hat, and not the kind she preferred, but a brimmed variety that flattened her hair and made her feel very American.

She scanned the entry to the patio and spotted Michael as he slipped past the hostess and walked straight toward her. A hat also covered his dark hair, and sunglasses hid his eyes and most of his features from those in the restaurant. Gwen stood as he approached and didn't back away when he greeted her with a hug and a kiss to the cheek as if they were old friends. "So good to see you again," she said, avoiding the use of his name should anyone be listening.

"Thank you for meeting me." He waited for her to sit before taking his seat. He looked around the room. It wasn't lunch or dinner hour so the restaurant wasn't busy. The closest group of people was well out of hearing range.

"I assumed you wanted some privacy," she said just above a whisper. "I hope this establishment meets your needs."

He glanced around again. "I'm hoping this is the only time we meet in private."

The waiter arrived and took their drink order. They ordered a couple of appetizers and let the waiter know that they weren't there for a meal.

Once his soda arrived, and the waiter walked away, Gwen started asking questions. "Tell me, Michael...should I call you Michael?"

"Let's stick with Mike for today. For some reason my fans don't think of me as a Mike."

Gwen smiled and continued. "What do you know about Alliance, Mike?"

"I know you have the ability to find a companion for my needs. My temporary needs."

"You make us sound like a call service."

Michael smiled, and shook his head. "That won't be one of my needs."

Ahh, yes. The confirmation she needed of his sexual orientation. But just in case she was mistaken, she prodded him one last time. "I'm told you can have any *woman* you want. Why come to us?"

Michael leaned forward and peered over the top of his sunglasses. "I can have any *woman* I want. I'm coming to you because although I don't want one, I need one."

"I see."

He slid his glasses up on his nose and kicked back in his chair. "I'm an actor, Miss Harrison. I pretend to be something I'm not every day of my life. My wife will be required to do the same."

"That's understood. All my clients understand the rules."

"But mine will have to do it in front of the public eye. She will have to be as skilled as I am in convincing people we're happily married and that ruse must not fall until after the divorce."

Gwen noticed the waiter approaching and shifted their conversation to the weather. Once the food was on the table, she continued. "How long will you require a wife?"

"A year…maybe slightly longer. My filming schedule is massive over the next eighteen months, which will take me out of the country quite a bit."

"All of which will make it easier for you and your wife to live a life apart from each other."

"Yes, but when together, we need to be the perfect couple. She will be kissed in public, held in front of the cameras, and passed off as my lover."

The entire time they talked, Gwen thought of Karen. How apt she was for this role. Karen could have been an actress if she were so inclined. Her liberal views on sexuality and ability to get along with kids from the street just as equally as the political elite made her the perfect choice for Michael.

"Why are you doing this?"

"I have my reasons," he said. "Millions of them. My publicist won't even be privy to what I'm doing. Only you and your client will know the truth."

Gwen sat forward and picked at some of the food. She took the time to explain the contract he'd have to sign, and the payment schedule they would set up. "I have papers I need you to fill out. I will probe into your life, Mike. And I will find out things about you you'll probably not wish me to know." Gwen thought of Samantha, of how easily she told prospective clients that their lives were a book for her to read and she never skimmed the pages.

"You'll only find what I wish you to find," he told her, his smile cocky.

It was her turn to lower her sunglasses and force his gaze to hers. "By the time I'm done, I'll learn the name of your first lover. Some of our clients have bigger secrets than yours to keep. If you're willing to open wide, I'm happy to help."

"The media can't find out that information. What makes you think you will?"

"The media wants a story. I want to protect my clients and make certain I'm not setting someone up for abuse. My goals are more personal, Mike." She pushed her glasses back up and let him ponder her words.

"I like you, Gwen. Are you married?"

Gwen tilted her head back and laughed. "No, and no thank you." Samantha had met her brother when she was hired to set him up with another woman to marry. But Blake had never met any other woman, and the two of them were nearing their third anniversary. She was not Samantha and nothing like her brother.

"Go ahead and look," he told her. "It will be refreshing to have someone to talk to who knows all my secrets."

"Your wife will know them, too."

"I would assume so. How soon will I be hearing from you?" he asked.

"I already have a woman in mind."

"Trustworthy?"

"All of our clients are that. This one in particular might be the only one who wouldn't be…what do you call it, *starstruck*? With you. Your celebrity status might be news to me but not with any others in our database."

"I understand that."

"If the woman I have in mind agrees to meet with you, how soon can we set that up? And how quickly do you want to marry?"

"This is Hollywood. Everything, and I do mean everything, is carefully choreographed. I'd want a 'chance' meeting, a slow burn of a courtship, and then an undeniable attraction and undying love." As Michael explained his needs, his voice lowered an octave and the charm Hollywood paid dearly for swept up her spine.

Too bad he's gay.

"So one month…tops?" she asked with a grin.

"Yeah, that should work. I'll time it as I'm finishing filming in New York. Do you think we can work within that time frame?"

As long as Karen agreed.

"Not a problem."

Chapter Three

The sound of the shutter clicked as the camera captured image after image of the two leaving the restaurant. The man kissed the woman on the cheek and they went their separate ways.

From where he sat, he saw the make and model of the man's car, snapped a picture of the license plate, and swung his lens to the woman. She removed her sunglasses while searching in her purse. She glanced around, as if aware someone watched.

"I'm watching," he whispered to himself. "Get used to me."

He lowered his camera as the man sped by, oblivious.

And when the woman pulled away…he popped a piece of candy into his mouth and followed.

———

Gwen dialed into the long distance call and waited through the double rings. After a quick cordial conversation with Tamara, the housekeeper at her brother's estate, Gwen was put on hold while she went to find Samantha.

"Hello?"

"Oh, it's so good to hear your voice. How is Albany?"

"Wet," Samantha said, laughing. "How is Tarzana?"

"Hot and dry."

"How is everything there? How's Karen?"

"She's great. In fact, she's part of the reason I called. I need a background check on a prospective husband for her. Have you heard of a Michael Wolfe?"

"The actor?"

Why was it everyone knew the man but her? "Oh, good, you do know him."

Samantha no longer took care of the daily activities of Alliance since her marriage, but she knew the people to contact for background checks. The higher the profile, the harder it was to find anything of substance. If there was any dirt to find, she'd find it.

"Everyone knows him, Gwen."

"So Karen has told me. Do you have time to look?"

Samantha laughed. "You've lived here, you know I have nothing but time. There's more staff on this estate than there are people on your block. If I leave a towel on the bathroom floor it's picked up before I get out of the shower."

Gwen remembered. Domestic help filled the halls of the home of a rich duke. And although she wasn't much of a cook, she wouldn't take three decent meals a day in return for privacy again anytime soon. Gwen glanced up at the camera she knew was hidden in the corner of the room.

Almost private.

"So what does this have to do with Karen?"

"She's a suitable match. He needs someone attractive enough to convince his fans that he's found the right match. If he's as sought after as everyone tells me, he could have anyone."

"He could," Samantha told her.

"Karen's beautiful. They'll make a very handsome couple. Karen isn't rattled by his celebrity status. I doubt there are many women in our database we can say the same about."

"I agree."

Gwen kept listing Karen's attributes. "Her closest friends are you, Eliza, and myself. If she needs to bend our ear about her marriage we can be there for her without her slipping to someone talking with the media. She understands the stakes better than most. She only has to convince the kids at the Boys and Girls Club that she's helplessly in love."

"She might be the perfect match," Samantha agreed. "That is, if everything checks out."

"Oh, I think so. They'd get along very well."

"She hasn't met him yet?"

"No. I'll wait until you're done before introducing them. How long do you think you'll be?"

"Give me forty-eight hours. Michael Wolfe. How exciting. You know what that means if this all works out, right?"

Gwen blew out a breath, anticipating Samantha's reference to what was coming next. "It means I'll finally get some privacy around here." Gwen loved sharing the home with another woman her age, but the last thing she wanted was for anyone in the family to feel sorry for her. They all knew she'd never lived alone.

"You don't fool me, Gwen."

"I don't know what you're talking about. Oh, would you look at the time? I have a few more phone calls to make. Do be a dear and give my brother a kiss from me, will you?"

"Leave the acting to Michael. You suck at it."

Gwen chuckled, sent her love, and hung up.

"Hey, Gwen?" Karen called from the back of the house.

Gwen followed Karen's voice and found her staring out the kitchen window.

"What do you make of that?" Karen pointed in the backyard, beyond their fence. A crane on the street behind them was hoisting a large wooden box over the edge of the house.

"I've no idea."

"I know the old owners were foreclosed on. The 'for sale' sign went down a couple of weeks ago. I wonder what the new owners are doing."

Gwen opened the back door. The sound of a dozen male voices speaking in a minimum of two languages filled the kitchen. Gwen walked through the back door and peered over the fence to the neighbors' house. The wooden box hung on a large cable that tilted close to the eaves of the house. She held her breath when someone from the other side of the fence shouted for whoever operated the crane to stop. Karen moved to Gwen's side and stepped up onto a lawn chair to get a better look.

"Do you see anything?"

Their small backyard was fenced with a combination of cinder blocks and wood. The fence that separated the two properties stood no more than five feet tall. A few trees helped separate the space, but no matter how you looked at it, the backyard privacy was nonexistent.

"I think it's a hot tub."

The wooden box swung in midair, the hydraulic hum of the machine holding it hiccupped, and the tub jolted about an inch closer to the house.

"I hope it doesn't fall into the roof," Karen said.

"I'm guessing that's what everyone over there is worried about, too."

Neither of them could stop watching the swinging box until the crane set it safely on the ground.

"What are we doing down here? Your room is the perfect place to watch," Karen said.

Gwen moved back into the house. "Suit yourself." Watching the neighbors, especially colorful ones, was a nice source of entertainment, but Gwen hadn't seen any men in their neighbors' yard worth gawking over.

After a short time spying, Karen returned to their joint office and sat at her desk. "You know what this means, don't you?"

Gwen was scanning the entertainment section of an online magazine, searching for information on her newest client. "No, what's that?"

"Mrs. Sweeny is going to smell up the block."

Gwen pinched her eyes shut. Their neighbor, Mrs. Sweeny, greeted all neighbors and newlyweds with a batch of her completely unpalatable pasta and clam sauce. The smell alone would make the hungriest dog sprint in the opposite direction. Even the cats.

"We'll be sure and close the house up tight and keep the air running as soon as we scent the first boiling noodle."

"If all she did was boil noodles, no one would complain."

"True." Gwen noticed a picture of Michael on the arm of another actress. Each time she found him he was with someone new. "I spoke with Samantha. She's checking out Michael's background."

Karen swiveled in her chair, giving Gwen her full attention.

"I somehow doubt she'd find much of anything we don't already know about the man."

"Or what we assume about him," Gwen added.

"Do you know where he lives?"

"Moved to Beverly Hills about a year ago. Before that he had a home in Hollywood Hills." All of that was on public record.

"Secluded?"

"You know how most of those homes are in Beverly Hills… completely unseen from the street. Unless the owner wants to flash and flaunt."

"My guess is Michael wouldn't want his *home life* flashed." Karen shrugged. "I can live with that."

Gwen regarded her friend. "I'd think you'd enjoy some privacy. Between the cameras and noisy neighbors, we don't have much here."

"I like being around people."

Karen volunteered at a local Boys and Girls Club and probably spent half her income on disadvantaged kids. Although Samantha had done a complete background check on Karen long before Gwen started working at Alliance, Gwen didn't feel it was her place to dig into Karen's past. If Michael had specific questions about Karen, Gwen would have Samantha call him with the details. As Gwen's co-worker and roommate, she thought that eventually the other woman would open up to her. If she didn't, then that was her business.

"What will you do with the money…if in fact you and Michael marry?" Their female clients who were willing to marry rich men did so for a very steep price. A minimum two million dollars with a twenty percent commission to Alliance was in the contract. The groom agreed to take care of every expense his new bride needed, including everything from a new wardrobe to a new car. Living arrangements were determined early in the negotiating phase. Some husbands lived with the wives, though never in the same bedroom. If the couple became attracted to each other, it was understood that Alliance would have nothing to do with any resulting paternity suits. If the couple stayed married after the agreed upon time, Alliance was paid as per the agreement and it was up to the couple to dissolve the prenuptial contracts.

There were a few clients, very few, who were actually looking for love. In those cases, couples were matched based on their profiles and desires for a romantic interest. Both parties agreed to pay Alliance for their background checks and all expenses associated with the match…and a finder's fee.

Samantha had started Alliance over five years ago. Several couples had met, married, and divorced their spouse, leaving as friends. So far, eighty percent of the couples they matched for love were still married. Only about twenty percent of the couples who married for money had endured past their contracts and had children, or were otherwise wed for life. The rest divorced as planned.

Samantha and Blake being among the twenty percent.

"I'll invest half of it. Make sure I'm set later in life."

"And the other half?"

"I've been thinking of opening a house for runaways. A place where every child can escape to and feel safe. A place for kids to go when they have nowhere else."

If there was ever a time Gwen wanted to probe it was now. "That sounds like a lot of work."

"Anything worthwhile usually is. There are a lot of homeless teens out there getting into all kinds of trouble just to keep food in their mouths." Karen turned away, which signaled to Gwen that "sharing time" was over. "Besides, an ex-wife of a celebrity might be able to convince others to make donations to help with the kids. It's worth a shot."

Karen had a huge heart. "Let's hope Michael's background checks out then."

Gwen's phone rang, saving Karen from more questions.

"Hello?"

"What's going on in the backyard?" Leave it to Neil to skip any "how do you do's" and get right at the meat of things.

"I'm sorry?"

"Your backyard? The motion detectors are off the charts but nothing is coming up on the video feed." Neil's short tone and quick questions made it difficult to respond in a warm or friendly manner.

"We have new neighbors. They've craned in a Jacuzzi."

"The people directly behind you?" he asked.

"Yes."

The line was silent for a few seconds. "Neil? You still there?"

"I need you to step outside."

"Why?" she asked as she left her chair and started walking toward the back door.

"I need to run a test."

Gwen opened the back door and walked into the yard. "Has anyone ever told you you're paranoid?"

"Most people avoid saying things to me that piss me off."

She smiled. "I like annoying you."

Neil laughed...well, more snort than laugh.

"Was that a laugh, Neil?"

The man rarely smiled, but when he did, her body went numb and she lost herself in his gaze. Too bad he wasn't standing with her so she could see him instead of imagine him.

"There you are," he said, not answering her question.

Gwen waved, knowing the camera had found her.

"Walk to the back fence."

Gwen tiptoed and avoided sinking her heels into the soft grass. "Are you there?"

"I am. Can't you see me?"

"I need to readjust the equipment. Get a better angle."

"I'm going back inside now." The men in the yard behind them were starting to peer over her way. She waved, smiled, and returned to the house. "If you're done...I need to get back to work."

"I'm...I'm...How's your leg?"

Gwen paused inside the kitchen and glanced at her foot. "It's fine. Thank you for asking."

"Good. Uhm, I'll be there in an hour to check the cameras."

She'd look forward to it. "Paranoid," she told him again.

He snorted a second time and hung up the phone.

Chapter Four

I shouldn't be here.

But damn he couldn't stay away. He knew the static on the motion detector was most likely due to normal neighbor behavior, a passing cat, or even the wind.

Gwen was right. He was paranoid.

He couldn't stop his paranoia any more than he could stop thinking about her, about the terror in her eyes as he pulled his gun and pointed it at her.

Getting close to an assignment, which is how he needed to look at Gwen…at all the Harrisons, made him weak. Distance… he needed to find it and keep it.

So what the hell was he doing driving to Tarzana to check on a woman who didn't want or need his help?

Ignoring his own internal warning bells, Neil pulled into Gwen's driveway alongside her car and frowned. Why did she insist on parking outside the garage?

Purposeful strides took him to the front door. He knocked twice and stepped back so Gwen or Karen could see him clearly on the monitor by the door.

Neither woman answered. He knocked again, this time louder and longer.

"Coming…"

Gwen opened the door a little too quickly and without enough effort to assure him it had been locked. "Oh, hi."

She stood back, letting him in.

"Did you even look to see who was here?"

"You told me you were coming."

"But did you look?" He moved past her, ignoring the floral scent of her skin that reminded him of spring.

She disregarded his question, confirming that she hadn't checked. When she closed the door, she didn't lock it.

I'm going to need a dentist if I keep grinding my teeth together.

As Gwen moved to leave the foyer, Neil stepped into her path and grasped her hand. Like a child, he moved her hand to the lock on the door and held it there. "Forgetting something?"

She smiled up at him and moved even closer. "I doubt anyone would attempt anything with you here, big guy." Her pale blue eyes sparkled as she taunted him.

"Your brother asked me to keep an eye on you, Gwendolyn."

She lowered her voice and twisted the lock under his hand. "I like when you use my full name, Neil. Makes me think you care."

Any other woman and he'd flatten her against the wall, press his body to hers, and slide into her sultry voice and flirting eyes.

He released her hand and forced his eyes away from hers.

Damn woman!

"Where's Karen?"

"Running errands."

Gwen was alone…with the door unlocked and her car parked outside the garage. Why not just wear a fucking sign that said *"I'm here. Come and get me"*?

I hate this neighborhood. Too damn hard to manage. The neighbors are only feet away…cars driving by. No locked gates.

He worked his way to the back of the house and out the door. The camera positioned in the backyard had been strategically placed along an eave line. Without asking, he moved to the side of the house and tried the side door.

Unlocked!

He found a ladder and returned to the yard. He set his laptop up on the patio table and moved the camera back where he wanted it. He cleaned the dome of the motion detectors and checked the lines.

The new neighbors had placed a hot tub in the center of their small yard. Wood was stacked around it, letting him know that there were probably going to be more people around, maybe even a small construction team.

Neil made a mental note to swing around the block and check out a few cars…and their license plates.

"Finished up there?" Gwen asked from below. Neil hardly noticed that she watched him from the doorway.

Once both his feet were on the ground, he asked. "Have you met the new neighbors?"

"Not yet. Up until today, I haven't seen anyone there since it sold."

"It was a foreclosure, wasn't it?"

Gwen nodded. "That's what Eliza told me. I never met the old neighbors."

More eyes, so long as they were friendly eyes, were better than less. A nosy neighbor was more likely to call the police if they saw anything suspicious.

"So what's all this really about, Neil?"

"Doing my job."

"You sure that's all?"

He was about to answer when Gwen crossed her arms over her chest in a sign of defiance. "This doesn't have anything to do with the possibility of Karen leaving, does it?"

He set the ladder back down. "Karen's leaving?"

"Maybe. You hadn't heard?"

"Heard what?" He really needed to eavesdrop on the Tarzana conversations a little more often.

Gwen lowered her voice. "I might have found a match for her. If it all works out Karen could be moving in a couple of months... maybe sooner."

"You're serious."

"It's what we do."

A muscle in his jaw started to twitch. He tried to relax and failed.

"You're staring at me, Neil."

He rubbed his chin, set the ladder back up, and checked to see if another feed had been placed in the wiring so he could install another camera. To make damn sure he could see every inch of the small backyard.

He spent the next thirty minutes checking and rechecking the security equipment. There was static in one of the external audio feeds, and he made a note tell the electricians to replace them.

The entire time he moved about the house he kept thinking of her living there alone.

Lady Gwendolyn Harrison, a pampered daughter of a duke, and the most stunning woman God ever graced the earth with, had no business living alone in this cheap neighborhood only blocks away from murderers, rapists, and thieves. Neil had listened to the police scanners enough to understand the neighborhood demographics.

No wonder writers crafted tales of keeping captive princesses safe in ivory towers.

"You've tested that lock three times." Gwen graced him with her pristine white teeth and brilliant smile.

"It sticks."

"Ah, huh."

"When will you know about Karen?" He twisted the lock a fourth time.

"We'll finish the background check, and then have them meet. We should know if it's going to work in a couple of weeks. Maybe sooner."

Enough time to add a couple of cameras...update a couple of things. He didn't like the amount of motion the outside detectors were picking up. He stood in the yard, completely still, and the damn things were going ape-shit crazy. Glitches like that made people ignore the signals.

He tapped the control panel used to set and unset the alarms. "What's your distress code?"

"Zod."

"What numbers?"

"Nine six three."

"When do you use that code?" He was drilling her, but he didn't know what else he could do.

"If someone was here threatening me and telling me to turn off the alarm. I know the drill. Nothing is going to happen. I'm a big girl."

"You're a tiny girl the neighborhood paperboy could snap like a twig if he wanted to."

"Tommy would do no such thing. He's a good boy."

The edge of his lips lifted ever so slightly.

"Is that a smile I see on Neil's lips?"

He forced his lips to a thin line.

"Oh, my mistake." Gwen hid her own grin.

"I'll call tomorrow with details about who will come to fix a few things." He returned his equipment to his bag. "Lock the door behind me."

"Yes, sir." She gave him a mock salute.

"I'm serious, Gwen. Your security habits suck. Your brother isn't going to let you live here alone if you don't start taking things seriously."

Her playful grin fell and Neil knew he'd used the wrong words to get her to move over to his way of thinking.

"My brother is not my keeper."

"He owns the house."

"Samantha owns the house. And she'd never make me leave."

Neil's jaw started to twitch again.

"Perhaps I need to remind you that I'm not a child."

His eyes did a quick sweep of her body. "You don't have to remind me of that."

She took a step toward him, placed her hand on his arm. "I'll try and be better about locking the doors."

He nodded, not willing to let her know how much the thought of her living there alone distressed him. He opened the door to let himself out and called over his shoulder. "And park your car in the garage."

———

"Oh my God, Gwen, get up here!" Karen laughed as she yelled from upstairs. "Quick."

Gwen hustled up the stairs and found Karen hovering over her bedroom window. She'd pulled the curtains back enough to peek out.

"What is it?"

"Look!"

Gwen switched positions with her roommate and narrowed her eyes. It was late at night and the neighborhood was dark... except for the light coming from the new neighbors' hot tub. A couple of days had passed since their arrival. In the Jacuzzi sat two people, and from what she could see one was a woman and the other a man. If Gwen had to guess, she'd say that they were an older couple. Maybe retirement age. "What am I looking for?"

"Just keep watching."

Gwen was about to leave her spying perch when the woman stood to move to a different spot.

"She's naked."

Karen started laughing. "Ewww!"

"We have naked neighbors…" *I never saw this back home.*

Karen peeked beside her all the while giggling. "Look how hairy he is."

Gwen averted her eyes. "We shouldn't stare."

"They shouldn't parade around naked."

"They're in their own yard."

"Surrounded by two-story houses." Karen flashed a brilliant smile. "That's the crazy crap you never get when you're locked behind security gates at an estate."

Gwen couldn't argue with that. She took another quick look.

The phone rang and both of them jumped.

"We shouldn't stare."

Karen continued to watch while Gwen answered the phone. "Hello?"

"There's noise coming from the backyard." Neil skipped pleasantries and started issuing orders. "Make sure the doors are locked."

"You know, Neil, normal people say hello when they call on the phone. A little 'hi, how do you do,' stuff like that."

"The motion detectors are off the charts." There was frustration in his voice.

Gwen purposely hesitated to say anything.

She heard him sigh. "Hello, Gwen. Can you tell me what's going on over there?"

Isn't that better? "Why hello, Neil. Nice of you to call. Nothing's going on. Our new neighbors are enjoying their hot tub. Perhaps their tub is interfering with your equipment."

"I should come over and see for myself."

"Don't you dare."

"Why not?"

"I do not need my new neighbors thinking I've invited people here to gawk at them." That wouldn't be the way to introduce herself.

"Gawk? Who said anything about gawking?"

Gwen peeked through the shade again, catching the unwelcome sight of the hairy man's backside. "Apparently their hot tub is clothing optional. They opted out."

"They what?"

"They're enjoying the jets naked. And I'll not have you coming over to stomp around my backyard with them out there. If something needs repair, then you can come over tomorrow."

"They're naked?"

"That's what I said. The doors are locked and the alarm is set. We're fine, Neil. I promise."

"Fine. I'll be there in the morning."

"Suit yourself. I won't be here, I have an early appointment."

"Fine."

"Good night, Neil."

He clicked off the phone. Apparently saying hello and good-bye was too much to ask for in one conversation.

Chapter Five

Gwen visited the corner bakery where she picked up her morning tea and biscuits before meeting with Michael for the second time.

The skeletons in his closet weren't unexpected, and none raised any alarms for Samantha, Karen, or Gwen.

Karen was cautiously excited.

Since Michael checked out, it was his turn to approve of Karen's portfolio before they met.

She drove through the locked gates of his estate, which was located well off the main streets of Beverly Hills. A star map purchased for a small price would point out Michael's estate, but a tourist would have to scale a twelve-foot block wall to see his yard.

The stone drive reminded her of home. But that was where the similarities ended. The Spanish influence of the architecture was evident everywhere her eye was drawn. Bougainvillea climbed up the columns of the entry, welcoming guests in shades of purple and red. Arched windows and doors reminded Gwen of one of the many missions sprinkled along the California coast.

Michael walked through his front doors with open arms. "Lady Harrison."

He kissed both her cheeks.

"Gwen, please. No one calls me Lady Harrison unless they want something."

"We both know I want something. Come in."

"Your home is beautiful." She was expecting something modern...sleek.

"Not what you expected?"

"Am I that transparent?" Inside the home the visual delights continued. Expansive walls filled with luscious art led to vaulted ceilings with iron chandeliers.

"It's the closest thing to a Spanish villa this side of the border... well, that I've found anyway."

"It's lovely, Michael." *Karen's going to love it.*

"I'm sure if everything works out you'll be here often enough to enjoy it."

He led her to a great room with massive windows allowing a view of a garden courtyard. The sound of water flowing drew her eye to a fountain in the center of the yard. Splashes of color mixed in with trees and shrubs.

"I thought you'd lean toward a modern décor."

"Hard edges and black and white lines...not me. For some of the characters I've played, maybe." Michael indicated for her to sit. "I come from a small town where people take more pride in their yards than they do their cars. I guess some of it sunk in."

"I'm sorry to admit this, but I've not seen your films."

"So you told me. What about the woman you're showing me? Has she seen my films?"

Gwen centered her attention on her client. "Karen knew who you were the instant I uttered your name."

"A fan?"

"Fan would be short for fanatical. Karen isn't enamored with anyone. Well, perhaps a child with a sad story to tell. But not fame. Not even money believe it or not."

He leaned against his chair and crossed his arms over his broad chest. "Then why would she agree to this marriage?"

"She wants the money this agreement will make her, Mr. Wolfe, but not so she can live a life of opulence and grandeur." She spread her arms wide indicating the room they were in. "This isn't a life she wants permanently."

"I've yet to meet anyone who wouldn't want this."

Gwen reached into her case and removed Karen's file.

Michael took it and glanced at the photo. "She's beautiful."

Gwen shrugged. "And if you were attracted to women you might be tempted to keep her. But we both know that will never happen." Samantha's background check did find the name of his first lover, but not many after. Michael had done a superb job of keeping his personal life personal.

Michael offered her half a smile and flipped the page. "Mind if I read this?"

"Of course not. That's why I'm here."

"Can I get you something to drink?"

"Water would be nice."

He stepped into the kitchen and brought back a bottle each of sparkling and plain water. She took the plain and told him to take his time.

While Michael looked over Karen's information, Gwen moved into the courtyard to give her client all the time he needed.

The file contained a snapshot of Karen. What her interests were, where she spent her time. Her work, up until Samantha brought her into Alliance, had been managing an assisted living home for young disabled patients. On the surface, Karen was a bleeding heart, always helping someone less fortunate than her. Her only family was an aunt who had recently married a rich gentleman who had been in the process of hiring Alliance to find him a young bride. He wanted the bride to tick off his children and grandchildren. All of whom were fighting over his wealth. Karen set up her Aunt Eddie with Stanley and everything turned out remarkably well.

"This woman sounds like a saint," Michael said from the doorway.

"I'll be sure and tell her you said so."

He moved to a chair adjacent her on the patio. "Seriously. No one can be this clean and be real." He tossed the papers on the table. "What's she really like?"

"Everything in there is true."

"Fine. I get that. But what's she like?"

Gwen thought of telling him that Karen was a kind and witty girl whom he would adore…but instead she decided to tell him something else.

"Last night, while watching the evening news, Karen called me upstairs to spy on our new neighbors."

Michael's brow drew up. "Spy?"

"Apparently our new, very old, and quite unattractive neighbors have decided that their backyard oasis…which is clearly visible from all the homes around them, is their own personal nudist retreat."

Michael's smile was slow to come, but then he started laughing.

"Karen is not a saint. Yes, all we've put in there is true. She is exceptionally bright and funny. Her clever tongue never seems to fail her, even when life erupts. I realize you're the movie star in this equation, but Karen is the prize. And when your agreement with her is resolved, I'll lay my bets now that you'll always be friends."

"When can we meet?"

Gwen lifted her chin. *Perfect.*

An hour later, they stepped out of Michael's home as he walked her to her car.

She glanced around the door, searching for the cameras that she felt were watching. There was nothing visible.

"What are you looking for?" he asked.

"Where are your security cameras?" The ones on her home were tucked under the eaves but no such device could be seen under Michael's.

"I have a camera on the gate but that's it. I have an alarm system."

Gwen turned a full circle. "I would think you'd want tighter security."

"Is that going to be a problem for Karen?"

She shook her head. "No. Not at all." Gwen looked behind her again. *Neil's paranoia is rubbing off on me.*

"Eliza!" Gwen walked into Eliza's hug with both arms. "My goodness it's wonderful to see you. How is the First Lady of California?"

Gwen stepped aside and let Eliza into the house.

"I'm stupid busy," she said as she moved past Gwen. "Who knew that Carter's job would be so damn taxing on me?"

"Sam and I both warned you about your position."

Eliza tucked a strand of her dark hair behind her ear and tossed her purse on the coffee table. "I thought you were exaggerating. There's at least one political dinner a week, sometimes two depending on who's in town. Ladies' luncheons…with ladies I don't even like. I could do lunch all day long if it were with you guys. Ribbon cuttings, trips to DC."

Yet even as Eliza pitched her fit, she smiled.

"Do you want your old life back?"

"Not unless I can take Carter with me. He's loving his job. It's going to take a lot of work to turn things around for our state, but if anyone can do it, he can. So how are you?"

"I'm good. I assume Samantha told you about Karen?"

Eliza's eyes lit up. "Do you think it's going to happen?"

"I'd plan on attending two weddings this year, if I were you." Blake made Samantha marry him in Vegas the first time and had made up for that mistake every year since.

"How exciting. Has Karen met him yet?"

"Their 'chance' meeting should happen within the hour. She's at the Boys and Girls Club right now where he is going to make an unexpected PR stop."

"I wish we could watch."

"That would be too obvious. It's up to the two of them now."

Eliza glanced around the room. "Will she still work here? Or have you talked about that?"

"Most of her work is online or on the phones, so we're going to work it out from Michael's place."

"Which means you'll be here all by yourself."

Gwen pushed off the couch. "Oh, please…not you, too?" She walked into the kitchen.

"Me too what?" Eliza followed her.

Gwen removed a chilled bottle of Chardonnay from the refrigerator, lifted the bottle for Eliza to see. "Is it too early for wine?"

"It's never too early for wine."

Good. Because the "you're living here alone" conversation needed wine. "I'm getting tired of people treating me as if I'm a child incapable of living on her own. Shortly after you moved out Karen moved in. I've loved the company. But I don't need a keeper."

"I don't think I said anything about a keeper."

Gwen saw the doubt in Eliza's gaze. "Samantha brought up me living alone and Neil hasn't stopped coming over to check on me since the news of Michael and Karen broke." She uncorked the wine, poured two glasses, and handed one to her friend.

"I'm sure having Neil over isn't a hardship…for you."

Although Gwen had never confirmed her feelings for Neil to Eliza, her friend had always guessed they were deeper than those of a friend. Besides, she would never say anything in a house Neil listened in on, that might clue him in to just how often she thought of the man.

"It's nice outside. Let's go out back." Where the audio feeds weren't as clear as Neil liked.

Once outside and seated with their wine, Eliza started in. "OK, Gwen…what's up?"

"Having…*him* around isn't a hardship. It's a constant reminder that I've not had one lover since I moved here. My love life may not have been ideal at home. In fact, it was downright boring after a while, choreographed affairs that usually ended a week after they should have."

Eliza sipped her wine. "Where did you meet the men you've dated?"

"Friends of the family, sons of men my father worked with when he was alive. Boring, predictable. Not once did I have the urge to carry on with any of them."

"You make it sound like there were a lot."

"Not that many. These past months I realize how sheltered I've been. Living here, although it couldn't be more different from Albany, is still an extension of that shelter. Eyes are always on me. I've even taken to looking over my shoulder lately."

"That might be your subconscious talking. You're used to the security of people being around…of cameras and alarms."

Gwen played with the stem of her glass, chasing the condensation with her manicured nail. "That isn't real life though, is it?"

"It's been your life."

"A sheltered life I don't need and don't want."

Eliza sat forward and lowered her voice. "No one knows more than me what it feels like to have unwanted security guards watching your every move. But you can't ignore the fact that your brother is titled and very rich. You have a trust fund worth more money than I'll ever see and there are people out there that wouldn't think twice about getting to you to get to that money. You want independence. I get that. Lord knows you're more street-smart now than when you first moved here. But in order to shake off all this security, you're going to have to prove you can take care of yourself. And not just to your brother and Neil...but to yourself."

Gwen knew her friend was right. Looking over her shoulder was part insecurity and part paranoia. Both of which made her seek the refuge of her home or even the privacy of her car. If she were ever going to get her own life, and stop riding on that of her brother's, she'd have to start making some changes.

"You're right."

Eliza smiled, satisfied with herself. "So, we have an island wedding to plan."

"And you're in charge of the dresses," Gwen said with a laugh. She'd picked out the yellow bridesmaid gowns they'd worn last year for Blake and Sam's Texas wedding. Eliza hated them and offered to pick out the dresses for Aruba. Eventually Gwen would get an opportunity to redeem herself. Blake and Samantha repeated their vows every year.

"It's an island...I'm thinking simple. Beach ceremony. Island food...flowers."

Gwen thought of the sea gently lapping on the shore and being carried off in the sunset. "Sounds lovely."

"Good. I'll pick out the dresses and everything to go with them here and we'll travel to the island a few days early to finish any details needed. This ceremony is going to be smaller. Samantha wanted only family and close friends."

"They can't all be grand."

"Not when you get married every year."

Gwen rolled her eyes. "I'd settle for once, thank you very much."

Eliza finished her wine and stepped inside to get the bottle. "You want to get married?"

"I don't want to live my life as a spinster." Being Auntie Gwen...the woman who never married. Never had a family of her own. No. She didn't want that as her legacy.

"It wouldn't be hard for you to find a husband, Gwen. You just need to put yourself out there. Waiting for *you know who* to make a move that might not ever come is a waste of your time." Eliza topped off Gwen's glass and refilled her own.

"I'm not waiting for anyone."

"I see right though you. If you're serious about taking charge of your life, you might try starting with a date."

Gwen hated that her friend was right. Hated it even more that a coward lurked inside her head and kept her from finding the nearest pub and picking up a man...even for one night.

Chapter Six

Moisture gathered on the palms of Karen's hands. She'd be lying if she said she wasn't nervous.

"Miss Jones?"

Karen forced her attention to the study group at her table. There were four girls and three boys with open math books and paper sitting in front of them. Two of the boys were busy texting on their phones while one flirted with the oldest girl at the table.

"I'm sorry, Amy, what did you ask?"

"Is this right?"

Karen glanced at the paper and noticed Amy's mistake instantly. "Add the fraction again."

Helping the kids after school with their math, or English, or whatever schoolwork they had was something she could do to help these kids stay in school. They were good kids…kids from broken families, or parents who had to work second jobs to make ends meet and couldn't be around to help their kids with their homework. Kids who needed a safe haven from the streets on which they lived.

Karen always spotted those kids. The ones who didn't have enough food, who kept the world from knowing that they lived in a car, or on the street…or a lean-to structure beside someone's yard. Homeless kids…kids ready to give up on a normal life and reduce themselves to drugs…to dropping out of school.

Amy pushed the paper in front of Karen again. "Perfect."

Jeff, the club director, walked toward her. His grin spread across his face and Karen could swear he was skipping. "Karen, can I talk to you?"

"Sure."

The unusually excited tone of Jeff's voice had the kids looking between them. "Boys. Let's see if you can get at least two problems done before I get back."

One of the boys ignored her and continued playing on his phone. The other two straightened up, pulled their homework in front of them, and picked up pencils.

"What's up, Jeff?" she asked as they walked away.

"I just got a call from a man named Tony. Says he works with a celebrity who wants to come by today and check out our facility."

Her heart skipped. "A celebrity?"

Jeff nodded. "Tony said the actor is looking for kid charities to spend some of his money on. Needs the tax write-off or some such thing."

Well that's original. She wanted to roll her eyes but didn't. "Really? What does this have to do with me?"

"He wants someone who's been here awhile to show him the place." Jeff shuffled his feet with excitement or maybe it was nerves, Karen couldn't tell.

She shrugged, trying to act uninterested. "You've been here awhile. Why don't you do it?"

Jeff stood a little taller. "I'll be with you...but you know the kids better than anyone here. If anyone can plead their need it's you."

"Fine. Let me know when *moneybags* gets here." *And the Oscar goes to...*

She moved back to the kids at her table and checked their work.

"You know, Juan, if you ever want to move past algebra you're going to have to do some of the work," she told the one teen at the table who acted like he didn't want to be there.

"I'm never going to use this stuff."

"You don't know that."

Juan stopped leaning back in his chair and glared at her. "Yeah, I do."

He was probably right, but she'd take a bite out of her own tongue before telling him that. "So where do you hide your crystal ball...the one that tells you the future?"

Juan smirked.

"C'mon. I'll spring for pizza on Friday after your test if you come back with a C or better."

The other kids at the table perked up.

If she thought for a minute that Juan wasn't capable of obtaining a C in his sleep, she wouldn't have added the pressure. The kid wasn't unintelligent, just cocky and uninterested.

His friend smacked him upside his arm. "C'mon, Juan. I can help."

Juan picked up his pencil and started solving for x.

Twenty minutes and several problems later, the noise level in the room started to rise. Karen and the kids at her table looked toward the entrance.

Wearing designer jeans and sunglasses that probably cost enough to feed every kid there pizza for a week, was her future husband. Michael stood next to Jeff and a shorter man Karen didn't recognize.

When Jeff motioned for her to come their way, the kids started whispering.

"Oh, my God. Is that Michael Wolfe?"

"Michael who?" Karen asked. *Might as well make this good.*

"The actor," Amy said, her face unable to contain her excitement.

Karen pushed away from the table. "Action flicks, right?"

"Seriously, Miss Jones, you don't know?"

Karen winked at the girls. "I go to the movies, too. He's just a person, no better than you or me." Making the kids believe they were just as valuable to society as Michael Wolfe might be difficult, but not impossible.

She offered a polite smile when Michael caught her eyes.

"Here she is," Jeff said. "Karen Jones, this is Michael Wolfe, who I'm sure you recognize, and his manager, Tony."

"Action flicks...right?" She asked, extending her hand.

He took her palm in his and sandwiched it with his other hand. *Oh, the two-sided handshake. Very convincing.*

"That's right."

She turned to Tony. "Nice to meet you."

"Mr. Wolfe wanted a tour of the place, Karen."

"Sure. Anything to help the kids. You don't mind meeting some of them, do you Mr. Wolfe?"

"Michael. Please call me Michael." He tucked his sunglasses into his shirt and looked around the room. It seemed everything and everyone stood silent as he walked between her and Jeff. "I'd love to meet the kids, Miss Jones."

She thought of suggesting he use her first name, but that would be *way* too easy.

A couple of the braver girls followed behind them while others huddled together in the corners whispering.

The kids' goo-goo eyes weren't going to leave them alone. Karen placed a hand on his briefly and stopped their progression through the club.

"Hey, guys?" she called to the kids in the room. "We're going to give Mr. Wolfe a quick tour of your club but he's *promised* to stick around after to meet you. So why don't you go back to what you were doing, OK?"

Most of the kids kept staring, but some moved back to their work or to playing whatever it was they were playing before Michael walked in.

"I don't think Mr. Wolfe promised anything, Karen," Jeff said under his breath.

"Yeah he did…he said he'd meet the kids. Right, Michael?"

"That's what I said." He smiled and stared at her. His gaze would have been unnerving if this were a chance meeting.

He's gay, she reminded herself.

"Have you ever been in a Boys and Girls Club?"

"No, I haven't."

She walked him through the game room. Several couches and chairs, beanbag chairs, and pillows were thrown about. "Our mission statement really does define what we do for the kids. To enable all young people, especially those who need us most, to reach their full potential as productive, caring, responsible citizens." Karen had memorized the statement a long time ago.

"We accomplish that by having a safe place for kids to hang out after school. Kids love video games so we have that here for them." There was a big-screen television she had personally bought for the club along with two gaming stations. A few older arcade games were lined up along the walls. "There's also table tennis and a pool table when the video monitor isn't working for them. We have a yard outside I'll show you when we get there."

"How many kids come in?"

"It varies. We've had up to a hundred kids signed up to come in daily…but double that who only come in periodically."

Michael looked at the kids who were trying to act uninterested but failed. "They have to sign up?"

"For our insurance purposes they do. We have a pay-what-you-can system. Most of these kids aren't able to pay. We rely on donations and outside fundraisers."

"The kids themselves do some of the fundraisers," Jeff added. "We had a car wash last month that brought in a couple hundred dollars."

"A couple hundred doesn't sound like it would pay your power bill."

"It doesn't," Karen said, surprised at the level of interest in Michael's voice.

"We help the kids after school with their homework and school projects. It's mainly teens but sometimes we get kids that are eleven or twelve." Karen walked by her math table and glanced at Juan's paper as she did. "You're never gonna get that pizza if you don't get past problem six, dude." There was laughter in her voice. She really did want the kids to do well.

"Yes, Miss Jones."

She walked Michael into the kitchen. "The kitchen is fully functioning. We provide snacks and occasional meals. The truth is, there are plenty of kids out there who don't get a solid meal at home. Every one of them knows they can find something here. Most are too embarrassed to say they're hungry."

"How do you get past that?"

"We let them know when we're providing meals, and none of them miss that day."

"Why not provide a meal every day?"

Karen met Michael's eyes. "Funds."

"Oh."

He held the door to the back open and she walked through. Jeff had fallen behind with Tony, who was asking about details of what it cost to run the club.

"There's a basketball court and a yard where the kids play. We try to organize scrimmage games for them. Seems the only way to get them off the video games."

He watched her now, and she was highly conscious of the smile on her face.

"Sounds like you love it here."

"The kids are great. Not all of them are disadvantaged. Just misguided. I like to think we keep them off the streets and away from drugs and gangs."

He placed his sunglasses over his eyes. "Do you have a lot of that here?"

"We've had a couple of problem kids. But we deal with them as soon as we know anything about it. Two or three times a month a youth counselor is available. I think of this place as a safe haven for these kids. We have no tolerance for bullying and don't judge."

"Interesting."

Jeff stood several yards away, well outside of hearing range. The teens lingering in the yard talked among themselves.

She lowered her voice. "Kid charities to spend your money on?"

Michael looked behind them. "Worked, didn't it?"

Karen laughed. "So, what do you think?"

He shook his head. "I think Gwen was wrong. I think you are a saint. You do all this for free?"

"That would be the definition of volunteer."

He chuckled. "Oh, a smart-ass…you'll fit right in."

She pointed a finger to his chest. "Saintly smart-ass. Get it right. Does Tony know why you're really here?"

He shook his head. "Only you and I…and Gwen."

Jeff and Tony were walking their way so Karen quickly changed the subject. "Well, what do you think?"

"I like it. There are plenty of youth charities out there help-ing kids after they've fallen down the wrong path. This one seems to want to get a hold of at risk kids before they tumble." Even if Michael was acting the part, he did it successfully.

They walked back into the main room, where none of the kids had moved.

Michael leaned down and whispered in her ear. "Time to turn on the charm."

And he did.

Karen found a stool for him to sit on as he encouraged the kids to ask questions. "Where do you guys go to school?" he asked them, helping to break the ice. "What do you like most about school?"

Several kids told him they liked going home.

Amy told him she liked coming to the club after school.

"What do you like least about school?"

"Algebra!" Juan said from the math table.

"Just think pizza party, Juan. Makes solving for x easier," Karen called from the back of the room.

Several kids laughed.

"Pizza party?" Michael asked.

"Miss Jones bribes us with pizza if we do good on our tests."

"Do *well* on your tests, Steve," Karen corrected him.

"If I had a tutor as stunning as Miss Jones when I was in high school, I would have had straight A's." Michael kept eye contact with her throughout his exchange. "No bribes needed."

The kids around them hooted and whistled.

"It's been a long time since you were in high school, Mr. Wolfe. Things have changed." She was teasing him, making him work a little harder.

From the playful expression on his face, he enjoyed the banter.

The kids were laughing and at least one had a cell phone out as he took pictures.

"I tell you what, guys…if someone here can convince Miss Jones to go out with me, I'll do better than pizza."

The kids were eating this up.

"Oh, my God, Miss Jones, Michael Wolfe just asked you out!"

"You've got to go, Miss Jones."

Michael chimed in. "Yeah, Miss Jones."

"Does it always take a room full of kids to make women go out with you, Mr. Wolfe?"

Michael cocked his head to the side. "No. But it helps."

There were no less than four cell phones out. She was going up on YouTube before she managed to get home. She just knew it.

"C'mon, Miss Jones."

"I tell you what. Why don't I give you my number and we can talk without an audience?"

"I can live with that."

She looked around the gawking eyes in the room. "Can I borrow someone's pen?"

Someone shoved one in her face. She walked up to her future husband, grasped his hand, and did what she was sure no one had ever done to him before. She wrote her number on his palm. When she finished he took her hand in his and kissed the back of it.

His eyes were laughing.

Something told her that the next year of her life was going to be a boatload of fun.

And if the kids could get more than pizza out of the deal…she was all in.

———

"This was exactly what I needed," Karen said from across their table.

Gwen smiled and lifted her drink into the air. "Might be the closest thing you get to a bachelorette party if Michael moves as fast as I think he will."

Karen and Gwen sat across from each other at the Hard Rock Café on Sunset. Gwen had decided to take Eliza up on her suggestion. *Put yourself out there. Date. Meet someone.*

If she wanted to meet someone other than a boring, responsible man who could be counted on to show up on time but never make her feel excited about his presence. She'd had predictable and utterly dull men in her life before, she needed to look outside of the ballrooms where she conducted her business.

The bar was packed. The patrons were all drinking, laughing, and forgetting about their problems.

"He's really a nice guy. The kids loved him."

Gwen glanced around the room, but didn't notice anyone watching them. "I'm sure his celebrity status will make the kids look up to you even more."

"An added bonus."

"To a successful relationship," Gwen said, clicking her cocktail to Karen's.

"I can drink to that." They sipped their drinks. "I can't believe this is really happening."

"Wait until you see his house."

Karen smiled as she peered beyond Gwen. "Over here," she said as she waved.

Eliza joined them, tossing her clutch on the table. "I wasn't sure I'd find you in this zoo. Could they pack more people in here?"

"Probably."

"It's good to see you," Eliza told Karen. "I hear congratulations are in order."

"Not yet…but it is starting to look that way."

Eliza flagged down a waitress and ordered a martini. "I see not a lot has changed," she said after the waitress left.

"What do you mean?" Gwen asked.

"We're sitting in a bar and your giant shadow is lurking in the back of the building." Eliza tossed a peanut in her mouth.

"My shadow?"

Eliza looked to the right of the bar. "Yeah. The man who acts like you're a job but can't seem to leave you alone. If it was anyone other than Neil I'd be afraid he was a stalker."

Gwen twisted around in her chair. Sure enough, perched at the edge of a seat on the far side of the bar, sat Neil.

"What's he doing here?"

His eyes found hers for a brief moment before she looked away. "I think that's obvious."

Her back teeth started to grind. "I don't need a babysitter."

"I don't know, Gwen. The last time we sat in a bar I remember a certain someone getting drunk and a couple other someones getting into a fight."

She'd never live that down. Gwen and Eliza went to blow off steam in a Texas bar. The cowboys were full of "yes, ma'am" and "howdy, darlin'." They danced and carried on...and yes, she drank a little too much. When one of the cowboys mistakenly took her smile as an invitation for intimacy, Neil erupted from the bar to teach the cowboy the meaning of the word no.

It was the first time Neil had defended her honor, and though she hated to admit it, she got a kick out of how ticked off he became when another man looked at her. "That was last year."

"What's changed since then?"

Nothing! It didn't matter how much she flirted with the man, or how obvious she was about her attraction. Neil didn't bite.

"Everything." Gwen stood, ready to put Neil in his place. "If you'll both excuse me for a minute."

She pushed her way through the crowd as if on a collision course with Neil. He kept his lips in a thin line as she approached and gripped the longneck bottle at his side.

Slipping between the woman on the stool next to him and Neil's massive frame, Gwen slapped her hand on her hip and growled. "What are you doing here?"

He blinked, once, and picked up his beer. "Having a drink."

She wanted to scream. "Having a drink," she repeated.

He tilted the bottle back, took a swig.

"I know what you're doing, Neil. And I don't like it. I don't want or need a bodyguard."

"That's debatable."

If stomping her foot would knock some sense into him, she'd stomp better than a farm girl in a vineyard.

Poking a finger into his chest, she moved closer. "Do you have any idea how difficult it is to have a love life with a two-hundred-thirty-pound bodyguard standing in my way?"

A muscle in his jaw tightened. "Two hundred and fifty."

"Ahhh!" She did scream now.

He lifted his beer again, but before he could take a swig, Gwen grabbed it from his fingers and tilted it back herself.

In a move that would make Eliza and Karen proud, she pushed the empty beer bottle back into his hand and slid between his thighs.

His jaw twitched again.

The strong musky scent that was pure Neil invaded her senses. She dropped one hand to his thigh and left it there. "This is how I see it, Neil. You have two choices. Either back off or step up."

Gwen squeezed his thigh before vacating his personal space and marching back to the girls.

A satisfied smile stretched over her face.

Chapter Seven

What the fuck just happened?

Gwen's shapely butt swayed back and forth as she worked her way back to her table.

He didn't have time to process Gwen's ultimatum before he heard someone calling him.

"Mac? Is that you?"

Neil froze. His name from the past caught in his throat, making him think twice before turning around.

He waved his empty beer to the bartender, hoping whoever called out wasn't looking at him.

"MacBain?"

He glanced over his shoulder. "Rick?" he said in shock. The last time he'd seen Rick...

Thick heat sealed in the scent of dirt, blood, and death. The Blackhawk carried what was left of his men to safety. Five of them made it out, and one of those would take his last breath before the chopper landed.

It was his fault.

Rick slammed his hand into Neil's and pulled him into a man-hug. "Damn, it's good to see you."

"You look good," Neil managed, thankful the bartender was quick with his drink.

"You look angry as ever." Rick "Smiley" Evans, Smiley to those in their unit because of the never-ending lips that smiled regardless of the sky falling around them, ordered a whiskey, and sat in the now vacant stool at Neil's side.

"How long has it been?"

Neil glanced over Rick's shoulder, noticed Gwen laughing.

"A few years." Five years, eight months, and a handful of days.

Rick shifted in his seat. "That's a tableful of trouble if I ever saw one. Friends of yours?"

Neil averted his gaze, and focused on his old colleague. The last thing he wanted to do was explain Gwen to Rick. Hell, he didn't know how to explain Gwen to himself. "What are you doing in LA? I thought you didn't like the West Coast."

Rick took his drink in his hand and the smile he always wore fell.

A chill ran down Neil's spine.

"I hate this plastic scene."

"So why are you here?" Something told Neil he wasn't going to like the answer.

Rick emptied his glass with one swallow. "Looking for you."

Ah, fuck!

Rick dropped a twenty on the bar and stood. "Let's find a quieter place."

Neil's jaw ached. He had no desire to leave Gwen, but knew Rick wouldn't suggest they talk if it wasn't important. He glanced Gwen's way one last time before following Rick out of the bar.

There were plenty of bars to fade quietly into throughout LA. They found one, ordered a couple of drinks, and faded.

"Billy's dead."

"What?" The hair on Neil's arms went up and stayed there. Billy Thompson was a redneck from the woods of Tennessee, and one of Neil's men. His grandfather was notorious throughout his hometown because of the moonshine he pumped out of a home-made still. A skill he passed on to Billy who shared his bounty in mason jars. Redneck he was, but Billy could track a king rat through a rain forest and take it out with a shot through the eyes from a mile away. His place on the team was invaluable.

Had been invaluable.

"How?"

"The official report said suicide. Post traumatic bullshit."

"That's crap." Shit rolled off Billy better than most of them. Last Neil heard, he'd married his high school sweetheart and was trying to put his military days behind him.

Rick took a drink. "That's what I said. The fact there was a report to hack into told me our guys were watching him."

"Why?"

"His wife disappeared. Rumor in his town was that she left with someone other than Billy. The official report was he drank himself stupid and jumped off a cliff."

Neil sat forward. "If Billy's wife ran off with another man he'd hunt them down and bring her back."

Rick smiled. "Exactly."

"So what do you think happened?"

"I think someone tossed him off that cliff. And whoever did it either has his wife, or killed her and no one has found her body."

"What makes you say that?"

"His wife, Lucy, worked at a local restaurant, waited tables. The day she disappeared someone saw her in the restaurant parking lot talking to a man. A man who wasn't Billy."

"Where did you get that information?"

Rick shrugged. "Several people were happy to share. It's a small town, people lower the volume on their TVs to hear their neighbors fighting. Cheap entertainment. The next day Lucy doesn't show up for work."

"And?"

"Billy comes home from his shift at the mill. The report said some of her clothes were missing, but her mother said the only thing missing was her purse."

"Did Billy file a missing persons report?"

"So the local yahoos can find her? What do you think?"

"I think Billy could find her faster."

Rick nodded. "Exactly. Except Billy stays home...doesn't look for her. There are three phone calls to his residence, all from pay phones. Who fucking uses a pay phone?"

"People who don't want to be seen."

"Exactly."

"When Lucy doesn't show up for work and her boss calls, Billy says she's ran off."

Neil's jaw twitched. "You think someone had Lucy and was calling Billy...taunting him? Threatening him? Demanding ransom?"

Rick pointed his beer in Neil's direction. "That's exactly what I think happened. Only I don't think they were after money."

"I don't think Billy had any money."

"Exactly. Which is why I think they were just fucking with him...making him bleed on the inside, ya know?"

"Jesus. That's sick."

"Some kids hunting came across Billy's body at the bottom of a ravine."

"Hidden?"

"No. On a path...or just off one. Whoever did this wanted him found."

Neil rubbed his jaw. "So you want to hunt down whoever did this to Billy?"

"Damn right, but that's not why I'm here talking to you."

"Oh?"

Rick's cold, hard stare met Neil's. "They found a dead raven shoved inside Billy's coat."

The chill up Neil's spine turned to blocks of thick ice.

Gwen twisted her pillow over a third time, finding the cool spot, and forced her eyes closed. Still, sleep eluded her.

He'd left. Walked out without as much as a backward glance. One minute he was standing guard, the next he was gone.

All she could say to herself was…*I pushed him to it.*

Karen and Eliza both suggested she move on. Regardless of the heat between them, if Neil never made a move things would never get off the ground.

Yet as they left the bar, Gwen could swear someone was watching her. Maybe Neil decided he needed to be stealthier.

Eliza suggested she take a couple of self-defense courses…buy a gun. If only to feel better about living alone. Leave it to Eliza to see through some of Gwen's armor. Gwen wasn't making a big deal about living alone, but the truth was, she'd never done it. Eliza had already shown her how to use a gun. Up until Eliza's marriage, there had always been a firearm in the house. Eliza's parents were murdered when she was a young girl. The man responsible promised to kill Eliza, too. Her friend had grown up in a witness protection program and carried a handgun for her own protection. Karen moved in shortly after Eliza moved out. With Karen around and the never-ending presence of Neil, Gwen didn't feel the need to own a gun.

But maybe she'd look into it now.

Through the etched glass of her *I'm fine on my own thank you very much* facade, she wasn't completely comfortable by herself.

The next day Eliza flew back to Sacramento and Karen went on her first official date with Michael.

At ten in the evening her phone buzzed, signaling a text.

I like him. Going to stay the night.

Gwen smiled and texted her back. *Call anytime if you need me.*

Karen's reply was an emoticon smiley face.

And so the evenings home alone begin. Gwen set the alarms, thought of Neil, and went to bed.

In the morning when she worked her way into the kitchen for tea, she noticed the back door open an inch. She could have sworn she'd shut it, but maybe she hadn't. The offshore winds, otherwise known as the Santa Anas, were tossing leaves around the backyard.

She was sure the motion detectors were going crazy and yet Neil hadn't called.

He wasn't going to call.

He'd made his choice.

"A week from Friday," Karen announced when she strode through the door midday.

"Welcome home."

Karen beamed. "We're getting married a week from Friday."

Gwen moved from her desk where she was searching the Internet for self-defense classes, and hugged Karen. "How exciting."

"We're going to fly to New York, grab a judge, and hide out in France for a week. I've never been to France."

"It's lovely this time of year. Do you *parlez vous*?"

"What about 'I've never been to France' did you not understand? I don't poly vu anything other than English and the occasional teenage gutter talk." Karen flopped on the couch and tossed her feet up on the coffee table. "I can't believe this is happening."

"Tell me everything."

Karen blew out a breath. "He took me to this hidden gem in Brentwood. The waiter knew him. The patrons craned their necks to get a glimpse of us. I asked him how he managed to go to the bathroom without someone following him. He told me he did it like women, in pairs." Karen laughed. "The fame doesn't bother him. He ignored the stares and eventually I found myself ignoring them, too. I talked about the kids at the center. He talked about his latest movie. Our conversation was entirely superficial while we ate. When we got in the car we headed to his house."

"Isn't it beautiful?"

"It's amazing. Not as stuffy as I thought it would be."

"It felt very welcoming to me."

"Once we were alone, we talked about the next year…if it all worked out. We watched a chick flick. I suggested one of his movies, but he said he never watches them. Can't stand to see himself up there. He likes drinking wine but pretends to like beer in public. Did you see his wine cellar?" Karen rushed the events of the evening together in her excitement.

"No, I didn't."

"Huge, brick walls, iron table…racks and racks of wine I know nothing about. That's one of the reasons we picked France. There are a couple of vineyards he wants to visit and what better excuse than a honeymoon?"

"I agree. So why did you stay the night?"

Karen smirked. "Some guy with a camera followed us out of the restaurant. When I left this morning, he clicked a few pictures. Michael knew he'd be there, waiting."

"There will be more of that."

"I know. It's only a year. Well, sixteen months. Crazy to be planning the divorce before the wedding, but Michael has the timeline down to the hour."

Gwen narrowed her eyes. "Is all of this for publicity?"

Karen shrugged. "I'm not entirely sure. He talked about his family, how they didn't know about him. He thinks his mom suspects, but not his father. A couple of women he'd dated, for the camera, made it clear to the media that there wasn't a sexual relationship, which I think started some inside rumors. The industry is rather tight-knit according to Michael. I'm not sure if he's doing this to save his macho rep, or to buy himself some time. He has three huge films he's involved in over this next year…and another two for the next. The millions he makes per film is enough incentive for him to get married."

"That's what I thought. Doesn't matter anyway. So long as you don't have any romantic ideas."

"He's sexy as hell but he rubs me like a good friend or a brother. No worries about me falling for him."

"Good." Gwen pushed off the couch. "You're going to have to show me a few things in our files. Though I doubt there will be much activity while you're prancing around France, you never know."

"Let me change my clothes first." Karen left the room and headed upstairs.

Gwen bookmarked the page she'd been looking at on the Internet and clicked into Alliance's main client files.

"Ewwh! Gwen, get up here," Karen yelled.

Gwen laughed as she walked toward Karen's voice. "Our naked neighbors at it again? They were up late last night."

Karen stood in the door of her room, not at the window.

Gwen followed Karen's stare.

The window in Karen's room was open a few inches and on a flower box was a mass of black feathers. "Is it a dead bird?"

"A crow, I think."

Gwen moved closer. Sure enough, the crow looked like it had attempted to peck inside the screen. The beak was caught partially inside while its body lay in the gardenias.

"I hate birds, Gwen. Bad Alfred Hitchcock flashbacks."

Gwen chuckled. She removed her shoe and tapped the end of the beak until it was free of the screen. She popped the screen free, and then using the tips of her fingers, Gwen managed to pick up a feather and quickly toss the bird to the ground below. "I'll put it in the trash."

"Thanks," Karen said shivering. "Ewwh."

Gwen chuckled as she left the room. "And everyone thinks I'm the weak one around here," she said under her breath.

Chapter Eight

Gwen drove through the gates of her brother's Malibu estate and parked her car in the circular drive. She waved at one of the groundskeepers and let herself into the house. "Hello?" she said as she walked inside.

The sound of soft heels meeting the tile floors preceded the housekeeper.

"Lady Gwen?"

"Hi, Mary." Gwen removed her sunglasses and set them with her purse on the hall table. "How are you?"

Mary had worked with her brother for as long as he'd lived in this house. She was the main cook and would sometimes help with other domestic chores. There was a full-time live-in maid and groundskeepers who went home in the evenings. And of course, Neil.

It was killing her not to look for him. He was probably in the guesthouse...if he was there at all.

Gwen told herself she didn't care. She was on a mission.

An independent mission.

"Did Samantha tell you I was coming?"

"She did. Will you be staying for lunch?" Mary asked with hope on her face.

"Bored, Mary?"

"To tears. I can hardly wait for them to come home."

They walked together down the massive hall to the kitchen. The kitchen and breakfast room opened to a great room with huge floor to ceiling windows. Beyond the swimming pool and patios was a breathtaking view of the Pacific Ocean.

"I'd be happy to stay for lunch so long as you'll join me."

Mary raised her eyebrows. "Wonderful. Any requests?"

"Anything that isn't prepared in a microwave would be super." Learning how to cook hadn't been part of Gwen's upbringing. Since moving to the States, she'd had to learn to fend for herself, and that meant plenty of ready-made microwavable meals.

"Coming right up."

"Wonderful. I'll be in my brother's study if you need me."

Mary smiled as she wrapped an apron around her thick waist. Gwen heard her humming as she left the room.

Blake's study was a painted in dark masculine colors with built-in bookcases and a desk that sat center stage. Brown leather chairs flanked the desk, with a couch and wet bar on one end of the room. Considering how much Blake despised their father she found it entertaining how the space reminded her of the larger study in Albany where their father used to spend all his time. The very same one Blake now used when in Europe. He ran his shipping business from both continents and did so quite successfully.

Not that he needed to any longer. Their father left his estate to Blake once he married and had an heir. Gwen and her mother were given small stipends on which to live. Small by their standards, large by anyone who hadn't lived in a country manor all her life with jets at her disposal and a clothing allowance that could feed small countries. Blake didn't feel the division of funds was fair so he added to her trust fund, not that she asked him to. Gwen knew her brother loved her. When he transferred the money into her accounts, she realized how much he'd sacrificed to obtain their father's millions. She also realized how different her father and brother had been.

Living in the small Tarzana house was a choice. One Gwen really did enjoy. But now that she knew Neil wasn't going to watch her every move, she needed to make certain she was safe.

Gwen crossed to where her brother hid his walk-in safe. The paneling on the wall looked like the others in the room, but when she placed her finger on a digital reader, the wall moved and a steel door stood in its place. A palm scanner opened the next door and she was inside.

Only four people had access to the safe: Blake, Sam, Neil, and herself. Gwen kept some of her own jewelry and funds in the secure space but that wasn't why Blake gave her access. At twenty-four feet by twenty feet, and impermeable from the outside, it doubled as a safe room. When Blake and Samantha took a private vacation, Gwen stayed with her nephew and Sam's disabled sister Jordan. Blake wanted to be sure that if there was ever a problem his family would be protected.

Gwen walked into the room and opened a drawer.

Inside, four handguns of different shapes and sizes sat next to open boxes of ammunition.

All she had to do was figure out which one suited her best.

She lifted the gun that looked like one that Eliza owned.

Always treat it like it's loaded. Eliza's words drifted in Gwen's mind.

She checked the chamber, found it empty, and noticed the clip sitting beside it.

"What are you doing in here?" Neil's booming voice made her jump. She turned toward him, gun in hand.

She noticed his gun in his hand and pointed toward the floor. "Good Lord, Neil, you scared me half to death."

He reached behind his back, holstered his gun, and stepped into the room. "Answer the question."

The sheer size of the man dwarfed the space. She turned away from him, doing her best to ignore his presence.

"What does it look like I'm doing?" She picked up the clip, tested its weight.

"That's not a toy."

"I'm quite aware of that."

"What do you need with it?"

"Nothing. Probably. But between Eliza and Samantha's advice, I've decided I should have something at the house should I ever need it." Samantha had agreed with Eliza's advice when they'd last spoken on the phone.

"You'll likely shoot off your own foot." He moved closer.

"Thank you for your vote of confidence but I'm sure I'll be fine." After putting the gun and clip down, she lifted a revolver. She'd only held Eliza's revolver once and couldn't remember how to check the chamber. She wasn't about to ask the man who just mocked her.

"Have you even held a gun before?"

She put the revolver back, skipped over the second larger revolver, and lifted another gun that was similar to the first. "Eliza taught me, remember?"

Neil grunted. "None of these are what Eliza carries."

"These look the same."

"Different calibers, different mechanisms."

He stood next to her now, close enough that she felt the heat of his body.

She closed her eyes. *I really have to stop torturing myself with this man.*

"They shoot bullets, don't they?"

"Of course."

She grabbed the first gun and the clip. "Then I'll be fine." She turned to walk away, and Neil placed a hand on her arm, stopping her.

His grip was firm at first, and then softened when she met his hazel eyes. "Eliza shoots a .38. That's a .45 and will knock you clear across the room when you squeeze the trigger."

She couldn't remember what Eliza shot, but apparently, Neil did. Gwen glanced at the gun.

"I'm not leaving here without a gun, Neil."

His hand barely rested on her arm now, but he didn't move away.

"Fine." He let her go, knelt on the floor, and opened another drawer. He removed a black case, opened it, and proceeded to place all the guns, clips, and extra bullets inside.

"I don't need them all," she said.

He cocked his head to the side. "You need to leave with the right one. You won't know what that is until you fire all of them."

"Oh."

They stayed for lunch, appeasing Mary, and then drove to an outdoor shooting range tucked in one of the many canyons of the California mountains.

The range was relatively quiet and it didn't take long to realize that she was the only woman there. A couple of men sent her an appreciative glance, but after noticing Neil at her side, quickly looked away.

The concrete ground was littered with shell casings, making it difficult to walk in high heels. Once they entered the area where the guns were being fired, Neil handed her ear protection. The sounds of the blasts were muffled, and Gwen had a hard time hearing what Neil was saying.

He set up their guns at the far end of the run and rested his hand on the counter. "I want you to try this one first." It was the largest revolver in Blake's drawer.

Its sheer size intimidated her. "Why that one?" Did he want to scare her away from guns?

"It's the easiest to shoot."

She huffed out a laugh. "I doubt that."

"I take my weapons seriously, Gwendolyn, and would never lie to you about them."

The fact he used her full name made her question her doubt.

She glanced at the gun and decided to own up to her lack of knowledge. "I've forgotten how to open and load it."

Neil brushed against her and picked it up. He pressed a button and swiveled out the round chamber in the middle. "There are six shots." He picked up the bullets, one at a time, and added them. "Once it's loaded, it's live. You don't have to pull this hammer back to shoot, but if you do, it helps with accuracy."

"How does it help?"

"It takes more pressure on the trigger to fire the weapon than one of these guns." He pointed to the guns with clips. "The added pressure messes with your aim, unless you're a good shot."

He handed her the weapon and nodded toward the targets on the field. Unlike the paper targets she'd used before, this range was full of swiveling metal that made clanging noises when hit.

The gun felt heavy in her hand. Heavier than the others.

Neil hesitated before moving into position behind her. He wrapped his arms around hers, holding her hands in his over the gun as he positioned them to his liking.

She swallowed. The thick feel of him holding her, even like this, made her breathless. The desire to lean into him made her dizzy. But she refrained. Every other time he'd been close to her, she'd practically jumped in his lap.

Not anymore. It was Neil's turn to make the moves. That is, if he wanted to.

She wasn't sure why he brought her to the range, outside of his instruction. Of course he could have suggested an instructor if he wanted to keep his distance.

But that wouldn't have been Neil. He didn't allow anyone to do what he did better.

"Ready?" His voice was muffled.

"What?"

"Are you ready?"

She nodded and closed one eye to see the target at the end of the barrel.

Neil cocked the gun and released her hands. He inched back, but she still felt his body against hers.

She focused on the beat-up red rotating triangle, sucked in a breath, and squeezed the trigger.

The blast kicked her back into Neil, but it wasn't that bad. In fact, it was better than what she remembered about Eliza's weapon.

"Did I hit it?" She hadn't paid attention.

"No."

Now that she knew what the gun would do, she cocked the hammer herself, took aim, and fired.

The triangle zipped in a circle.

She glanced up at Neil, whose eyes smiled even if his lips didn't.

She fired again and hit the same target twice.

Neil pointed farther out on the range. "Shoot there."

The second set of targets took a couple of extra shots to hit. But soon she found herself plucking away at them as if she'd done so for years. Excitement shot up her spine.

One corner of Neil's lips lifted.

You really are sexy when you smile.

"Try it again. Without cocking the hammer."

She concentrated harder, her tongue poked through her teeth as she fired the weapon. Sure enough, she missed her target, but at least it wasn't off in the bushes, which made her feel good.

They went through several rounds with both revolvers before Neil moved to the pistols. The smaller one felt like Eliza's but

Gwen's accuracy wasn't as good. After a few shots, Neil took the gun in his hand, narrowed his eyes, and squeezed. His arms didn't so much as move with the kick. He missed his target.

He readjusted his aim and fired again.

Gwen watched as he fired six shots, all hitting their targets at the far end of the range.

"The sights are off. I'll have to adjust them at home. It's shooting to the left of what you're aiming." He handed her the gun again. "Try and adjust for the gun's issue and hit something close."

She managed one out of five targets.

They finished with the gun she'd nearly taken home. Neil warned her about the kick and braced her body with his. She did her best to ignore the warm feel of him at her back and shot.

The gun tilted her back, into his arms.

"Wow." Her arms vibrated with the force of the gun.

"I told you."

She set the weapon down, not willing to shoot it again.

"Giving up?"

She narrowed her eyes and found him smiling down at her.

"You're taunting me."

"Maybe. But if you needed to use it, I don't want you unprepared."

He wrapped his arms around her again and picked up the gun. He held on to her as she shot the gun two more times, helping absorb the impact. The following rounds came close to their targets, but missed. When the clip was empty, Neil stood behind her with his hands on her shoulders. For a moment she stood still, enjoying the feel and scent of the man she'd fantasized about relentlessly since they'd met.

The range had emptied out, leaving only the two of them.

"Not bad, Harrison."

She laughed. He'd never addressed her by her last name. "Harrison?"

His hands softened on her shoulders. "In the military, we often called each other by our last names. Seemed appropriate with you out here lighting up the place."

He'd never, not once, said a thing about his military days. That he did so now felt intimate somehow.

"So they called you MacBain?" she asked, removing the plastic glasses she wore to protect her eyes.

"Mac. They called me Mac." His voice had softened, making it difficult to hear him. She tugged the earmuffs away and twisted in his arms.

He offered a smile, one seldom seen.

"Well, Mac, thanks for the lesson."

He hadn't moved away. His hands rested on her forearms. This close, she could see his eyes even through the dark sunglasses. They stared directly into hers.

Her heart kicked in her chest, firing signals throughout her body. Neil lifted his hand to her face, traced his thumb alongside her jaw.

She wanted his kiss so much she could taste it. For one brief moment, she felt him move into her. Then something snapped, and he moved away. His gaze, his body, his hand.

"We should go."

Gwen wanted to call him out. He wanted her; Lord knew she wanted him. So why did he hesitate?

What was so broken inside of him that made him pull away?

Chapter Nine

The silent ride back to Malibu ate at him.

His gut ached. The floral scent of the shampoo she used found a comfortable place inside his head and took root. He'd never again look at the froufrou shampoo section in the store and not think of Gwen.

He'd tortured himself when he'd wrapped his arms around her. Her tiny frame fit perfectly against his. Not that it mattered.

But it did. He knew it mattered. The only way he was going to escape her was to leave. Hire someone to take his place at Blake's side, pack his one bag, and disappear.

And what about the raven left with Billy's body? Was it a warning? A warning that wouldn't mean anything to anyone other than the remaining members of Neil's team?

More reason to pack up and leave.

But who could protect Gwen better than him?

Neil knew the answer before he bothered booking a flight.

He didn't need anyone thinking he cared about her, thus making her a target.

She stared out the window at the passing traffic on the freeway. She should have been riding in the back, where the tinted windows would obscure her face. But Gwen refused. Said he was no more her driver than she was his maid.

"Do you think about it…your time in the military?"

Her question came from nowhere. He wasn't sure how to answer it. "Neil?"

"Sometimes."

"Was it awful?"

He gripped the wheel, recalled the smell of her hair, and ignored the memory of burnt flesh and blood. "War is hell."

"I can't imagine. The only violence I've witnessed was my brother breaking the nose of a boy chasing me in school. And you and Carter fighting those men in Texas."

He felt his spirits lift. He'd enjoyed teaching the man hitting on Gwen a lesson in propriety. He flattened his lips and said, "Violence doesn't solve as many problems as it creates."

"You're probably right. The threat of violence does tend to keep people in line, however. Take today for example. We spent the day firing weapons. I doubt anyone would mess with you but I realize how I might be considered vulnerable. If the people out there who would do me harm knew I had a weapon, my guess is they'd look for an easier target. Don't you agree?"

"Some." *Purse snatchers and cowards.*

"I don't imagine I'll ever have the need to use the gun for its intended purpose. It does feel right to have one, however."

That, he completely agreed with.

Short of that ivory tower he thought of putting her in when he saw her, owning a gun was better than nothing.

"You'll need to keep it at the house."

Gwen nodded. "I didn't think to carry it with me."

He pulled off the highway and onto the street leading to the Malibu estate. "A Taser fits inside a purse. It's legal for you to carry."

"One of those electric zapper things?"

A rare chuckle rose in his throat. "Yes. One of those."

She smiled at him and damn if he didn't want to melt into that smile and forget every awful thing about his life.

"Do you have one?"

"No." He didn't need one. "But I'll get one for you."

"That would be lovely, Neil."

Only a lady would say a Taser as a gift was *lovely*.

Neil parked behind Gwen's car. He placed the larger revolver she liked the most inside her trunk along with an extra box of ammo.

She opened the door, and tossed her purse inside. "Thank you, for today. I feel better knowing I have the proper weapon."

He liked the ivory tower idea better. "You're welcome."

Neil stepped away from the car, intending to give her room to drive away.

"Oh...uhm, the alarm on the house?"

"Yes?"

"All the doors and downstairs windows have to be closed in order for it to set properly, right?"

He paused. Stepped closer. "That's right."

"Don't freak out," she warned him.

When a woman suggested he not "freak out," it meant he had reason to.

He lifted his hands in the air and forced the tension away from his shoulders.

"OK...well, I found the back door opened, just a little bit, when I woke up the other day. The alarm said it was engaged."

"The alarm won't set if a door is open."

"That's what I thought. With all the interference lately, I thought I should mention it."

"Are you sure the alarm was armed?"

"Positive. I checked it twice. Though I think the cameras and outside motion detectors are overkill, I do think a home alarm is wise."

"Did you set it before you came over today?"

"I did."

He fished his cell phone from his pocket, clicked on his mobile app of her home. "Karen's not home?"

"No."

The alarm said it was set, and the cameras didn't indicate any issues. He didn't like it. Any of it.

"I'm coming over."

Surprisingly, Gwen didn't argue.

"I have a few errands to run," she told him. "Do you mind looking into it without me there?"

He preferred it, actually. The distraction of her being there might make him miss something. "Not a problem."

"Thank you," Gwen said as she drove away.

Yet the farther Gwen drove away from him, away from the safety he knew he could provide, the less control he felt.

He hated a lack of control. Made him weak.

———

"So Blondie has a gun," the man said to himself as he witnessed the two leave the range.

His camera recorded them, found the subtleties of their behavior that he would analyze later.

MacBain wasn't acting alarmed. Didn't even realize he was being watched.

"You're slipping, dude."

He doubled around to his perch above the Malibu house and watched as she left alone.

He knew, without a doubt, that she hadn't mentioned the dead bird in her conversation with Neil.

If she had, he would never have let her leave.

Time to up the ante.

———

Kenny Sands, the owner of Parkview Securities, met Neil at the Tarzana house.

"This doesn't make sense." Ken stated the obvious.

Neil had run test after test. Sure enough, the back door no longer tripped the alarm. Yet when on a chime mode, a feature that let the homeowner know when a door or window was being opened, it made noise.

"There's been an unusual amount of noise in the backyard motion detectors, too. I thought I fixed it last week, but it seems to light up anytime the neighbors use their hot tub."

"That shouldn't affect it." Kenny picked up his cell phone. "Hi, Jane. I need you to send a team to 5420 Cherry Lane." He paused. "No, have them bring a full truck. We're replacing the wiring to the back door."

Neil moved into the backyard, looked around, and found nothing out of place. He walked to the back fence and looked over to the other side. There was a base around a Jacuzzi complete with a small bar set up. Lucky for him the naked neighbors liked to tub in the dark.

It was midday.

He glanced up at the second story of Gwen's home and noticed an open window.

Neil walked into Karen's unusually warm bedroom. He moved through it to the window and tugged it closed. The view to the naked neighbors wasn't ideal from this perch so he moved to the next room over.

Gwen's room was filled with soft colors and plush textures. Feminine, just like the woman. The space smelled like her too.

He peeked out the window. "Nice naked view." He'd laugh if it weren't screwing with his surveillance.

Something flashed in the corner of his eye. He looked beyond the houses to the hillside that separated Tarzana from Woodland

Hills. It was one of the nice features of the location of the house. There was one row of houses behind Gwen, and then a park.

For Neil, it was both a blessing and a pain. A blessing that there were fewer neighbors, a pain because anyone could be hiding in the acres of brush.

He searched for the source of the light but didn't find anything.

While Kenny's men worked, Neil took a walk around the neighborhood. Paying close attention to the house directly behind Gwen's. The shades were drawn and two newspapers were stacked on the front porch. There wasn't a car parked in the driveway. From the look of the neighborhood, most of the residents parked a car in the driveway or on the street. Very few houses had empty space in front of the garage doors.

Neil attempted a smile and walked to the door and knocked twice. No one answered.

He tried to look inside the bay window to the front room. They had blackout shades making it impossible to see anything inside. Blackout shades were a staple in Vegas, but in suburbia? Not so much.

Why would people who parade around the backyard naked hide from the front yard?

Neil knew he was as inconspicuous as a semi truck in a parking lot full of Smart cars. So instead of walking around the house, he moved away from the front door and back around the block. For the most part, the neighborhood was quiet. As much as he hated the fact that he couldn't control it in every way, it could be worse.

He turned a full circle, looking around.

He felt naked walking the streets in the wide-open world without the security of an AK in his hands.

How fucked up was that?

It didn't help that Rick had dropped a load of shit on his door two days ago. They were both putting out calls to the fourth man who made it out alive.

So far nothing. Mickey wasn't taking calls, or wasn't around. He could have gone back in. Units like his seldom left the military, making it a career for life.

He hoped to hell Mickey had gone back in. The thought of something sinister happening to him…to any of them, made Neil sick.

And Billy was dead.

How did anyone get past him?

Back at the house, the wiring for the back door had been replaced, the motion detectors in the backyard swapped out. Neil and the men who worked for him simulated several break-in scenarios, all of which screamed the alarm and notified Neil's phone and the monitors Dillon watched over at his base.

Neil checked the time, it was nearly five. He considered waiting for Gwen or Karen to return, but remembered Gwen's ultimatum in the bar.

Back off or step up.

She couldn't have made herself more clear and after spending the day at the firing range, she'd probably think he was stepping up.

And that couldn't happen.

He checked the GPS on Gwen's car, which he'd slipped under her hood when she'd purchased the car.

She was inching through traffic on the freeway, but headed home.

Neil made a point of pulling out before she saw him.

On his way to Malibu, he sent her a text, telling her the monitor and alarms were back up and running correctly. Told her to let him know if there were any more problems.

She didn't call.

He noticed when she arrived home. He watched her walk through the house, and then check the back door. A look of disappointment crossed her face as she moved into her office and turned on her computer.

Neil left the audio feeds on and listened to every sound in the house. A one-sided conversation on the phone led him to understand that Karen wasn't coming home again that night.

According to a conversation with Blake earlier that week, Neil learned that Karen would be moving by the following weekend.

Gwen living alone meant the noises of the Tarzana home were going to be his constant companion. Someone needed to look out for her.

Chapter Ten

"You can always back out." Gwen and Karen sat tucked in a private back corner in a Ruth's Chris steakhouse.

Karen shook her head. "No way." She lowered her voice. "The money's already in the trust."

"Doesn't matter."

Karen smiled. "It's going to be a great year, Gwen. It's like a long paid vacation where I get to meet new friends and spoil the kids at the center."

Gwen felt it was her duty to give Karen the out if she wanted it. In theory, getting married for a short time for a lot of money sounded doable...until one said "I do," then there were doubts.

Gwen lifted her glass of champagne and clicked it to Karen's. "To a fabulous year."

"Hear, hear."

They drank and Gwen continued. "You'll be back before Aruba, right?"

"Of course. That's on a Friday?"

"Yes. Why?" Gwen had confirmed the dates with Samantha and Blake, who were planning on going straight to Aruba from Albany.

"Michael told me his Fridays are almost always free. Even if he can't stay in Aruba, he can make it for the day."

"That's a bit of a flight for a day trip."

"Apparently he doesn't think so. Says he does that kind of stuff all the time."

"Eliza and I will be there early. You're welcome to join us if you can."

"I'll try. I assume your mother is coming?"

Gwen hadn't thought of her in a while. "I can't imagine her not showing up. Although I don't think I can stand one more pitying glance from her."

"What do you mean?"

"Always the bridesmaid, never the bride."

"Oh." Karen buttered a piece of bread. "I'm sure she just wants to see you happy. Most mothers do."

"If only I could have a fiancé by that Friday…then she would keep her comments to herself."

Karen raised her eyebrows. "You have a handful of men in a database at home to consider."

Gwen smiled. "I hadn't thought of that." And if she started to interview men to be her date, how would the man watching over her feel about that?

"On the other hand, I'll be invited to all kinds of industry parties over the next year. You never know who I'll meet."

The waiter arrived with their food. The rich aroma of the steaks washed over the table. There was something about being able to cut into a filet with a fork that made the dining experience even better. After refilling their glasses, the waiter left.

"Have you heard from Neil?"

Gwen used the excuse of chewing her food to keep from answering the question quickly.

"Not a word."

Karen shook her head. "What's his deal anyway? He was a marine, right?"

"He was."

"I guess that explains why he's head of your brother's security. But you'd think that would mean he'd be at Blake's side twenty-four seven. Even if that meant following Blake and Sam to Europe."

"The only times he's traveled to Albany were for personal parties and events. Otherwise he's stayed here."

"To keep an eye on the house? Seems over-the-top, if you ask me."

"Blake told me they had been friends before he hired him to be his bodyguard. Samantha indicated that Neil had some kind of loyalty to my brother, though I don't know what for."

Karen bit into her steak. "God this is good."

"The best."

"Do you think Neil saved your brother's butt in a fight or something?"

"My brother doesn't fight." Not with his fists anyway.

Karen laughed. "All men fight if they need to. It's in their DNA."

"I completely disagree. I've met men who cried over paper cuts."

Karen rolled her eyes. "OK...I mean men like Blake and Neil. Blake wouldn't stop his fists from flying if someone pushed him."

"I suppose you're right. I don't know what transpired between them that led Neil to work for my brother. I suppose someday I'll find out." Maybe it was time to ask her brother...or ask Samantha to find out for her.

"Neil seems so angry all the time."

Gwen felt the need to defend him. "Guarded. Not angry." She remembered the expression on his face when he'd fought the cowboys in Texas. His hazel eyes turned a dark shade of gray and the muscles in his neck strained with every heated breath. Now *that* was angry.

"Guarded, angry…whatever. I don't think I've ever seen him smile."

"It's devastating when he does." Gwen felt breathless just thinking of Neil's smile.

"Oh, man, do you have it bad. I hope you're not wasting your time with him."

"Can I tell you something?"

Karen leaned forward.

"The other day, after we went to the shooting range…I swear he was going to kiss me."

Karen blinked. "And?"

Gwen shook her head. "I don't know. He backed off. Snapped away really. Like I bit him or something. Do you think he's not taking advantage of what I clearly told him he could have if he were to ask, because he works for my brother?"

Karen shook her head. "No. Absolutely not. If working with your brother was an obstacle to getting to you…and he wanted you, he'd quit."

Gwen sighed. "I guess that means he doesn't want me."

"The man follows you around, and guards you as if you were made of glass."

"An obligation to watch over me isn't the same as wanting me."

"You said yourself he nearly kissed you." Karen sipped her wine.

"Then ran away. I've not seen him since that day."

"Something is stopping him, Gwen. Find out what that something is," she said. "And you'll find the problem."

Karen was right. "Do you think there was a woman…someone who hurt him?"

"You never know."

Gwen picked at her food. "Even if I do find out, there's no guarantee he'll come around." The thought depressed her.

"True. But will you live with never knowing whether things might have worked between you? So long as he works with your brother you'll see him all the time."

"I don't know what to do," Gwen admitted.

"You have one life, Gwen. And you're a romantic if I've ever seen one. You should follow your heart."

"So wait for him?"

"Waiting is passive. I'd never advocate you pine away for a man who wasn't showing interest. I suggest you set a time limit for yourself. And then move on. I know you told him to get a hint the other night...but you're not ready to move on."

"Not after the firing range."

Karen smiled. "Just promise me we won't be having this conversation next year at my divorce party...OK? If Neil hasn't stepped up, I'm going to kick your ass to move on."

"I can drink to that."

They did.

They finished their meals and stepped into the parking lot. Since Karen had started dating Michael the media and plenty of freelance photographers were often close by snapping pictures of her.

"Looks like the paparazzi took the night off," Karen said.

Gwen removed her keys from her purse as they stepped to her car. "I still feel like someone is watching me," Gwen said.

"I'd say you're paranoid, but I have to agree. Ever since Michael and I started to date I always feel eyes on me." Karen turned in a circle. "If someone's watching tonight, I think the stealth eyes are on you. The guys following me don't care if I see them."

"Neil?"

She giggled. "You think?"

Perhaps he did care.

Karen walked around to the passenger side of the car and squealed. "Eweeh."

"What?"

Karen backed away from the car and looked at the ground. "What is up with the suicidal birds?"

At her feet was another dead crow. This one larger than the last.

"Do you think someone knows you don't like birds?"

Karen's eyes widened. "Oh, you don't think...oh, yuck. You think this is here on purpose?"

Gwen reached down and moved the bird a few feet away. "Two dead birds in as many weeks. I guess it could happen."

"That's sick."

"C'mon. Let's go home."

That night they locked all the doors and checked all the windows...twice.

The news of Michael and Karen's wedding was everywhere by Friday evening. The media followed them to New York and reported them leaving via private jet, compliments of Lord and Lady Harrison, to take them to France.

Samantha insisted on lending them the plane. A flight to France for a honeymoon was a simple token for the newlyweds.

By Sunday evening, the media that had been attempting to get information from Gwen had left the neighborhood. There had been three phone calls over the past thirty-six hours. One from Eliza "checking in" and Samantha called to see if Gwen "needed anything."

And then there was her mother.

"You should return to Albany."

"That isn't going to happen, Mum."

Linda had always been very proper and direct. "You're not equipped to live alone, Gwendolyn. Blake and Samantha aren't even there."

"Mother, please. I'm not a child." *Lord, Neil must be loving this conversation.* That was of course if he was listening. Gwen glanced at the video monitor and rolled her eyes.

"What if I told you I was lonely?"

"I'd suggest you find a lover." *That ought to quiet mother.*

"Gwen!"

"What?"

"One does not simply find a lover."

Gwen laughed. "You're right. One chooses a lover."

Linda paused on the line. "Is that what you've done? Is there a man in your life?"

"If I told you there was would you leave me alone?"

"I'd insist on meeting him," Linda said.

"In that case I won't tell you."

"You were never this difficult when you lived here."

No. She was always perfect...the perfect daughter, the perfect sister. Perhaps that was what attracted her to Neil. He wasn't perfect. His edges were hard, rough, and complex.

"Gwendolyn? Are you still there?"

"Yes. Exactly where I plan on staying."

"Oh, very well. But be prepared for a proper amount of guilt when I see you in Aruba."

Gwen laughed. "I'd expect nothing less. Love you."

"I love you too, dear."

Gwen smiled as she hung up the phone.

Neil turned the Taser over in his hands. Damn thing was pink.

He felt a genuine smile on his lips when he looked at the thing. Only Gwen would carry a pink Taser. At first he thought, Hell no...I'm not buying a pink weapon.

But it was for Gwen, his little blonde fireball that held a gun with purpose and pride. *His?* He really needed to get her out of his mind as *his*.

His phone rang, removing pink Tasers and Gwen from his mind.

"Yeah?"

"Hey, Mac."

"Rick."

"Looks like Mickey is back to his day job."

"Confirmed?"

"Shit, Mac. You know that's impossible. When you're in deep, no one knows crap."

Neil remembered. Their last assignment was cloaked so dark he and his men didn't know what there were doing until they were in the air. There were no official orders, no files. What happened in Afghanistan didn't happen. Not officially anyway.

The deaths of his crew were "training accident fuckups."

"I'd feel better knowing where he was."

"You and me both, buddy."

"Where you headed now?"

"Billy's."

"It could be a trap." He should go with him.

"I don't have a wife, Mac. My family thinks I'm crazy and stays away as it is. There's no emotional garbage this asswipe can use against me."

Neil rubbed a hand over the stubble on his chin.

"I could use some backup, man."

Neil glanced at the Taser in his hand. Maybe it was time to move on. "I need to secure a few things first."

Rick blew out an excited whistle. "Hot damn. I knew I could count on you."

"Where are you now?"

"Washington State. Let's hook up in Colorado in four days. That give you enough time?"

He looked around the empty walls of what he called home. "Yeah."

"Rock and roll. It'll be like old times."

Neil thought of the ones who didn't make it home. *Let's hope not.*

As much as Neil wanted to leave the acting to the man Karen had just married, he needed to step up and put an end to any romantic ideas Gwen had about him. He was going to play with her mind and break anything that might have been between them.

He had to.

His conversation with Smiley reminded him why men like Neil didn't have normal lives. Look what love cost Billy.

Two hundred Taliban soldiers armed to their teeth, willing to blow themselves up for their cause didn't take Billy out...but add a woman to the mix, and his friend was dead.

The chances of finding Billy's wife alive were less than zero.

Being responsible for his own life Neil could live with.

Not Gwen's.

Neil worked his way to the back of the estate and let himself in the kitchen. Mary sat at the kitchen table with newspapers and glue everywhere.

"What are you doing?"

"Not cooking. I can tell you that."

The newspaper clippings were pictures of Karen and Michael from every tabloid in LA. He noticed one of Karen and Gwen eating in an outside café.

"It's a scrapbook for Karen. Can you tell I'm bored?"

Mary was a good woman.

"Women like these things," Neil told her.

Mary picked up a paper and looked at the one below. "Yeah, they do."

Gwen was art at the end of a camera lens, Neil thought.

He looked closer.

The girls were standing beside Gwen's car. Gwen had something black in her hand.

Neil grabbed the paper.

"Hey, you'll mess up my system," Mary scolded.

He read the caption bellow the photo. *Lady Gwen isn't as fragile as she looks as she clears a dead crow from Karen Jones's path.*

Every muscle in Neil's body tightened. He twisted the paper in his hands. The article had been written a week ago.

"Jesus." Dead crows…Ravens. Rick's words filtered in his head. *They found a dead raven shoved inside Billy's coat.*

"Neil? What's wrong?"

"I've got to go." He ran from the main house to his. He checked the monitors and Tarzana feeds. Saw Gwen wearing a bathrobe and cleaning dishes.

He picked up the phone. Saw her answer it.

"Hello, Neil."

The backyard motion detectors were fuzzy again.

"Neil?"

"What's going on in the backyard?"

"Not this again. Remember what we talked about? A simple hello goes a long—"

"Damn it, Gwendolyn. Skip it."

"Do not cuss at me, Neil MacBain, or I will hang up the phone. There is nothing going on in my backyard." Now she was pissed. Something he didn't hear very often, but at least she answered the question.

"Are the neighbors in the Jacuzzi again?" There was a light glow from beyond the reach of the monitors.

"I don't know. I think so."

"Go check."

"Neil, this is silly. We both know there isn't anyone roaming my yard."

His hand clutched the phone so hard he heard the case around it pop. "Please, Gwen. Just check."

Gwen turned her back to the camera in the kitchen, tossed the towel in her hand on the counter, and marched upstairs.

"This is the last time, Neil. Next time the monitor goes nutty you're just going to have to come over here and check it out yourself."

Gwen walked into her room and out of reach of the video monitors.

Then she screamed.

Chapter Eleven

Gwen dropped the phone and backed away from the window.

Both her naked neighbors were floating facedown in the water. Lifeless. Her body started to shake.

She needed to help them. Pull them out of the water. Call 911. Something.

"Gwen? Gwen? Fuck, Gwen?"

She heard her name. Didn't know where it was coming from.

The phone.

She dropped to her knees and the alarm in the house suddenly started to scream.

She jumped and turned toward the door of her room. Half expecting someone to be standing in it. It was empty.

"Gwen?"

Her fingertips found the phone. "Neil?"

"Jesus, Gwen."

"They're dead, Neil." Her breath came in short pants.

"Who?"

"The alarm. My alarm is going off." Her whole body shook. *What's going on?*

"I tripped the alarm from here. The police are on their way. Who's dead, Gwen?"

She looked toward the window. "The neighbors. In the Jacuzzi. I need to see if I can help them."

"No! Fuck. No, Gwen, listen to me! Stay inside. Stay in your bedroom. Lock the door."

"But I can help."

"Damn it, Gwen, no. You have to trust me. Where's your gun?"

Gun? Why do I need the gun? It was hard to think above the screaming alarm filling her house. Neil was frantic, which wasn't keeping her calm. Didn't she need to be calm?

As she asked herself those questions, she opened her bedside table, found her weapon, and grasped it. "I have it."

"Is your bedroom door shut?"

She scrambled to it, closed it with a loud bang. "It is. Do you think someone is here? Is someone here?" Was someone in her yard? She'd felt a set of eyes on her for weeks now. Did Neil know something?

"Hold on."

She glanced outside again but kept her body shielded from the window.

Only her bobbing neighbors were visible. Lights from several neighbors' houses went on. Probably because of the noise coming from her house.

She stepped away from the window, and pointed the gun in front of her as she looked in the bathroom, checked under the bed, her closet. Nothing. She released a shuddering breath.

She heard Neil talking to someone else through her phone. "Directly behind the residence. My client sees two bodies in a backyard hot tub."

Gwen scrambled into the middle of the bed and listened to Neil barking information and orders. His tone was deadly. One she'd never heard him use before.

"Gwen?"

"I'm here."

"Hold on."

Like she could do anything else. She asked herself why she wanted to live alone. This wasn't independence...this was fear. Raw unadulterated fear. Seconds ticked into minutes.

Her body jolted as the screaming of her alarm went silent. "Did you do that?" she frantically asked Neil.

"Yes. I'm in my car. On the way. Don't open the door for anyone."

She already heard sirens approaching from outside. "But the police."

"For no one. I'll let you know when I'm there." It was a twenty-minute drive under the best of conditions from Blake's home to hers. She didn't think she could wait that long.

"What's going on, Neil?" Something was wrong. Very wrong.

"Ten minutes."

There were flashes of lights behind her house. She crawled to the window and noticed the flashlights of the police as they roamed the neighbors' yard.

"Gwen?"

"The police are here." One of the uniformed officers moved to grab one of her dead neighbors from the water. Another man stopped him by pulling him back. The officer tossed something in the water, and the water sparked.

"Oh, God."

"What?" Neil asked.

"The police are trying to remove my neighbors but the water... It's charged. It just arced."

"Electrical current?"

"I guess. How is that possible?"

"Is there a power line down in the water?"

She looked around, didn't notice anything out of the ordinary.

"No." She heard the horn of Neil's car. "Be careful."

"Are you still in your room?" he asked.

"Yes."

Minutes ticked by at a painfully slow speed. Finally, Neil said, "I'm pulling onto your street."

She squeezed her eyes closed and thanked God he was close.

"I'm coming in now."

She heard him running up the stairs.

One urge from his foot and the door popped open, cracking the wood as it crashed against the wall.

Gwen flung the gun on the bed and jumped into Neil's waiting arms.

He held her. His massive arms wrapped around her in a cocoon of safety.

"It's OK."

She held him tighter. Buried her face in his chest.

"Shhh, it's OK."

"I've never been so scared."

"I'm sorry."

"Miss Harrison?" Someone called from downstairs. "Tarzana Police."

Neil loosened his hold and held her face in one hand.

Real fear traced Neil's brow. He tried to smile and failed miserably.

"Miss Harrison?"

"Up here," Neil answered for her.

The heavy feet of the officer made it up the stairs. He glanced briefly at the door and then at the two of them. The officer, a kid not much older than twenty-five, looked around the room.

"Miss Harrison?"

Gwen nodded, not trusting herself to speak just yet. Neil still held her and she wasn't about to push away.

"I understand you saw the bodies and notified the police."

"I was on the phone with her and sounded the alarm by remote access," Neil said.

The officer raised a questioning brow. "Remote access?"

"That's right."

Gwen's gaze slid to her blinds.

The officer moved into the room and looked out the window. "You can't miss that. You spy on your neighbors often, Miss Harrison?"

Neil's arm tightened around her. "You're out of line, officer." The anger in Neil's voice was thinly reined.

"Duly noted, Mr.…?"

"MacBain," he answered. "C'mon, Gwen, let's get you out of this room."

Gwen was still shaking as she made her way downstairs with Neil holding her up.

When she closed her eyes, she saw her neighbors bobbing in the bubbling water. How long would she live with that image as company?

Neil perched himself at the edge of the couch and sat her down beside him.

Another officer had made his way into the house. "Are you the homeowners?"

"I am."

"You reported the bodies?"

Gwen blinked twice. "So they are dead?"

The officer looked at Neil and nodded once.

Bloody hell.

The officer upstairs called his colleague.

"I need to talk to the police. Are you going to be OK here?" Neil asked.

Gwen wrapped her robe closer to her body. "I'll be fine."

"Where's your cell phone?"

"In my purse, why?"

"I need you to call Eliza, get Carter on the phone if you can. I need him to clear a path for me to see what happened over there with my own eyes."

Gwen cringed. "Clear a path? I don't understand. It's probably an unfortunate accident."

Neil looked around the room, spotted her purse, and brought it to her. "Just call her."

Eliza's voice might help to calm her down, even if Gwen had no idea why Neil insisted on sticking his nose into the investigation.

While Gwen removed her phone from her purse, Neil walked up the stairs to the officers in her bedroom.

The phone rang twice before Eliza picked up. "Hey, Lady... what has you calling this—"

"Eliza?" Gwen heard the distress in her own voice.

"Oh, no, what's wrong?"

Gwen closed her eyes; saw the bodies. "My neighbors...they're, they're..."

"They're what, honey?"

She swallowed. "Dead."

Eliza gasped.

"I was washing dishes. Neil called, pissing about the monitors in the backyard." Recalling the events now made her remember the distress in his voice. More than normal.

"And?"

"The monitors have been acting up a lot. They don't work when the neighbors are in their hot tub for some reason."

"The naked neighbors?"

Naked and dead neighbors. Gwen sucked in her bottom lip and refused to let tears surface. "Neil told me to go check if they were in the tub. I was pissing mad at him, Eliza. Ordering me around. I told him it was the last time I was running up stairs to look down at my neighbors. And then…then I looked. Then the house alarm went off, and Neil was ordering me to lock the door and wait for him."

"Oh God, Gwen. That's awful."

"Neil needs to talk to Carter. Is he there?"

"He's not. But I'll call him and tell him to call Neil's phone right away."

"OK…thanks, Eliza."

"I'll call you right back."

Eliza hung up and Gwen held her phone in her lap. Lights flashed out her front and back windows.

Two people were dead. Gwen wasn't sure she could live in this house alone after all.

———

"You noticed something abnormal on the surveillance system?" the sarcastic, wet-behind-the-ears cop asked.

Neil lied. "Yes."

"What?"

"I'll have my assistant make a digital file for you to examine." What Neil needed right now was to get out of the bedroom and over the fence into the neighbors' yard to check out the scene himself.

"Did you know the victims?"

"No."

"Miss Harrison?"

"You'll have to ask her."

"Who are you to Miss Harrison?"

Neil narrowed his eyes. "Her security."

"This is hardly an upscale neighborhood, Mr. MacBain. Sounds like the security system you have here and the surveillance is over-the-top."

Neil's jaw twitched. "If you'll excuse me, I need to investigate the scene."

"Private security isn't cleared, Mr. MacBain. I'm sure you know that."

Neil clenched his fist.

The cell phone ringing in his pocket directed his attention somewhere else and kept him from committing a felony.

"MacBain," he answered.

"Neil? It's Carter. What's going on?"

Neil turned his back to the cops. "Gwen's neighbors are dead."

"That's what Eliza just said."

"Mr. MacBain, this is an active scene, we don't—"

"I need clearance from whoever's in charge of Tarzana PD to check out the scene. And I need it before they fuck it up over there."

The officers looked at each other with slight smiles on their lips. *Cocky kids.*

Neil heard Carter talking to someone before he got back on the phone. If anyone could arrange his clearance, it would be the governor.

"I have someone on it. Eliza just called Dean." Good. Dean was a detective with the LAPD, and a close friend of Eliza's. "Do you think it's a homicide?" asked Carter.

"I won't know until I look. Hope the hell not."

"Mr. MacBain?"

"I've got to go," Neil told his friend. "Call Blake, tell him Gwen's safe."

"Will do. I'll call back if there's a holdup."

After Neil hung up, the officers started questioning him again. "Where do you live?"

Where he lived wasn't relevant and answering these kids' questions while the uniforms were running around outside was a waste of valuable time. Neil cut them off. "I'll talk to you after I've seen the area."

He returned to Gwen's side. She hadn't moved an inch from the couch.

"You all right?"

Her blonde head started to nod and then she shook it. "You don't think this was an accident."

Neil didn't confirm or deny.

"That's why you told me to stay in my room, get the gun."

Those few moments when she'd screamed and didn't respond to him on the phone were the longest in his life. He ran out of his house and broke every traffic law to get to her. Rick's words repeated in his head. *I think they were just fucking with him...making him bleed on the inside, ya know?*

Neil glanced at the officers as they walked down the stairs and out the back door.

He shoved his hand into his pocket and removed the crumpled up paper clipping of Gwen and Karen and the dead bird.

"What was this about?"

Gwen smoothed the paper on her lap. "Karen and I were eating dinner. She found the dead bird on the ground by the passenger side of the car."

"You look upset in the picture."

"We...we were a little worried. Karen found a dead crow outside her window in the flowers a few days earlier. She hates birds so she asked me..." Gwen kept talking but Neil didn't hear her.

Two...two dead crows?

"The crow in the window I didn't think much of. But this looked bigger to me, like a raven. I looked it up. Ravens aren't indigenous to this area."

"I have Raven in my sights, Mac." Billy was holding a sniper weapon and Neil was about to call the order to fire, save all of them the trouble of moving closer so they could get the hell out of there.

"Damn." Billy pulled back.

"What?"

"Kids. His kids jumped in his lap."

"Wait. We'll get closer. Make it clean." Less collateral damage.

"Neil?" Gwen's hand was on his arm, bringing him back.

"Why didn't you tell me about this?" He needed to get her out of there.

"We thought this was about Karen. A sick fan of Michael's."

It could be Gwen floating in a pool of water...and not the neighbor.

"Karen?"

"She hates birds. We found them in *her* window and on *her* side of the car."

"Mr. MacBain?" The officer nodded toward the back. "You've been cleared."

Thank you, Carter!

"Go upstairs, Gwen. Pack a bag. You're not staying here."

He didn't wait around for an argument. He moved out the back door and scaled the block wall.

The bodies had been pulled out of the water and were covered with sheets. The dozen officers in the yard were poking their flashlights around.

"Who's in charge?" Neil asked as he walked to the back of the hot tub.

"I am."

Neil looked over, and noticed a uniformed officer. "First on scene?"

"That's right."

Which meant he was waiting for someone of higher rank to show up and take over. "What do you know?"

"Each victim has burn wounds, one on the hand, the other the side of the face."

Electrocuted. "Where did you cut the power?"

"At the box."

Neil stood, moved to the side of the yard. Two cops were looking inside the box. One of them took pictures.

"Neil?"

Neil turned and saw Dean and his partner Jim walking his way. "Thanks for coming."

"Excuse me." The lead officer pushed his way between them.

Dean and his partner flashed their badges.

"You're out of your jurisdiction, detective."

Dean pointed to Gwen's house. "Do you know who lived in that house?"

The officer shook his head.

"The governor's wife. Anything that happens within a mile of this house is my jurisdiction. Now tell your guys to back off, they're trampling the scene."

The officer took Dean's advice and walked away.

"I love saying that." Dean's easy smile spread over his face.

"What happened?"

Neil brought them up to date. Omitting all information about the ravens. For now.

Dean looked around. "You think it's a homicide?"

"When's the last time you heard of a couple frying in a Jacuzzi?" Neil asked.

They walked back toward the tub. The other cops were standing aside.

Jim lifted a tarp. Neil didn't see what was underneath, and didn't need to.

"Electricity travels though the body and out just about anywhere. Frying everything in between."

"The water was still charged when the uniforms arrived," Neil told them.

He knelt down to the service door of the tub. One of the officers had already opened it. "Do you have a flashlight?"

Jim handed him one.

Neil peered in. Any possibility that this was an accident dissipated when he spotted the dead birds.

"What the hell are those?"

"Ravens."

Chapter Twelve

"Run, hero...run."

Playing with his prey was more addictive than crack. No wonder gangbangers couldn't keep their asses out of jail. They were all high and doing shit like this...well, not quite like this.

This was fucking genius.

He watched as Neil scaled the back fence and ran into the house. One suit followed him, while the other directed the minions.

He popped a sour candy in his mouth and watched the entertainment.

His binoculars followed Neil pulling the girl from the house and shoving her in his car. Neil tossed a bag into the backseat, and slammed the door closed.

"I thought you didn't care, MacBain. Thought you were leaving your princess."

He laughed, shoved more candy in his mouth. Now that Mac had proved the woman meant something to him, it was time to take her away.

Mac didn't deserve to be happy. None of them did.

Gwen fell into an exhausted heap on the bed in one of Blake's guest rooms.

Downstairs Neil appeared to be mobilizing for some kind of war. He and Dillon moved all the surveillance equipment into Blake's study, along with several large black boxes Gwen assumed held weapons.

She'd given up asking Neil for details. When he'd run into the house and found her packing a suitcase instead of a bag, Neil shoved a bare minimum of clothes into a satchel and rushed her to Malibu.

Dean followed him into the house and the two of them talked for half an hour before Dean left.

All Gwen wanted to do was sleep. Refill her energy reserve and sort out what had happened on this never-ending night.

She took a long, hot shower before climbing into the plush, welcoming bed. As she closed her eyes, she forced the images of hot tubs and death from her mind and focused on the memory of Neil's embrace.

———

It took Neil some time to remove the tracking locators for his phone, and on the cars they would be leaving in that night. He set the house system to produce static for ten minutes when he was ready to move. He was doing everything possible to leave the house and keep anyone from knowing about it.

After returning from the Tarzana home, his first thought was to hold Gwen in the ivory tower known as the Malibu estate, and find the man responsible for the neighbors' deaths…for Billy. Yet as he moved his equipment into the house and rebooted the system, he noticed two stealth cookies locked onto his system.

His state-of-the-art system had been hacked. Hacked so damn well that Neil couldn't find a physical bug. It had to be there, but he couldn't see it.

He knew now the reason he never found a problem with the Tarzana lines was because the problems manifested from the outside. The equipment used was beyond his knowledge. Every year the military came up with even more spectacular stuff to make their jobs easier. Ever since the invention of a bug, engineers worked to make them smaller and harder to detect. Well, this one he detected. Neil just couldn't find the damn thing.

With the news of Billy's death and the trail of dead ravens following Gwen, Neil knew he wasn't dealing with just anyone.

Whoever was behind the hot tub murders had a background in intelligence.

Since Billy was dead, Neil had to assume the person could overpower Billy physically as well.

Sitting in the Malibu house was a trap. Neil knew that now. Who knew how extensive this man's reach was?

Neil's brief conversation with Blake was met with resistance.

"I'll fly Gwen back here. She'll be safe at Albany."

Neil didn't agree. The only safe place for Gwen was at his side until he caught this dirtbag and took him down.

"She's safer here. With me. And before you suggest it, no. Don't come home early."

"Bloody hell, Neil. You expect me to sit here while people are ending up dead there?"

No. He expected Blake to come back as soon as the plane could lift off. But that would bring more people to watch over…more people for the killer to go after.

"Remember when we met, Blake?"

Of course he would. It had been the lowest moment in Neil's life. Six months had passed since he'd limped what was left of his team to safety. Three team members had been blown into so many pieces Neil couldn't identify them. Billy and Smiley carried Linden out, his left leg severed mid thigh. He died on the way home. His body couldn't handle the blood loss.

Neil never thought he'd have survivor's guilt.

Yet he did. He was alive and his men were dead...all because he said to hold the shot until they got closer.

"I remember."

Neil pulled in his memories, tried to keep what he said as cloaked as possible. Chances were, the man responsible for tonight was listening right now.

"What did I do the next day...after I sobered up?"

They'd met in a bar. And not a place Blake would normally walk into. Blake had returned to the States after his father's funeral and wanted to remain anonymous while he proceeded to get hammered.

They toasted each other for hours. Two strangers hating life and commiserating with a bottle. Neil had spent six months drinking to forget. He remembered saying that much to Blake.

Neil still wasn't completely sure just how much he'd told Blake about his time in the military. But somewhere at the end of the bottle, Blake pushed the wrong button.

"So that's it," Blake said. "You're done with life. Gonna spend the rest of it in a shithole like this until you're one of those vets on the street with a fucking cardboard box?"

Neil took a swing, connected his fist with Blake's jaw. Blake was on him in seconds. Managed a few good hits, too, but even drunk Neil outmaneuvered the man and had him pinned in seconds. He could have taken the fight further but the problem was, Blake was right.

Neil let Blake go and walked away.

In the light of the next day, once the fog lifted and his headache stopped screaming like a bitch, Neil remembered Blake Harrison and his shipping business. He also remembered Blake saying he thought his personal phone line was bugged but that none of the men he'd hired found a thing.

Within a couple of hours, Neil had a residential address for Blake Harrison and was on his way to Malibu.

He hid under a hat, posed as a gardener, and got on the property without even a dog sniffing at his feet. For a man as rich as Blake Harrison, his security was shit. Neil's own grandmother could walk on the property and jack his phone line in her sleep. And Nana was in her seventies.

Neil found the tap on the phone, removed it, and waited for Blake to come home.

Neil cornered Blake before he made it to the front door.

"What the hell?"

Neil tossed him the small tap disguised as a line clip.

Blake scrambled to catch it.

"That's your tap." It was Neil's way of apologizing for taking a cheap shot the night before. And maybe a thank-you for waking him up. Because while he was locating Blake, sneaking onto the man's property and taking out a tap, Neil remembered how much he loved to live. And he forgot…if even for a short period, he forgot about dead friends and body parts.

Blake stared at his hand, turned the clip over a couple of times. "No shit."

Neil turned away. Ready to walk from Blake's life forever.

"Hey. How'd you get in here, anyway?"

Neil huffed. "Your security is shit, Harrison."

"Want a job?"

Neil took the job. But not for the money. Neil had money… blood money is what that felt like. Blake invested Neil's salary into his own company under Neil's name. "A retirement fund," Blake had told him.

But Blake was a fucking ATM. The man turned leaves from a tree into hundred dollar bills.

And Neil took on the man's security.

Working helped heal some of the pain.

"I remember," Blake said on the phone. And then he was silent.

"Then you're going to have to trust me. And you're going to have to stay there. Keep your family safe."

"Gwen is my family."

"I know." But to Neil, she was so much more.

———

A hand covered her mouth when she woke. The room was pitch-black.

Gwen started to struggle, kick, and scream.

"Gwen! Shhh, it's Neil," he said in a hushed whisper.

She stopped struggling, but stayed on alert.

"I need you to listen when I let you go. Can you do that?"

She nodded.

He released her mouth slowly and spoke quickly.

"We need to leave the house. We have to go now." Neil was dressed in dark colors much like a midnight thief.

"Why?" Gwen matched his tone, keeping her voice low.

"No time to explain. You need to trust me. Do you trust me, Gwendolyn?"

His eyes were hard, searching…

"I trust you."

"Good girl."

He lifted his weight from the bed and picked up a small gym bag from the floor. "Here." He shoved some clothes into her arms as she left the bed.

"Why are we whispering?"

"The house is tapped."

She hesitated. "Tapped?" If her heart beat any faster, it would be a problem.

"Not now, Gwen. Don't turn on the lights. Get dressed, hurry."

She sat on the edge of the bed and pulled on the black pants he'd handed her. "Exercise clothes?"

"Easier to move in." He went into the connecting bathroom and rummaged around for less than a minute. She kept her back turned to him as she pulled a spandex bra over her head and followed it with the skintight shirt. She remembered packing the clothes earlier when she left the Tarzana house, thinking that she could use a little yoga to help ease her mind.

Neil returned, tossed a few things into her bag, and followed them with the nightgown she'd just taken off.

A hundred questions inundated her mind. Why were they running? Who was after them? Where were they going?

If someone had penetrated the secure fortress that Neil created for her brother and his family, then the enemy must be formidable.

She glanced at the clock. It was two thirty in the morning and something told her that life was about to change forever.

In less than a minute Neil swung her small bag over his shoulder and pulled her to her feet. "Not one word until I say."

She'd never seen Neil like this. His eyes appeared to see everything, even in the dark. The intensity of his stare and the taut muscles twitching under his snug shirt proved he was more alert than a cheetah ready to strike.

Neil kept to the shadows inside the house and out. They skirted through the courtyard and quietly made it into the garage. A second town car sat beside Blake's with Dillon behind the wheel.

Even standing right next to the car, Gwen found it nearly impossible to see the driver. She narrowed her eyes as they moved to the second car and he shoved her in the backseat. He took her head in his hand and gave a gentle nudge down to the seat.

Gwen took the hint and lay flat in the seat. From then on, the only thing she saw was the back of Neil's head.

He pulled on a stocking cap...all black. They backed out of the garage along with Dillon in the other car. Both of the cars inched up the drive in the dark.

Neil drove on a winding road, taking the turns faster than normal. Gwen braced herself to avoid being tossed around.

Adrenaline pumped as quickly as the car's speed. Gwen had to admit, if only to herself, it wasn't fear that charged her. It was excitement.

Even without an explanation, she knew Neil was protecting her and doing it so fiercely it sparked an unexpected flame of desire.

She shot her hand out as they rounded another corner.

Bad time to get turned on, Gwen!

It didn't help that before she woke up, she was dreaming of him. He held her with those arms of steel and leaned into her with parted lips. Then Neil woke her.

They hit a bump on the road and Gwen fell to the floor with an "Oomph!"

"Are you OK?" Neil asked as the car slowed.

Gwen scrambled back onto the seat. "Yes."

"Just a little farther," he said. "Then we'll switch cars."

"Can I sit up?"

"No. Not yet."

She stayed down and matched his silence with her own.

A lifetime passed in the backseat before Neil slowed the car down and pulled it off the road.

Neil slammed the car into park and jumped out. He opened her door and reached for her hand. Her stiff muscles protested as she stood and moved to a different vehicle.

What felt like forever was less than an hour. While Neil opened the trunks of both cars and transferred objects between them, Gwen sat in the front seat and stared into the night. They were parked in a commuters' park and ride lot with a dozen cars surrounding them.

Gwen waited until they were on a narrow highway without a car in sight before she uttered a word. "Neil?"

He glanced at her and then looked back at the road.

"What are you doing?"

His fingers gripped the wheel and for a full minute he didn't say a thing.

"Backing off wasn't an option."

At first, Gwen didn't understand what he meant. Then she remembered her ultimatum in the bar.

Gwen folded her hands in her lap and rested her head back on the seat.

All of her questions and more importantly, all of Neil's answers, could wait.

Chapter Thirteen

Heat-sensitive night vision goggles captured the cars as they crawled out of the Malibu driveway.

Both cars indicated the heat of the driver and heat in the backseat.

He scrambled from his perch, tossing the candy from his hand, and jumped into the front seat of his car.

Looked like MacBain was taking matters into his own hands.

"Wouldn't be good if you rolled over on your back and gave up, now would it?"

Both cars were identical, the license plates removed. His tracking was down.

Even a stupid man knew not to turn on his cell phone if he wanted to hide. Sooner or later he had to turn it back on. But the man wasn't in a hurry. In fact, he could do this all year.

The cars split up, going in separate directions. He took a chance and followed the car going east.

The other moved west.

The sun glistened on the horizon as it rose over the eastern sky.

Dark sunglasses kept Neil from staring directly into it. On his right, Gwen's head slumped against the passenger window and the even rise and fall of her chest told him she was fast asleep.

He kept his speed only a couple of miles over the posted limit. He didn't need something as simple as a speeding ticket breaking his cover.

The deserted highway stretched for miles in front of him. The only thing to break up the dirt landscape was the occasional high desert mountain range off in the distance.

And Gwen slept.

He was proud of her for what she'd done or maybe more importantly what she hadn't done. She could have insisted on knowing what he was doing, argued with him...but she hadn't done that. Gwen followed his instructions to the letter and he left Southern California without a good-bye.

Neil swept his gaze up and down her lithe frame. Dressed like a cat burglar, she'd never been more beautiful. And even though he never said one word to her about his naked thoughts about the two of them, someone else had figured it out.

Figured it out and used it against him.

Stay out of Vegas, Mac, he told himself. His poker face needed some work.

Gwen moaned beside him. A throaty sound that tightened his balls and made him squirm.

She blinked her eyes awake and stretched. "Good morning," she murmured.

Her simple greeting made him want to smile. "Good morning."

"Where are we?" She looked behind them.

"We'll be in Nevada in about half an hour."

"Nevada? Is that where we're going?"

"Driving through."

"Oh."

He waited for several breaths before he spared her a glance. "What...no questions?"

She smiled and something inside him burst. "Somewhere last night, between you dragging me out of bed and throwing me in the back of the car, and falling asleep once you stopped driving like a madman, I decided to take each moment as it comes."

"You're not going to ask me where we're going?"

"Would you tell me?"

No. The less she knew the easier it would be for her to keep where they were a secret. A stop at a gas station could result in a simple conversation that would blow their location.

"That's what I thought. Which is all well and good for a little while."

He only needed a little while. He hoped.

"Did you tell anyone where we're going?"

"No."

Her brother would worry, and her mother would be frantic.

"Are we going to call—"

"No," he interrupted. "We can't call…not until I say. The phones in Malibu were bugged."

"If you knew that, why not just remove them?"

"If the man following us thinks some of his toys are still in place he'll hear only the information I want him to."

"Then how are we going to tell Blake and the others that we're OK?"

"Leave that to me."

Gwen rubbed her forehead. "You think someone is after us?"

In the rearview mirror, a car approached. Neil kept his speed steady and squelched the urge to stay ahead of the car.

"I *know* someone is after us."

"Why me? I've not made any enemies here, or anywhere that I know of."

The car moved up on them fast and sped around.

Neil sighed. "Whoever they are, they weren't after you…they're after me."

"Then why did they murder my neighbors? How does that affect you?"

Neil swallowed, thankful his sunglasses hid his eyes.

"He was making it clear that he could get to you just as easily." It could have been her facedown in a bathtub. Lifeless.

"That's crazy, Neil. The house is wired from top to bottom."

"Yet the back door was open and the system was armed. Anyone could have come in."

"That still doesn't explain why someone would use me to get to you. You work for my brother and hardly give me a second glance."

He glanced…more than glanced. Someone had noticed.

"Neil?"

He decided a defensive tactic was best right at that moment. "We're stopping at the next open gas station. You can use the restroom, but don't talk to anyone."

As Gwen glanced out the window where not another living soul could be seen…not even abandoned houses were on the road he chose, he knew what she was going to say.

"I don't see anyone after us out here."

"Your accent will give us away if the man following us finds our trail."

"I hadn't thought of that."

"Leave the thinking to me."

The half smile on Gwen's face fell. *Oh, damn. Wrong thing to say.*

"I'm blonde, not stupid."

"I didn't say you were stupid."

"You told me not to think."

"No, I said leave the thinking to me. Bad choice of words. Until I figure out who's out there, and know you're safe, you need to trust me."

"I believe I've proven my trust in you by making the cloaked exit from my brother's home in the dead of night. I didn't do that by *not* thinking. I did that by making wise choices and trust. Both of which take thinking." She glared at him now, her brows tight together.

He gripped the wheel hard and searched for the right words to dig him out of what he'd just said to her. She wasn't a soldier under his orders. He'd do well to remember that. Finding his softer side was impossible when it wasn't there. He avoided deep conversations with women for this very reason.

"I'm sorry." *There. That should make her happy.* He dared a glance.

Not happy.

Instead of stepping deeper in the pile of shit he'd spewed from his mouth, he reduced himself to silence.

Painful silence.

The filthy bathroom provided little relief. But it was better than a bush on the side of the road. Although it killed her, she didn't utter one word while at the petrol station. She knew Neil was right about her talking to anyone. Her British accent gave her away better than her blonde hair and high cheekbones.

As for Neil's silence…he had no idea how proficient she was at the *silent game.* The British were known for their cool, dry humor and patient silence. In her family anyway. Americans were the ones who spoke excessively. She had to admit that chatting with her friends was much more entertaining here than back home. Eliza called Gwen on everything. In fact, Eliza had made the first comment about Gwen's attraction to Neil.

The big jerk.

Let me do the thinking.

She rolled her eyes as she pulled a paper towel from the holder so she could open the dirty door. No use coming down with whatever disease the bathroom was incubating.

The hot Nevada morning was even warmer in the black spandex clothing covering her body. The thought of taking anything off in the bathroom left her ill, so she decided to wait until they stopped for the night.

Besides, she wasn't even sure what clothes were in her bag. Neil had packed most of it.

She had grabbed a pony clip to tame her hair before running out the door, so at least her hair wasn't lying hot upon her back.

Neil finished pumping the gas and returned the spout while she took her place in the car.

In the center console were two steaming cups. The smell of coffee filled the interior of the car.

Neil took his seat, fastened his belt. "I know you like tea, but they only had coffee."

"Don't most Americans drink coffee in the morning?"

Neil pulled away from the pumps. "Yes."

"Then I *think* it's best I drink coffee. Ordering one coffee and one tea might give us away."

"Humph!" he said, with a grin on his face.

Chapter Fourteen

"What do you mean we're sleeping here?"

Neil had pulled the car far off the road and tucked it behind an outcropping of rocks that littered the Nevada desert. They'd driven until dusk and from what Gwen could tell, they were driving as slowly across the Nevada desert as humanly possible. No, make that meandering through the desert. They'd started out heading east, then north, then back to the west on a major highway for a short time then northeast again. And since she was hell-bent on winning the silent game, Gwen kept her mouth shut.

That was until now.

Not even the fast food Neil had tossed her raised her tongue.

"Yes here."

She looked out the window at the jutting cliff that rose to the left of the car.

"I don't see a hotel."

Neil backed the car up to the cliff, put it in park, and jumped out of the car.

From the trunk, he removed a pillow and blanket and tossed it in the backseat. "You'll sleep in the back," he said from the back door.

"You're serious."

"Problem, Gwendolyn?"

She pushed out of the front seat and glared at him over the car. "You know...I used to think you using my full name was endearing, now I realize it's thinly veiled sarcasm. Which might humor me after a shower and a good night's sleep, but I suppose that will just have to wait."

"We'll stay in a hotel once it's safe."

"And if I have to use the bathroom?"

He spread his hands open and looked around them.

Of course. Somehow, she knew the dirty toilets at the stations were a luxury.

"Did you at least remember a toothbrush for me?"

He moved back to the trunk and fished through her bag with a flashlight.

Gwen stood next to him to see exactly what he'd packed for her.

He pushed her knickers aside, a nightgown, socks, a real bra, a pair of jeans, and a couple of shirts. His hand wrapped around a hairbrush and deodorant before finding her toothbrush and a tube of paste.

"That's all you packed for me?"

"We'll find a place to wash what you have on."

She pushed him aside, grabbed his flashlight, and looked again. But no matter how far she dug the results were the same. "You expect me to wear two outfits and that's all?"

"One to wash, one to wear."

The expression on his face was a complete blank. She shone the light in his face and he turned away.

"Where's my makeup?"

"I'm sorry, *Gwendolyn*," he said dripping in sarcasm. "I thought finding safety was more important than packing your war paint. Besides, you're more beautiful without it."

"War paint?"

"A mask men put on their face before battle."

"Yes, yes, I know what war paint is. Why do you call makeup war paint?"

Neil pushed the flashlight from his face. "It's an American saying."

"Oh."

She batted a bug away from the beam of light and turned to the dark. After placing her toothbrush and paste in the backseat, she found an extra napkin from their pathetic dinner of warmed over hamburgers and fries and started to walk away from the car.

"Where are you going?"

She stopped, turned toward him, and raised her arm to the outside. "The ladies' room. What do you think?"

The flashlight kept her from stumbling over rocks and bushes.

"Watch out for snakes."

She hesitated but kept moving. *Of course.* He would have to pick a part of the world infested with poisonous snakes to hide out.

A large rock separated her from Neil. She was about to set the flashlight down when he called out. "And coyotes. They run in packs. If you see one, there are three surrounding you."

"Brilliant," she whispered to herself. She flashed the light in a full circle, assuring herself she was alone.

When she finished, she walked quickly back to the car. Neil leaned on the hood, his arms crossed over his chest.

"That wasn't so bad, was it?"

She grabbed her toothbrush and paste with a bottle of water from the car. "Not bad at all…if you enjoy relieving yourself with the snakes and coyotes." She swatted a bug from her arm before splashing water on her hands in a feeble attempt to wash them. After smothering the tip of the brush with minty paste, she shoved it in her mouth and tried to wash the day's greasy food away.

Neil was watching her, a smile on his face.

"What's so amusing?" She never saw the man smile yet he did now at her expense.

"Only you can make peeing in the bushes sound elegant."

"Did not."

His smile only grew with her agitation.

"Errr!" She moved behind the car, rinsed out her mouth, and returned to him.

The beam of light found his face again. "You're laughing at me."

"Relax, Gwen. I'm not laughing at you."

She swatted another bug and found three more ready to land on her.

Neil pushed off the car and took the flashlight from her fingers. He switched it off and plunged them into the dark. "There. No light, no bugs."

The light from the moon was barely visible as she cast her eyes to the sky.

She gasped. "Oh, wow."

"Beautiful, isn't it?"

"Magnificent." Undaunted by the city lights, the night sky held millions of stars. "I've never seen it quite like this." While staring at the sky, Gwen didn't mind their stop in the desert nearly as much as she had a moment ago.

"The desert has the best view of the universe," he muttered.

She leaned against the car and tilted her head back. After a few minutes she asked, "Do you ever wonder if there's something else out there?"

"Intelligent life?"

"Yeah."

Neil sighed. "I hope so."

She smiled at that. "Me too. I'd hate to think we're it."

"When I was a kid, I wanted to be an astronaut."

Gwen looked at him. "You did?"

"Yeah."

"Why didn't you pursue space?"

"I don't know. Lost interest. Moved on."

She understood that. "I wanted to be a ballerina."

"What stopped you?"

The hair on her arms stood up and the cool night made her shiver.

"You'll laugh if I tell you."

"I don't smile, so laughing is out of the question."

She giggled, completely unprepared for a joke.

Neil tried to hide his smile.

"I was too fat."

His jaw dropped. "You don't have an ounce to spare."

"I know. Never have…but prima ballerinas eat salad and question the dressing. I enjoy food too much." She returned her stare to the stars and rubbed her arms. "I still enjoy the ballet. The grace and beauty of the dance."

Neil shrugged out of his jacket and wrapped it over her shoulders. She snuggled into his side and surprisingly he kept his arm on her shoulders. "Thank you."

He gave a passing smile and looked up again. "I've never been to a live stage show. Outside of a rock concert."

"Really? Why?"

"Never occurred to me to go."

Her head rested on his shoulder as they talked. "I suppose the wealth I've always been surrounded by has afforded me many fine things in life. But you know something?"

"What?"

"I've never seen this, a night sky so crisp and clear with stars that look like the finest diamond in a bright light."

"The best things in life cost nothing."

True.

A star shot across the sky. "Did you see that?" she asked.

"Yeah."

She closed her eyes and wished they'd make it home safely.

"What are you doing?"

She opened her eyes and found him staring at her. "Making a wish. C'mon, make a wish upon a falling star…surely you've heard of that."

"Ahh." He was smiling again and the sight took her breath away.

"Are you going to make a wish?"

He shook his head.

"Why not?" She turned to him, his hand rested on her arm.

"I don't believe in wishes."

She huddled under his coat. "It's only a small fantasy, or desire, to wish for something. It's meant to be fun."

His smile fell and his gaze slid to her lips.

"It's OK to have fun once in a while, Neil."

She caught his eyes again, and drowned in his gaze. He leaned in and she made a second wish, his wish, that he not pull back this time.

Neil's hand moved up her arm and pulled her closer before her wish came true. There, in the middle of the desert filled with wild animals and a zillion stars, Neil kissed her. Hot, desperate kisses that filled every lonely pore of her body.

Gwen skirted her hands up his thick chest and clawed into his skin. She opened for him, accepting the feeling of his tongue alongside hers. She couldn't breathe, his embrace was so hard, but she didn't care. She could breathe later. Now was the time for feeling. As in how his hand found the back of her head and he guided her where he wanted. It was then she knew that she would give him anything should he ask.

Her dreams didn't prepare her for his touch. She pushed into him, felt his arousal, and wanted all of him.

If his kiss was any indication, he wanted her, too.

So why was he pushing her away?

His hot breath blew upon her cheek. "Gwendolyn," he sighed.

"I don't want you to stop," she confessed.

The arms that held her tightened.

"You're a distraction. Distractions get you killed."

Was he saying this to himself? Or to her?

"There's no one out here but us." And wild, hot sex, even on the hood of the car, was better than backing away now.

"We can't do this." He took her head in both hands and looked into her eyes. "Not now."

She could taste the argument on her lips.

She swallowed it.

I've waited this long. I can wait a little longer. Now that she'd sampled him, she'd taste him on her lips every time she thought of him.

———

Blake intended to follow Neil's advice. Until he'd heard that he and Gwen had left in the middle of the night and hadn't been seen since. At that point, Blake told his pilot to fuel his private jet and he kissed his wife and son good-bye.

Samantha hadn't been happy about being left in Albany, but a stomach flu kept her from using her power over him to let her come. If Neil's concerns were even half validated, Blake didn't need his family underfoot or in harm's way while he searched for his sister and bodyguard.

Once the jet set down on the west end of the runway and customs cleared him, Blake walked to the car waiting to take him home.

"Mr. Harrison?"

Not used to seeing anyone but Neil as his driver, Blake did a double take.

"First Class Services sent me." First Class Services was a company Blake had used from time to time. He needed to thank Sam when he talked to her later that night.

Blake nodded and ducked into the backseat. Dean was sitting on the opposite seat, a smirk on his face. "Welcome home, Your Grace."

Blake shook the detective's hand. "Knock that Grace crap off, Dean. What the hell is going on?"

Dean nodded toward the driver who inched off the runway.

"All their drivers are cleared before they get behind the wheel."

Dean sucked in a deep breath.

"I'm not sure what's going on, Blake. Eliza called me. Told me about the dead neighbors. We tuned into the radios of Tarzana's men…heard the calls going back and forth. They weren't happy about having to let Neil poke around and even less excited to see us arrive. At first glance, it looks like birds nested inside the hot tub's electrical system."

"And at second glance?"

"We don't have that yet. Homicide is going over the place with tweezers now. No one thinks it's an accident. Spontaneous electrocutions in hot tubs don't happen. Not unless the wiring with the tub had been tampered with. Which brings me to the victims themselves."

"What about them?"

"They were squatters."

"Squatters?"

"The whole damn country is filling up with them. People who move into abandoned or bank-owned homes and take up residency. Banks hate being landlords and many of the properties they've foreclosed on in the last five years are still vacant. People move in, get a bill or two in their name, and now the bank has to evict them. There are groups of people all over who organize squatting."

Blake shook his head. "So these people live free for what? Six months?"

"Or a year...sometimes longer. Only when a real estate agent comes around to inspect do they find the problem. Hell, San Francisco banks can own houses in Pacoima, and use San Diego agents to handle selling them. Needless to say, many times the agent never even sees the house. It's a mess."

"How the hell do they get the power turned on?"

"In this case, they were stealing power from the neighbors, Gwen and Karen included."

"Neil told me there were problems with the monitors at the house every time the neighbors used the Jacuzzi."

"And he never found the problem because he didn't have access to the neighbors' house. The fact that the squatters stole the power leads me to believe there could be a plausible explanation for their demise."

Oh, now Blake was very confused. "If that's true then Neil overreacted?"

"I'm not saying that yet. Neil doesn't strike me as an impulsive man. He's so damn quiet most of the time I don't have a clue what's going on in his head."

Yeah...but Blake remembered a time when Neil was as impulsive as a teenager getting lucky for the first time.

"Where the hell is he?"

"Don't know. He was ripping the place apart before I left your house. You'll see the mess he left behind. All his equipment is in your den. It's like he was setting up a fortress in there. Scared the shit out of Mary."

"And Gwen?"

"She was already upset about the neighbors. I came back yesterday morning and found them gone. Dillon gave me this." Dean handed him a handwritten note.

Dean
Keep all conversations outside of the Malibu and Tarzana houses. Everything I set up has been compromised.
I will notify you in seventy-two hours with more information.
If you don't hear from me, have Carter contact the Commander in Chief. Give them my name. And code name: Raven.
Mac

"Seventy-two hours?"

"Thirty-six as of this morning."

Blake ran a hand through his hair. "Commander in chief? Who is he talking about?"

Dean leveled his eyes with his. "I think he's talking about the president."

Blake's skin chilled. What the fuck did Neil drag his sister into?

Chapter Fifteen

Two consecutive nights of sleeping in the backseat of a small car was enough. Sure, it helped that Neil had managed to find two of the most beautiful places in which to camp, but enough!

The Nevada morning had taken her by surprise. The cliff they'd parked next to jutted hundreds of feet in the air with nothing but bright blue sky beyond. In the light of day, their impromptu campground felt less threatening.

Nothing prepared Gwen for Utah. She'd seen pictures, but had never been. The landscape was candy for her eyes. She sounded like a recording with her constant "brilliant, and stunning" being uttered from her lips.

The fierce winds that shaped the cliffs and vistas also blew their tiny car around.

"It's lovely," she said as they rounded another corner and one more picture worthy view met her eyes.

"It is."

He hadn't done more than brush his hands against hers since their kiss. He seemed to have found the comfortable distance he'd said he needed in order to stay alert. That didn't mean she didn't see him watching her every so often.

Neil had three days' growth on his face, and she loved it. Handsome, in his harsh way, he somehow softened with the beard.

His short hair made the beard look deliberate instead of lazy. She wouldn't even mind the scrape of it on her skin. Everywhere.

He had paid for everything with cash. Even Gwen, who hadn't watched that many movies about fleeing men and women, knew that credit cards could be traced. They were completely off the grid, as they say. No one knew them, no one would be able to find them like this. With anyone but Neil, the thought might frighten her. Instead, she felt liberated.

"Please tell me we'll find lodging tonight."

"We'll see."

"Neil, please. My clothing needs a good wash and I don't think you've slept more than an hour or two at a time."

"I don't need a lot of sleep."

"Oh, posh. Everyone needs to sleep. My attempts to clean up have been less than adequate. A bed and running water, please." She poured sugar into her request. "You know no one is following us out here."

He made a point of checking the rearview mirror.

"There's no one back there."

He sighed. "We need to buy a few things...before we check into a hotel."

She clapped her hands like a schoolgirl, jumped over the seat, and planted her lips to his rough cheek. "Thank you. I can't wait to be clean again." She settled back in her seat and counted the mile markers to the next town.

They found a corner store that seemed to have a little of everything. Like a mini Walmart, there was clothing for the whole family in a few aisles and groceries in the other.

"We won't be here long. Don't talk to anyone."

Gwen made a keying motion on her lips and smiled. He handed her two twenties. "I'll grab some food, you get whatever you need."

She hopped out of the car and practically skipped inside the store. After grabbing a basket and finding the shampoo aisle, she bought a couple of travel size shampoo and conditioners, soap, and a razor. She walked past the hair dye and stopped. She found a washable tint in both brown and red, tossed them inside. Lip gloss, bug repellant. *The important things.*

A woman walked past her and Gwen pretended to read the back of one of the boxes.

She wasn't sure how long she'd taken, so she headed to the register and noticed one more item she had to buy.

Condoms.

———

It never ceased to amaze Neil how people responded to the simple things in life after they'd done without them for a while.

Gwen's smile lit up her face as they climbed back into the car.

"Get everything you need?" he asked.

"I'm sure I forgot something, but I managed the essentials."

She unscrewed the cap of the small shampoo and brought it to her nose. "Lovely." She pushed it in his face. "Smell."

"Smells like you."

"Not yet, but soon."

He pulled out of the parking lot and watched the rearview mirror until they were back on the road. They'd find a hotel that wouldn't ask questions and he'd make a phone call in the morning once they were far away from the place they slept.

It was time to start leading his prey.

Being the prey wasn't an option.

Not any longer.

He still needed to work out how to keep Gwen far from the action when it went down. A couple of ideas swam inside his head, each nearly impossible for its own reason. He still had a few days to figure it out.

"You're frowning. What's wrong?"

"Nothing."

"I'd love to believe you, but my guess is you're trying to work out what to do next. We've left California, but we can't run forever. Though a little while might be fun."

He felt the frown on his face lifting. "You like running?"

"Come now, Neil, have you ever seen such a beautiful place in your life? I would never have seen this had you not dragged me out of the house in the middle of the night."

"There's nothing stopping you from taking a road trip."

"When there are perfectly good airplanes to take me where I want to go? I would never have chosen to take a car."

"Sometimes the journey is the destination."

"Hmmm," she hummed. "I like that. Anyway, you're worried about what comes next. Am I right?"

"Worried, no," he lied.

"Perplexed then?"

He didn't answer.

"Sometimes talking about it helps you work it out."

He couldn't tell her he planned to find an ivory tower for her, lock her inside, and then go fight the bad guy. Neil didn't think she'd sit back and let that happen. She was a lot better at the cloak-and-dagger life than he thought she'd be and would probably insist on coming along to help.

"Women talk, men think quietly."

"Is that your way of telling me to stop talking?"

"When have I ever been that polite?"

She leaned against the seat back and smiled. "Oh, you're quite right. You'd tell me to shut up if you didn't want to hear me any longer."

"Finally," he said laughing. "The woman understands me."

"The hell she does."

His jaw dropped.

"What?" she asked.

"You said *hell.*"

"Of course I said hell. I'm not a prude. I did live with Eliza, you know. The woman can make a sailor blush when she wants to."

Neil kinda liked that about Eliza. He supposed he admired her battle-tested spirit as well. Carter was a lucky man.

"You don't know how happy it makes me to hear you profess you're not a prude."

She ran a hand through her hair that she'd left loose since they'd pulled away from the store. "Oh, why's that?"

He nodded to the backseat. "I bought you something new to wear."

Gwen's face lit up, her grin nearly blinding him. Her seat belt was off and she was reaching in the back in seconds.

Her body stilled.

"What the?"

"You said you're not a prude."

She twisted back into her seat, his purchases in her hands. "You're joking."

The look of horror on her face brightened his. He for one couldn't wait to see her in his choice of clothing.

"Are these shorts?" She lifted the teenybopper shorts that only sported enough material to cover one cheek modestly.

"Those are shorts."

"They won't cover my knickers, Neil."

He'd seen her *knickers.* They'd cover a thong plenty.

The red and white checkered top was right off the queen of the Fourth of July parade.

"At least the shoes are cute," she said, dangling the pumps with a finger. "Cheap, but cute."

"You like?"

"It's appalling."

You can take a Lady out of the castle, but not the castle out of the Lady.

"That's what I was going for."

"Why?"

"You'll see," he told her.

"It better be good." She tossed the clothes back where she'd found them. "Or I'll choose an outfit for you." She leaned back and closed her eyes. "And I have a fondness for black leather."

———

Twenty miles outside of town, Neil stopped at a gas station and told her to change. She grumbled, but marched to the bathroom all the same. "And do something equally appalling with your hair."

He chuckled as he walked into the convenience store and bought a pack of gum and a pack of cigarettes.

Outside the bathroom, he leaned against the hood of the car… waiting. He kept checking his watch, wondering if she'd ever come out. He moved to the door and gave a quick knock. "Everything all right in there?"

"I look ridiculous."

"Scared, Princess?" he taunted her. Something he noticed worked on this trip. And here he thought he knew Lady Gwendolyn better than most. He hadn't known shit.

"I'm not scared."

"Uh-huh!"

He backed up to the car and waited.

Finally, the door to the bathroom opened. Her heeled foot carried her out the door. She tossed her bag of clothes to the ground and spun in a circle.

"Sweet Jesus," he whispered as he pulled his sunglasses off his face. He already knew her legs were long and elegant, but he had no idea how far up they went. The shorts fit like a second skin. When she turned for him, her ass did indeed peep out from below. She'd buttoned the shirt up high and kept tugging on it. A large portion of her hair was brushed to one side and put in a pigtail.

Yeah, she looked like a schoolgirl fantasy hooker playing grown-up with the heels.

Blood shot from his head to his cock.

"You're staring, Neil."

He swallowed and took a step toward her. The shoes brought her closer to his height, but he still had to look down at her by several inches. Gwen stood perfectly still as he reached out and unbuttoned the shirt until the creamy expanse of her breasts were clearly visible.

He licked his lips and ignored the feel of her soft skin as it grazed the backs of his fingers. He then gathered the edges of the bottom of the shirt, undid another button so only two were fastened, and tied the ends in a knot, tucking it under her ample breasts. With her midriff exposed, he stepped back and examined his creation.

"Perfect."

"For what? A twenty-dollar romp from the streets?"

A slow smile took over the muscles in his face.

"Oh, no, Neil you don't expect me to act like a…"

"Where's your sense of adventure, Princess?"

"I left it, along with my dignity, in the bathroom."

"I'm not asking that you parade around town like this. We just need to make walking into a hotel as believable as possible."

"I feel naked."

Almost. "We can sleep in the car again."

She dropped one hand to her hip. "That was mean."

"Your choice."

"Fine!" She walked toward him, stopped at his side, and pressed her breasts into his arm. "Black leather pants," she whispered in his ear. "Maybe a studded collar."

His temperature shot up ten degrees. *You're in trouble, Mac. Serious trouble.*

Chapter Sixteen

Eliza met Karen and Michael at the airport. Their "honeymoon" had been cut short by two days.

Michael suggested they return to France later between movies to make up for the interruption.

Karen ran into Eliza's embrace. "We came back as soon as possible."

"Thanks. I'm sorry we had to interrupt your vacation," Eliza said to both of them.

"Dead neighbors and missing people sounds more like something I'd find in a movie script than real life," Michael pointed out.

Eliza nodded. "I'm sorry. We haven't met," she said pushing her hand in front of his to shake.

"Oh...my bad. Michael, this is Eliza Billings." Karen introduced them, watched them shake hands. "Eliza, Michael Wolfe... my temporary husband," she whispered so only the three of them heard.

Michael winked at her. "No introduction needed for the First Lady of the state."

"Back at ya, movie star."

Michael smiled, already at ease in Eliza's presence.

They moved to a waiting limousine, with a security detail following them. Karen waited until they were in the back, the window between the passenger and driver sealed before she spoke.

"What happened?"

"I don't think any of us really know. That's why we need you to share any information you know to help us figure it out."

"I was in France. How can I know anything?"

"You've been living with Gwen…knew all about the neighbors' hot tub habits…you know plenty."

"All I know is Gwen and Neil have disappeared and the neighbors are dead. Michael and I laughed about the hairy naked neighbor throughout France. God, I feel bad now."

"How were you to know?"

She shrugged. "I didn't. The first time they were out there, I was all *come quick, Gwen. Look.*" She shook the once joyful memory from her head. "They're dead?"

Eliza's gaze moved from Michael to Karen. "Electrocuted."

"And it wasn't an accident?"

"No…or at least, we don't think so."

There was a hesitation in Eliza's voice. "You don't *think* so?"

"Neil phoned Blake shortly after it happened. Gwen called me. Neil sounded lethal."

"Lethal?" Karen interrupted. "Neil is never anything other than painfully silent."

"In Carter's words, 'I've never heard a more deadly voice in my life.' He had Carter call in a favor so he could investigate the neighbors' backyard after the police arrived. According to Dean, they found a bunch of dead birds in the Jacuzzi and Neil freaked."

Karen's body chilled. "Birds?"

"Yeah, ravens. We don't even have ravens in this part of Southern California."

Karen ran her hands up her suddenly chilled arms.

"Karen?" Michael asked...looking at her. "You OK?"

No! She was anything but OK. The memory of the dead bird, a bird she assumed was a crow but could have been a raven, on the sill and again at the door of the car at the restaurant. Now two people were dead.

"Karen?"

"Are you sure it was a raven?"

"A couple actually...why?"

"I think they were murdered. Neil needed to get her out of there." And there was no guarantee she was safe either.

———

"Chew this." Neil shoved a stick of gum in her mouth.

They were sitting on a dark road on the outskirts of town. From the looks of the lights in the distance, it was a small town with only a half dozen hotels at best.

"Why?" she asked, accepting the gum and making quick work of bringing the stiff substance into submission.

"Chew with your mouth open?"

She opened her mouth and tried. Then started to laugh.

"Sleeping in the backseat sound good to you, Gwendolyn?"

She tried harder. But chewing with her mouth open went against every grain in her body.

"Better?"

He nodded. "Now slouch."

She pushed her shoulders forward and thought of a hot shower.

"Good," Neil praised.

She sat, hunched in the passenger seat chewing her gum like a cow in a field.

"OK...good." Neil rubbed his hands on his jeans before gripping the wheel. "I'm going to go in and book the room. I'll use the name of Rex Smith."

"Sounds generic."

"It is. All you need to do is step out of the car and lean over the hood. If I look out at you, smile and think of every porn movie you've ever watched."

She gasped. "I've never—"

He stopped her denial with a look. "Do I need to remind you who's been listening to your conversations over the last year?"

"That is not fair! I simply said, once by the way, that I've yet to see an attractive man in any of those films." And it was a conversation on the eve of Eliza's wedding during which she was quite intoxicated.

Neil waited for her patient denial to end. "Like I was saying... think of the women in those films and play for the camera."

"Is there anything you don't know about me?"

His gaze dropped to her breasts and back to her face.

Heat rushed through her body.

"Plenty."

She diverted her gaze and stared out the window. "Well let's go. Clean sheets and a hot shower await."

As the last remaining miles passed, Gwen felt more comfortable chewing her gum with it nearly falling out of her mouth.

Neil drove through the town, twice, before settling on a small strip hotel with a vacancy sign.

"The show starts when we pull in the place. You're my night's entertainment and anyone watching needs to see it."

Gwen unhooked her seat belt and scooted closer. She rested her hand on his thigh and curled close. "This good?"

Neil stretched his thick neck. "Fine."

If she had to act the part, she might as well enjoy it.

———

A fan blew hot air around the reception desk of the motel lobby. Lobby being a loose term for the small space designed to register overnight guests. Neil rang the bell and kept his face as angled as he could from the camera pointing at him. Even dives like this liked some security. Chances were, the tapes were recorded over in a matter of days to keep from having to store data. Places like this didn't often feel the need to upgrade their systems so video files could be stored on a computer and nothing would have to be erased. The attitude "It's worked this well this long, no need to change it" often won at the end of the day.

Neil rang the bell a second time and glanced over his shoulder at Gwen.

She leaned against the car with one leg bent. Her hand waved in the air as she fanned herself and lifted her chin to the sky, pushing her breasts against the fabric of her shirt.

He had to admit she was sexy as hell.

The sound of the TV in the other room went down and Neil hit the bell a third time.

"Comin'," someone said.

A middle-aged man lumbered from the back room, his beer gut preceding him by about a foot.

"Sorry 'bout that. Didn't hear ya over the set."

Probably an old one with a turn knob and everything.

"No problem."

"Need a room?" No. He was standing there for his health.

"One night," Neil told him.

"Got a credit card?" the guy asked as he pulled his register book in front of him.

"Yeah…about that." Neil moved to the side and glanced over at Gwen.

Beer-Gut followed his gaze.

C'mon, Gwendolyn. Make it good.

Gwen met his eyes and turned toward the car. She stuck her ass in the air and leaned over the hood so her breasts spilled over the material of her clearly visible bra. After blowing him a kiss, she licked her lips in a slow easy fashion that would do a Vegas hooker proud.

"I need to pay cash," Neil said, nodding toward the show.

He turned to see the lust-filled eyes of Beer-Gut focus on Gwen.

Neil stepped in front of the view. "Don't need the charge coming up on the card...for others to see."

Beer-Gut raised his brow. "I'd leave the one looking and take her," he said.

"And give up the trailer? I don't think so." Neil pulled out a pack of cigarettes and tapped them in his hand.

The hotel owner looked over Neil's shoulder again and wrote in his book. "Want TV?"

"How about AC and a TV?"

"Fifty bucks."

Neil looked around. *For this dive?* He pulled the money from his wallet, added to it. "Don't need the missus, or her brother knowing I'm here."

Beer-Gut swiveled the book in front of Neil and he wrote his fake name.

"Room's around back."

Neil added another twenty, which disappeared into the guy's pocket.

Once he finished booking the room, Beer-Gut wished him a fun night and watched him walk out the door.

Neil walked straight toward Gwen and wrapped an arm around her thin waist. He nestled closer to her ear. "He still looking?"

He felt her lift a leg and slide it along his. "Yes," she said, nibbling his ear.

Heat shot to his dick. He kissed her neck and pulled her off before opening her door. And then, just because he couldn't stop himself, he pinched the cheek of her ass before shoving her inside.

Gwen squealed and sent him a wicked grin.

Once they made it to the back of the motel, he backed the car into the parking space and jumped out of the car along with Gwen. There was a row of twelve rooms, three of which were lit up. *Quiet night.*

"I can't wait for that shower," Gwen said as they walked to the room.

"Don't expect much."

"How bad can it be?"

The air conditioners shoved into the walls of the cheap motel struggled and gasped in an effort to work. It was still ninety degrees even after the sun set.

He swiped the key over the lock and waited for the green light. Something told Neil that the modern key lock was going to be the only luxury this dive would afford.

He opened the door. "Pretty bad."

The king-size bed sporting a dark green and red comforter filled the center of the room. There was a dresser to the right of the bed, another holding a chunky television, and a chair that looked like a petri dish. Topping it all off was the smell of stale beer and shame, all of which boiled in a temperature ten degrees higher than that of the outdoors.

The shock on Gwen's face twisted into a fit of laughter.

"Are you sure about this?" he asked.

She pushed around him. "Nothing is keeping me from a shower." As she moved into the room, her laughter elevated. Her gaze moved up the peeling paper on the walls to the dark splotch on the ceiling. "Good thing it's not raining."

Her giggle was starting to infect him. Despite the disparity of the room and the angelic nature of the woman in it, he found a smile on his face. Neil leaned down to the air conditioner and turned it on high. "I'll get our things."

Gwen glanced over her shoulder as she looked around the corner in the bathroom.

He swung her bag and his over his shoulder and grasped the case holding his weapons. He took one last look around the outside and didn't notice anything out of place. A dive in a two-stoplight town. He didn't think anyone was on their trail, but he wasn't going to make it easy on them if they were.

Neil tossed their belongings on the bed and kicked the door shut.

"Neil...can you come here?"

He moved into the tight space of the bathroom and found Gwen with a large sticklike bug in her palm.

"Is this a praying mantis?" she asked, laughing.

"I think so. Where did you find it?"

"On the less than clean towel."

The stained towel may have once been white, but now leaned toward a shade of gray. "You said a bed and running water." He reached over and turned the knob in the sink. "Water's running."

She laughed and handed him the bug. "I've slept among the insects for two nights. Kindly take this one outside."

The bug accepted his ride outside and sat on the railing before lumbering away. Once again, Gwen impressed him. Not only was she not squeamish about the bug taking up residency on the filthy towel, but instead of turning around and walking out the door of the dive, she laughed.

When he stepped back into the room she'd stripped the comforter from the bed and placed it on the dirty chair. She changed her mind and spread the cover on the floor.

"What are you doing?"

"The floor is filthy and everyone knows hotel bedspreads are never cleaned. No need to shower and end up with dirty feet."

This woman didn't cease to amaze him. Just when he thought she'd lost some of the Ladyship, the Princess in her came out to play.

"You shower first," he told her.

She rummaged through her bag and held up two bottles of hair dye. "Brunette or redhead?"

He loved her hair as it was. "You don't have to—"

"Neil. Please, look at me. I'm dressed like a common street girl. Surely a different hair color would aid in my disguise better than the clothes on my back. I'm not suggesting anything permanent. In fact, the box says this washes out within a week." She waved the boxes in the air.

He couldn't argue. "Surprise me."

She gathered her bag and disappeared into the bathroom. "Hot shower…here I come."

Chapter Seventeen

Blake waited patiently for introductions to finish before he encouraged everyone to sit so they could start to piece together all the information.

They met in Eliza and Carter's southern California home. Dean and Jim sat on opposite sides of the room. Karen and Michael faced each other across the living room. Carter hadn't arrived from Sacramento and planned on joining them the next day.

Blake glanced at Eliza, whom he knew better than Karen. He didn't like the fact they were talking in front of Michael, but it couldn't be helped.

Dean directed the conversation. "Eliza said you felt Neil was justified in hiding Gwen. Can you tell me why you think that way, Karen?"

"It started a couple of weeks ago. Right after Michael and I met. The more I think about it, the more I realize how off things have been at home."

Jim waved a hand in the air. "You need to start at the beginning."

"First were the cameras. Neil called on several occasions asking us to check the yard. The videos were fuzzy or something. Then I found a dead crow with its beak stuck in the screen. The window was open…which I don't remember opening. I could have forgotten, I guess. It's been so hot lately, we've had the air-conditioning on most of the time." She shivered. "I hate birds," Karen said with a grimace. "Gwen was great. Just knocked the bird free of the screen and tossed it to the ground below before throwing it in the trash. We didn't think of it after that."

"Until?"

Karen sighed. "Until dinner…a couple nights before we got married." Karen played with the diamond on her finger and smiled at her husband.

Michael winked at her.

"What happened then?" Dean asked.

"We went to dinner. On our way out we found another crow… Gwen called it a raven, by my side of the car. I thought the birds were on a suicide mission or something. Gwen wasn't convinced. Seemed to think the bird was there deliberately."

"Why?" Blake asked.

Karen glanced at Michael again. "Michael and I'd been seeing each other daily. She thought maybe someone found out I had a thing about birds and was planting them to scare me."

Michael sat up. "I've had fans do some crazy shit to get my attention in the past."

Dean directed his attention to Michael. "Do you have a restraining order against anyone?"

Michael shook his head. "No. I get my share of hate mail. Goes with the territory."

"I'm going to need copies of anything you have," Dean told him.

"I'll have my assistant drum them up. We keep everything in case of an issue like this."

Birds nesting in a Jacuzzi and causing some kind of electrical issue Blake could stretch…but three different incidences. His brain didn't stretch that far.

"So you think the dead birds are directed at you?"

Karen shrugged. "I hate birds. Serious phobia. I suppose if someone was determined to press one of my hot buttons, the dead birds could be directed at me."

Michael moved to the edge of his seat. "I've had missed calls and paper mail with strange 'gifts,' but I've never had anyone leave dead animals where I can find them."

"I've watched enough crime fiction to know that dead animals eventually progress into people. Do you think that's what's going on here, Dean?" Eliza asked.

Dean and Jim looked at each other, their nonverbal communication written on their faces.

"That's one theory."

"So it's not implausible that there is a rabid fan of Michael's out there who isn't happy with his relationship with Karen?" Eliza asked.

"Could be."

Blake shook his head. "Then why would Neil pull Gwen away?" Why leave the letter behind about contacting the damn president if he didn't call? And if he didn't call…did that mean he and Gwen were dead? He hated this. The not knowing. The inability to control the chaos of the situation.

"Neil must believe this has something to do with him," Jim added.

"Why? Why would someone use Karen and Gwen to get to Neil? Neil works with me." Blake stood and started to pace. "Why not go after Neil's family…someone he's involved with romantically?"

"Does Neil have a family?" Dean asked.

"I've heard of a grandmother. I think his parents are dead. I'm not sure." Damn if Blake wasn't sorry for not knowing that now. When he looked up, he noticed a look between Eliza and Karen.

"What?"

Karen glanced at Eliza, gave her a half smile. "You gonna tell him or am I?"

Eliza studied her shoes. "I-I, ah…not sure how to tell you this, Blake."

He felt a headache coming on. "What?"

"Your sister…Neil…"

His skin grew cold. "What?"

"They have this thing…"

"A thing? What the hell kind of a thing?" His blood pumped hard in his chest. Neil and his sister? How had he missed this?

"It's not a thing like you're thinking," Karen added. "They've never acted on it."

Acted on what? Now he was really confused.

Eliza tossed her hands in the air. "It's like this. She's always had it bad for him. I noticed in Texas last year. She never really opened up to me about it. But I'm guessing she said something to you, Karen."

Karen shrugged. "Yeah. I knew. It's not like she's been subtle. Neil, for whatever reason, hasn't ever acted on what is obvious to everyone."

Blake erupted. "Well it sure as hell wasn't obvious to me."

"You've been a little busy," Eliza said. "Either way. It's safe to say I think Neil cares for Gwen on a much deeper level than as a job. Otherwise why would he have reacted the way he did?"

Blake sucked in a deep breath. "Where the hell does Carter keep his whiskey?"

———

Gwen moved around the bathroom with a towel holding her newly dyed hair. She hand-washed her clothes and draped them over the towel rack and the edge of the sink. She wore her nightgown, the only clean item of clothing in her bag, and nothing else. She'd wanted a hot shower and ended with a tepid one at best. It was a blessing that the heat in Utah was in the triple digits, giving the water an extra degree or two within the pipes.

Once she finished washing her last pair of underwear, she turned toward the mirror. "Well, Gwen. Let's see what you look like with brown hair."

With all her brave words and intentions, she couldn't go red. Not yet. Baby steps, she told herself. The natural state of her platinum blonde hair would appear different with any darker color... so she chickened out and used the brown. And then didn't leave it in all that long.

She twisted the towel off her head and shook out her wet locks.

Not bad. Not fabulous, but not awful either. Without a hair dryer, Gwen used her brush to pull some of the wetness from her hair.

With nothing left to do, she opened the door and stepped on the comforter on the floor.

Neil sat on the bed watching the television, which was tuned to a local news station.

"Well? What do you think?" She spun in a circle.

Neil found the remote and turned down the set. He glanced at her head and then let his gaze slide down her body.

"I like it."

He didn't. She could tell, but he wasn't going to say anything against it.

She ran her fingers through it. "It's not awful. Probably looks better dry."

"How long before it washes out?"

"A few days." Which was the only reason she did it. "Bathroom's yours. There is laundry...everywhere."

"No helping that. The air conditioner isn't the best. Seems a little cooler in here to me."

Barely. But being clean made up for the heat. A fan over the bed spun and moved the air.

Neil moved around the bed and disappeared into the bathroom.

On second appraisal, the room was even worse than she thought. With hardly enough room to walk between the bed and the furniture, the only option was to sit on the bed. Gwen peeked outside and found only a glow of a distant room and a streetlight.

"At least it's quiet."

The local news talked about a break in the heat wave over the next few days, which was something Gwen looked forward to. The heat wore on her after a while. Perhaps it was her upbringing in Europe that made her intolerant to excessive heat.

The bed was surprisingly comfortable. The king-size bed.

There's only one bed.

The implications of that fact hit her and she smiled.

And when the shower turned off, she felt her skin heat with expectation.

A short while later Neil emerged from the bathroom. He wore only a towel around his hips. What she saw brought a gasp from her lips.

"Oh my God, Neil…I had no idea." She shot from the bed and stood at his side.

His glanced down at his own massive chest, which filled the doorway better than any man ever could.

"Impossible to escape the military without one."

The ink spread over his left shoulder and wrapped around his back. It wasn't a picture of a face or animal…or even a symbol she recognized. Rather it swirled and spiked and flowed with his skin. It was raw and urgent, just like the man. "What is it?" She traced it with her fingertips.

"A tribal tattoo. Some of us were on leave. Got drunk."

She couldn't picture him out of control enough to allow this. "Do you regret it?" She hoped not. She thought it suited him perfectly. The muscles on his back rippled under her touch.

"Too many other things in life to regret. This isn't one of them."

She couldn't stop touching him. Didn't want to. She ran her fingernail along the swirls as if the ink were a living thing. "I had no idea this was hiding behind your clothing." Mesmerized she reached the final spike below his rib cage and worked her way up. "What is it Americans say...go big or go home?"

His chest rumbled with a short laugh.

She followed her finger with her gaze. "You don't do anything partway...do you?"

"Do it right, or don't do it at all," he said under his breath.

She grinned now, and moved her gaze to his.

Her breath caught with the intensity of his stare.

She flattened her palm on his chest and licked her lips. One subtle movement of her hand and he caught it in his. For one awful moment, she thought he'd peel her off.

"I'm not an easy man, Gwendolyn."

"I never wanted easy."

She matched his stare and her breath quickened.

He released her hand and pushed his fingers into her hair. He studied her face, like only Neil did...as if searching for the answers in life. If she could give them to him, she would. There was a vulnerability in his gaze that she wanted to make disappear.

And when he gripped the back of her hair, and pulled her into his embrace, he took control.

His kiss was hard, almost a warning...she enveloped it.

The thick expanse of his chest rippled under her hand as she matched him for every kiss. She nipped his lip when he pulled back to kiss her neck and shoulder. He tasted her, using his tongue and teeth along her collarbone. The scruff of his chin felt delicious on her soft skin. He'd leave his mark on her, she knew. She loved the thought.

He released her hair and ran his hand down her back. When he reached her bottom, he squeezed her hard, and pulled her close. Under the towel, his erection already strained. As much as she wanted to see and feel that part of him moving inside her, she wanted this more. The torture of discovery and desire that made every pore in her skin weep for him. Only him.

Fingers found the bare skin of her backside. "Where are your *knickers*, Gwen?"

Was that laughter in his voice?

"Useless garment when going to bed...don't you think?" She scraped her teeth along the ink on his shoulder before swirling her tongue around his erect nipple.

He groaned, and brought her lips back to his for a deep kiss that reached to her toes.

His hand reached under her nightgown, his thumb grazed her breasts.

Gwen pushed into his touch.

"You're intoxicating," he told her. "And this," he tugged her nightclothes over her head, "isn't needed anymore."

His massive hands returned to her shoulders once she stood before him completely bare. Neil looked his fill, his lips lifted into a grin. "Incredible."

His stare brought a wave of power over her.

Slowly, he eased his hands down her chest. He cupped one breast and leaned in to taste. When his soft mouth found her, the world tilted.

He caught her before her legs gave way completely, and he lifted her to the bed.

Neil's eyes darkened as she stretched on the bed.

"Vixen."

He dropped one of his knees to the bed.

"Drop the towel, Neil."

It was on the floor in an instant. And she stared. Her body shivered. She knew he'd be large, given the size of the man...but bloody hell.

"Scared, Gwendolyn?"

She forced her eyes away from his intimate parts. "That is not fear on my face." She sucked in her lip, chewed it.

"Good." He fell onto her, setting one knee between her thighs and taunting her as he continued exploring her breasts with his tongue and mouth. Her body was a mass of sensation. The staggering weight of him felt like armor. Protective.

She'd always wanted this man, and now she knew why. With her heart and body working in tandem to please him, she finally experienced what it was to feel everything. Every touch...like how his fingers gripped her hip as they descended on her thigh, lit up her skin, her senses.

His thick heat pressed against her belly, begging to be touched. As he explored her body, she played with his as she'd always wanted to. The firm globes of his butt filled her palms. As she squeezed him, he tilted his hips into her.

She distracted him with a kiss, and slid her hand between their bodies and gripped him.

Neil tore his lips away. "Fuck, Gwen." He moved into her touch, dropped his forehead to hers. "I don't want to hurt you."

She loosened her grip, but stroked him softly. "That's never going to happen."

"You're not ready...not for what I'm going to do to you."

Her body flooded with moisture.

She opened for him. "Why don't you check?"

The hand that gripped her hip moved to her center and easily slid inside her. Her eyes rolled back. "Oh, please."

He stroked her again, added another finger. "You're ready."

"Maybe next time you'll take my word for it."

He played with her a little longer nearly completing her with his hand before chasing her orgasm away. She squirmed under him, trying to force all of him between her legs. He shifted on the bed, leaving her…and then returned with a condom.

"Finally," she whispered taking the packet from his fingers and opening it herself. "Allow me."

He knelt between her thighs as she sat forward and rolled the protection over him. She trailed her hands under him and down his legs before collapsing back to the bed.

With effortless hands, Neil pulled her hips up and toward him before teasing her a little longer by running his hands down her thighs and spreading the folds of her for his gaze. Only when she reached for him did he seem to snap out his trance. Taking both her hands in one of his he stretched them above her head and held her still.

"Last chance to back out." The words sounded painful coming out of his mouth.

"Don't you dare."

He smiled, lowered his body to hers. The thickness stretched her, filled her, and left nothing but mindless joy in its path.

"You OK?" he asked.

She opened her eyes, smiled. "I won't break, Neil."

Just when she thought she'd absorbed all of him, there was more. She was filled and completely enveloped him as he started to move. Slow at first like a runner warming up for a long marathon. Hot waves of desire bundled deep inside her started to tighten even more.

He wove his fingers with hers, kept her arms spread as he kissed her and possessed her all at the same time.

Gwen matched his pace and squeezed him with her thighs and the muscles deep inside her womb. Neil moaned and moved faster.

He plunged with such force the bed slammed against the wall and she wanted more.

She wrapped her legs around his waist and tilted closer. The tight spot of passion blossomed and spread until she ripped her lips from his to breathe his name. Her body exploded into a million stars like a desert night sky.

His fingers gripped hers as Neil followed with his release.

He came to rest on the side of her. Gwen kept her thigh over his hip, refusing to back far away. He kissed her knuckles and held her hand between them.

"I should feel guilty about that," he told her. "I don't."

"Glad to hear that. Otherwise I might have to tie you up in the night and purge you of such thoughts."

He laughed and smiled. She loved his smile, wished he'd grace her with one more often.

"You surprise me, Princess."

"Really? How's that?"

"You take bugs outside, flirt like a wicked woman, dress like a lady, and make love with your whole being."

If he knew she'd never made love like they just had…not even close, would she scare him away?

"Go big or go home," she said.

He laughed hard and released her hand to tuck her into his side.

For the first time since she'd met him she heard his breaths even out and Neil fell asleep.

Chapter Eighteen

"I have Raven in my sights, Mac." Billy's face was lowered over the rifle, his finger inched toward the trigger.

Mac twisted on the inside. *Squeeze the trigger. Damn it, just squeeze and take back all the pain.*

"Damn."

"What?"

"Gwen. His kids jumped in Gwen's lap."

No! That can't be right. She's not here. She's back at the tower. Safe. I locked her in myself.

Mac shoved Billy back, looked himself. Just like he thought. Kids were in Raven's lap. Not Gwen. *She's safe.*

Billy jumped up, turned an accusing finger his way. "You should have done your job. You didn't make the call and I'm a walking dead man."

Everything moved slowly. Boomer, Robb, and Linden followed Billy through the dark heat. They penetrated the compound, took out three in their path.

"This time we'll all come back alive," Mac whispered to himself.

Boomer and Robb moved in first, Linden close behind. The kid was there, just like before. This time Mac was ready for him. Only this time the boy ran to her...he ran to Gwen. Then blew them both to pieces.

"Neil! Neil!"

He jerked awake, his arms around something.

"Neil, wake up."

Gwen lay in his arms. Alive.

"Can't. Breathe," she gasped.

Neil released his vise grip. "Damn. Sorry. Did I hurt you?"

She sat up and ran her hands up and down her bare arms. "I'm OK. But you…" Gwen pushed his hair back. "That must have been an awful dream."

He pulled her back into his arms, gently this time. "Go back to sleep." He checked his watch. He'd slept longer than he had in years, but it was still only four in the morning.

Gwen wrapped her arm around him and intertwined one of her legs with his. "Do you have nightmares like that often?"

Not like this one. "Sometimes," he told her, hoping she'd not pry. His heart rate needed to slow down. The image of her blowing into a zillion pieces was fresh on his mind.

"You don't want to talk about it."

"I don't."

They lay there for a few minutes, neither of them talking, neither of them sleeping. Gwen ran her hand over his chest as if trying to calm him.

He kissed the top of her head and assured himself she wasn't gone. That Raven hadn't removed her from his life. Neil closed his eyes and tried to think of something pleasant.

Gwen's face as she came. Now that was a much better picture to take to bed.

Gwen ran her leg up his and between her touch and his memory, his body responded.

"Hmmm," she hummed. Her fingers moved lower on his stomach. "Let me erase the nightmare, Neil." He always thought her hands were tiny. Compared to his they were, but she found him, gripped him, and he shot to full attention.

Then he remembered the lack of condoms in his wallet and cursed under his breath. He stopped her playful fingers. "I'm out of condoms."

She shook off his hand and ran her fingers up his length. "Good thing I bought a whole box."

His brow drew together. "When did you do that?"

"At the store with the hair dye and the shampoo."

He grinned. "You planned on this the whole time?"

"More like hoped." She crawled over his body, her firm ass stuck in the air, as she dug into her bag on the floor. Sure enough, a box of premium condoms appeared in her hand. "See."

"When you told me you picked up the essentials, I should have known."

She grinned, and tossed her now brown hair over her shoulder. "So what do you say, Neil? Want me to chase away the dreams?"

Gwen sat back on her bent knees, her body bare for him to touch, to taste.

He reached for her. "Dreams are overrated."

———

They drove to the next one-horse town and ate at a dive. Gwen hadn't stopped smiling at him since they left the motel. For the first time in a long time, he felt like smiling back. She had a unique way of chasing away the darkness. If he turned his mind to his dream, his nightmare, he'd fall into the black abyss again. He didn't want that.

It didn't take a shrink to tell him his brain was working through the trauma of his past. Things he'd brushed away long ago and forced himself not to think about. He'd blamed himself for not calling the shot when he had a choice. Boomer, Robb, and Linden were dead because of it. And now Billy. And Gwen's neighbors.

"You're calling the detective this morning, right?" Gwen placed a dainty bite of eggs into her mouth.

He glanced at his watch. Still too early in California. "I am."

"Will that pinpoint our location?"

"I don't see the need for Dean to trace our location, but you can't be too careful. The conversation will be short."

Gwen swallowed her food. "So long as Blake knows we're safe. He'll worry otherwise."

They would all worry. Neil knew he asked a lot of them when he told them to do nothing for three days. It would have killed him to wait. In three days you can disappear into Mexico, Canada...or fly out of the continent altogether. He needed a week to get them where they were going...to keep Gwen safe. Then Neil could set his trap. Give Rick enough time to join him.

Right before he'd left, Neil sent a message to Rick telling him he'd have complete radio silence and that there had been a change of plans. If Rick moved on to the Smokey Mountains without him, he'd have to double back.

All of which would give Neil a little more time with Gwen alone.

After they'd made love a second time, he'd fallen into a restful sleep. He'd considered two safety zones for Gwen. One more indestructible than the other. Getting her to stay there without him... that would be the trick.

"I'll need you to make a phone call to Karen in the morning."

Gwen questioned him with a look.

Neil looked behind him. The morning crowd at the restaurant stayed close to the front door, giving them some privacy.

"You'll call. Just to assure her you're OK. Tell her where we're at."

"I'll what?"

"You'll tell her we're close to the Canadian border."

Gwen set her fork down. "We're nowhere close to the border."

"If our guy is listening…which I think he will be, that will buy us time."

She sipped her tea. "Time for what, Neil? What do you have planned?"

Trap the motherfucker and get him before he gets us. But Neil couldn't exactly tell Gwen that.

"Setting a trap."

"Isn't that hard out here like this? Shouldn't we find a place to stay?"

Neil shoveled a pancake in his mouth.

Gwen tilted her head to the side. "You already have a place in mind."

He nodded.

"Would this place have a bed and a hot shower free of wildlife?"

What a trooper Gwen turned out to be. "I think I can arrange that…eventually."

"Brilliant." She started to pick at her food again. "The bed last night was surprisingly comfortable."

"Food always tastes better when you're starved." Like the buttermilk pancakes he was putting away.

Gwen watched him bite into his food. She sucked in her lower lip and hummed. "Much better."

Her seductive stare took hold of his body.

"You're insatiable."

"Been called worse."

Was it getting hot in here? "Put that thought away, Gwendolyn. We need to put some miles between us and this dive today."

She lifted her glass of ice water to her forehead and placed the two together. "We need to stop…eventually."

He should probably be putting a filter over his actions with this woman, but he couldn't bring himself to.

Twenty minutes later, he turned on the prepaid cell phone and made the one call he would from it.

Dean picked up on the second ring. "Neil?"

"We're OK. Safe."

"You should have stayed here. We could have—"

"You can't protect us from this one, Dean. Your force isn't big enough. This guy is smart. Military, if I had to guess. Let Blake know Gwen's safe." He smiled at her over the hood of the car.

"Can I talk to her?"

"No time. You'll hear from one of us in twenty-four hours. Then we're silent for three days."

"Jesus, Neil. Tarzana PD is asking questions. I can only hold them off for so long."

Questions? What kind of questions? He didn't have time to ask.

"Twenty-four hours, Dean. Trust me. I know what I'm doing." He hung up and tucked the phone under the wheel of the car. Cell phone towers could pinpoint the call within a few miles. Hopefully Dean didn't look for a day or two.

"Ready?" he turned to Gwen and asked.

"Ready!"

———

Between the media attention after her marriage to Michael and the dead neighbors at the Tarzana house, Karen hadn't had a private moment alone in weeks. She didn't like the fact that Gwen had run off with Neil, regardless of what everyone else thought. Neil was a bit quiet for her taste. Hard to read. It wouldn't take a lot for Gwen to jump in the Neil truck because of her unrequited desire for the guy. But what happened when the sex grew stale and Gwen realized that Neil was running from the shadows of his past and dragging her along with him?

Karen reminded herself that if Neil was actually overreacting to the neighbors' final dip in the hot tub, then there was a real possibility of someone watching her…someone trying to scare her.

It worked. Karen was scared.

Then again, now that she and Michael were married perhaps the birds would stop.

Karen turned onto the street of the Boys and Girls Club for the first time since she said *I do*. She picked a quiet day as to not cause too much of a stir with the kids. Until they grew used to the fact that she was married to a movie star, she would keep her visits brief. Sooner or later, they'd realize she was the same person. Just one who hung around with the rich and famous.

She parked her car in her usual spot and twisted the key out of the ignition. Her gaze fell on the ring on her finger. Not overly huge, but not a chip off the diamond block either.

So far, the temporary marriage thing was a breeze. She didn't even feel guilty about saying "I do" when she clearly didn't. Michael described it as a yearlong role where they'd both get a payout in the end.

His publicist had shown up shortly after they arrived from France to congratulate them on their marriage. And then Michael's agent made a house call, too. His producer sent flowers and champagne and some of his actor friends insisted they have a reception. Karen agreed to do whatever Michael wanted. As she told him… *this is his movie, I'm only acting in it.*

She only wished that Gwen was back and all the dead bird crap was over before their party.

And what about Aruba?

What was wrong with her? People were dead, a couple were running from God only knew who or what, and here she was thinking of engagement parties and trips to Aruba.

Karen pushed out of the car. *The Hollywood lifestyle is already getting into my veins.*

Inside the walls of the club, the kids noticed her one at a time. The girls jumped up first and rushed to her side. "Oh my God, Miss Jones. I can't believe you're married."

"It's Mrs. Wolfe, now," said one of the kids.

Karen wasn't going to correct them. They decided not to change her name. Actors almost never changed their names for their spouses. If the reporters in the tabloids found out that Karen didn't make the change, they wouldn't think anything of it.

"Hi, girls."

Amy hugged her with open arms and Nita piled in, too.

"Is it true you went to France in a private plane?"

"We did. It was amazing."

"You're in all the papers. I told my teachers that you were you... Mr. Jenkins didn't believe me until the news van showed up here the day after you guys ran off." Amy's eyes brightened as she told her story.

By now, the boys started to meander closer. In typical teenage fashion, they listened with one ear in and the other on the buzz of their cell phones.

"Are you just here for a visit, or are you sticking around?" Steve asked.

"Trying to get rid of me, Steve?"

He pulled his eyes away from his cell. "Just wondering."

"I have to get a few things settled, but I'll be back. Think you guys can stay on top of your homework without me for a couple of weeks?"

Steve shrugged and several kids said they'd work hard.

Jeff walked from one of the back offices, grinning as he approached.

"I can't believe you actually married him!" Jeff hugged her.

"Think I should have held out for someone else?"

The kids started moving away. Still she felt their eyes on her as she and Jeff moved to the back of the room.

"Not sure if there is anyone who can compare to Michael Wolfe." Jeff lowered his voice when they were away from the kids. "You just met him, Karen. You sure about this?"

Ahh, how sweet. Who knew Jeff cared? Karen lifted her left hand and wiggled her fingers to flash her wedding ring. "Little late now to have second thoughts, Jeff. But I'm sure."

"I guess this means you won't be around anymore."

"Are you kidding? I'll be here more. Sure, I'll be taking a few more vacations...or trips. Michael has some shoots in some great locations this year. But I won't have to work at my day job. I told them I'd help out remotely for a while. Let's face it, Michael can afford me."

Jeff's smile fell. "Living in someone else's shadow gets old after a while."

Had she married Michael for love and forever, she'd do things differently. That wasn't the case...and therefore not something she needed to worry about. "I won't forget who I am. I'll be OK."

"As long as you're happy."

"Thanks, Jeff. I'm happy."

Jeff nodded to a back room. "There's something else I want to ask you about. Have a minute?"

"Sure." She followed him to a private room. "What's up?" she asked when he closed the door.

"I heard about your neighbors. I don't think the kids recognized the house on the news...then again, I don't think any of them watch the news."

Karen rubbed the chill in her arms. "Yeah...it's scary. They aren't sure if it's a homicide or a bad accident."

"Thank goodness you weren't home when it happened."

"My roommate wasn't so lucky. Actually, that's part of the reason I'm going to be MIA around here a little longer."

Jeff sat forward. "Why's that?"

"Some strange things happened before the neighbors ended up…well, you know. The police are looking at all angles. One theory is a fan of Michael's wanted to scare me."

"You're kidding?"

"Wish I was. The media hasn't heard that yet. And please don't be the one to tell them, Jeff."

Jeff looked offended. "C'mon, Karen. I'm not a sellout. Do you really think someone's out to scare you?"

"There were dead birds found by the bodies of the neighbors… another dead bird or two has made its way close to me since I met Michael."

"We know how much you *love* birds."

They'd arranged for a zookeeper to visit the kids six months ago. The zookeeper thought it would be fun to have a macaw in their animal mix. Every kid and every volunteer learned just how far Karen's disdain for birds went on that day. There had been screaming, cowering…feathers and the need for therapy by the time they zookeeper left. If Gwen had witnessed that scene, she wouldn't have concluded that Karen never cracked. Oh, she'd cracked plenty on that day.

"I hope to hell that's a mistake."

"Tell me about it."

"Shouldn't you have some kind of police protection?"

There had been some talk about that. Karen agreed to stay close to Michael's home and when she wasn't, she wouldn't go near the Tarzana house without an escort. If any more dead birds turned up, Dean and Jim would assign someone to her.

"I'm OK. But until we know all the details, I'll be keeping my distance from the kids."

"Much as we'll miss you, I have to agree."

Karen stood and swung her purse over her shoulder. "That means you need to stay on top of my math group."

He walked her out of his office. "I will."

Karen talked with the kids for a few more minutes and then made her way to her car. She'd started looking around her vehicle before getting inside. With the pavement free of dead crows, she unlocked the doors and opened the driver's side.

"Miss Jones?"

Karen turned to a familiar voice.

"Hi, Juan." She hadn't seen him inside but thought maybe he'd just missed the day. "How ya doing?"

As Juan came closer, the smile on his face started to fade. "So, you really married *that guy*?"

The way he said "that guy" made her pause. "The news got it right. Michael and I eloped last week."

Juan's eyes moved to her hand. "Everyone knows actors are all phony."

Hookay, looks like Juan didn't approve. "You met him, Juan. He's a nice guy."

"Didn't mean you had to marry him." Juan shoved his hands in his jean pockets and stared at the ground.

Damn, Karen. You're a fool. The last time she'd seen a crush on a teenage kid, she'd been one. How had she missed Juan's feelings?

Time to remind Juan that he was a teenager and she was a grown woman. "Michael and I are both adults, Juan. I married him for more reasons than he's just a nice guy."

"You can screw without getting married," he bit out with anger.

"That's out of line."

"Whatever." Juan twisted away from her and walked to the street. Away from the club.

That went well.

Chapter Nineteen

They stopped in a small town just inside the Colorado border and picked up camping supplies.

"I don't camp," Gwen whispered in Neil's ear. The closest she'd come to camping was sleeping in the backseat of the car they were dragging across the country.

Neil blinked in response, put the tent in his cart anyway, and continued down the aisle.

What did she expect really? That they would hit a hotel every night now that they'd enjoyed one? And how many days and nights were they going to be doing this anyway? So far Gwen hadn't pressed Neil for any details. She'd hoped that he would have opened up to her about his plans, but he hadn't. Not much anyway.

Gwen walked faster to keep up with him as he found the sleeping bags and started looking at them. "I'm not kidding. Lying on the cold ground holds no appeal to me."

Neil reached for a two-man sleeping bag, fixed his eyes to hers, and tossed it in the cart.

Maybe camping with Neil wouldn't be so bad. There wasn't room in the backseat for both of them.

With one side of her mouth curled up, she found a double mat to place in the bottom of a tent and added it to their supplies.

"I want a campfire." Cozy firelight and Neil? What could be better?

For a moment, she thought he'd veto her suggestion.

Then he added a bag of marshmallows to the cart.

In silence, they moved through the store. She added sweatshirts for both of them. His was triple extra large and hers a medium…both with a picture of the Colorado Rockies on them. Neil added a small pan and several cans of pull top food, soda, instant coffee, and water.

The clerk at the checkout chatted as he rang them up. "Looks like you guys are going camping?"

Gwen smiled, and remembered to stay silent.

"Looks that way," Neil said.

"You have bug repellant?"

"We're good."

"We try and go a few times a summer." The clerk looked beyond Neil to her. "Where you headed?"

Gwen noticed the muscles on the back of Neil's neck tense. "We'll figure it out when we get up there."

"Those are the best trips." The kid told them the total and bagged up their purchases.

"Have fun."

Neil grabbed the bags. "We will."

Gwen offered a smile and followed him out the door.

Once in the car she finally felt like she could talk. "Next time you go through the checkout without me. Who knew staying quiet could be so difficult? Not sure how you do it all the time."

He opened the door for her. "Practice."

As the road stretched out in front of them, so did the silence. And Gwen wanted a few answers.

"So how much longer are we going to go on like this?"

Neil narrowed his eyes. "Like what?"

"On the road…cheap hotels, and now I need to add camping. How many more days like this?"

"Not much longer."

"That's not an answer, Neil."

"Three, maybe four days."

That didn't seem like that long of a time. "Then what?"

"I take you someplace safe."

"Where will you be? Someplace unsafe?"

Gwen could see him shutting himself off from her. In an effort to bring back his smile, she placed her hand on his thigh. "Why don't we both go to where it's safe? Let the police handle whoever killed my neighbors. You do think they were murdered, don't you?"

"I know they were."

"How?"

Neil moved around a large semi truck having a hard time going up the steep grade into the Colorado Rockies.

"How, Neil?"

"I just know. You'll have to trust me."

"You think I don't? I'd think after last night, you'd know just how much I trust you." She kept her eyes on him even though his were on the road. "I'm not a child. I've gone along for the ride without too many questions at all. We can both agree to that, right?"

He nodded. Said nothing.

"How is it you know they were murdered and it wasn't just an accident?"

Neil hesitated before he answered. "The ravens. My l-last mission in the service was code named Raven. The dead birds you found were meant to taunt me."

"How does a dead bird next to my car taunt you?"

"Our guy's a coward. He uses women to get to the men."

"So when I didn't tell you about the dead birds, *our guy* as you call him, made sure you knew he was causing the problems?" She didn't want to think of a murderer as *our guy*.

"Exactly. He knew I'd take action."

"How many people knew about your *Raven* mission?"

Neil stretched his neck as he drove. Gwen knew she was pulling this information from him, that it didn't come freely. Now that she had him talking she wasn't about to let up. It might be the only time she learned anything.

"Very few. It was a covert mission. We were an elite group."

"How many men were in your company?"

"Seven."

She rubbed her forehead and tried to see what Neil did. "Six men went on the mission with you. How many others knew you were there?"

"A dozen…maybe less. The bigger the secret, the less people know about it."

"So it isn't likely you can ask your government to step in and help."

"The general rank and file of the government knows nothing about Raven. The secretary of defense, the president…one or two who answer directly to them, and that's it."

"Do you think one of the other six men are behind this?"

Neil glanced at her briefly for the first time in their conversation. A flash of pain met his eyes. "There are only three of us left."

Gwen's heart leapt. "Oh, Neil…I'm sorry."

"It happened a long time ago."

"That doesn't make it easier. They were your friends."

He nodded. "The best. Four of us made it out alive. One recently…died."

"You don't think that one of your friends did this…do you?"

Neil snorted. "That's like asking if you think Blake is capable of killing you."

"That's preposterous."

"Exactly."

"I've read my share of novels," Gwen said. "And it seems the hero is always trying to get into the head of the killer. What is motivating this guy? Why is he after you? Was there something about the mission you knew and the others didn't?"

"I led the mission. But we all knew our goal."

"Maybe someone is seeking revenge from the mission itself." Part of her wanted to ask what the mission was, and then she remembered Neil's restless night. Perhaps she was better off not knowing all the details.

Neil shook his head. "Raven was a person. And he's dead."

The conviction behind his words convinced her that he knew this fact because he'd seen it with his own eyes.

"Did Raven have a brother?"

Neil's jaw tightened. "He might have."

Yet her logic didn't make much sense either. "Of course, if Raven had a brother, how could he know about the code name? I assume Raven wasn't the man's real name."

"It wasn't."

"If someone is seeking revenge for Raven…and it's not directed solely at you, then your remaining colleagues might be at risk, too. Perhaps you should call and warn them."

He looked over and gave a brief smile.

"You've already done that."

He smiled again.

Gwen relaxed in her seat and stared at the landscape as it thickened with trees with the climb up the mountain. No wonder Neil was so quiet. There was a lot of information to process. Lots of possibilities, but only a few probabilities.

If none of the men in his unit were the killer and Raven was dead, that left someone loyal to Raven, or someone in Neil's own government who wanted him and possibly the others dead.

Gwen thought of what Neil had said about the recent death of one of the men. "Your friend who died...recently. What happened?"

"Officially a suicide."

Not unheard of from retired military who lived through combat. "You don't believe that."

Neil shook his head.

That left all of this up to a government conspiracy or Raven loyalists...

Government conspiracy ranked in Gwen's mind as impossible. If Neil mentioned a conspiracy chances were others would think he'd been in one too many gunfights. Post-traumatic stress had a way of making sane men paranoid.

There was no faking dead neighbors and birds left for her to find, however.

Yet in the back of Gwen's mind, she thought of Karen's phobia...and how originally they thought the dead birds were directed at her.

"I don't know what to think, Sam." Blake looked out over the city from the bay window of his West Coast office. "I trust him. I do."

"You sound doubtful."

"What if I'm wrong? What if something sprung loose inside of him and he's chasing shadows? When we first met, he was less than stable. Granted, he's done nothing since that made me question anything." He hated that he doubted Neil now. "The war was hell for him."

"Does he ever talk about it?"

"No. Only that first night, when we met. A bunch of his guys were blown to bits right in front of him. He blamed himself. That's all I know."

"That couldn't have been easy."

"No."

"There's one thing you can count on," Sam said. "If he is chasing shadows, eventually he or Gwen will realize there's no one there and they'll come home."

Blake ran a hand through his hair. "Not sure if that makes me feel better. I sure as hell don't want to think there's someone out there after them. And the thought of my sister falling for a guy chasing shadows..."

"Are you sure you're just not worried about your sister falling for anyone? Even Neil?"

Blake moved away from the window to his desk. "Maybe when she was twenty. Now I'd love nothing better than for her to find someone." A picture of Sam and Eddie sat on his desk and he pulled it closer. *I'm a lucky man.*

"Someone stable."

"Yeah." Even on a normal day Blake wasn't a thousand percent sure that man was Neil. He hated that he thought that way.

"Hmm. When will you hear from him again?"

"Dean said we'd hear something tomorrow. Then again in three days."

"That's a long time."

"It's forever. Dean said they're keeping the electrocuted neighbors case open as a homicide. They have more questions for Gwen and Neil and they're not happy they left."

"They don't suspect them, do they?"

"Jim and Dean don't. Can't say the same for their colleagues."

"It keeps getting worse," Sam said.

"It would help if we found the trace he talked about. Dillon hasn't found anything."

"Dillon doesn't have Neil's background in intelligence. Wasn't he special ops or something like that?"

Once again, Blake was reminded of just how smart his wife was. "He was."

"Hmm." Samantha sighed. "Want my opinion?"

Blake found a smile on his lips. "I can't believe I've escaped it."

She laughed. "Remind me to slap you for that later."

"Promises, promises."

"I think," she began, "that you need to give Neil the next four days. If you went looking for him now and led whoever might be out there to him you'd never forgive yourself. If there isn't anyone out there, then I think that will be evident by day four. Neil would never hurt Gwen. And Gwen...well, we all know how she feels about Neil."

"I sure as hell didn't."

"I tried pointing it out to you after Carter and Eliza hooked up. You, my Duke, just don't listen."

"I listen." Maybe not as much as he did before he had a wife. "Really?"

Sam took some of the daily burden of life off his shoulders. Even now, just talking to her helped calm him down like no one else could.

"I'm pregnant."

One minute he was broken up about Gwen liking Neil and the next...*What?*

"What did you say?"

Sam started laughing. "Wasn't the stomach flu after all."

Good thing he was sitting. "Pregnant? You sure?"

"Been there. Done that."

They'd been less than careful. Tempting pregnancy more than really planning one. But Eddie was toddling and they both wanted more kids. "Oh, Sam. I love you." He couldn't stop smiling.

"I love you, too. I thought I'd wait to tell you when I saw you again…but we both know I'm not good at keeping the pregnancy thing to myself."

"Want me to fly home?"

"Don't be silly. And I'm not getting on a plane until my stomach settles. I'll wait to say anything to Eddie until we're together."

Blake leaned back in his high back leather chair. "Eddie's going to be a wonderful big brother."

"If he's anything like his dad."

"I'm smiling…damn happy to know I'm going to be a dad again…and feeling guilty all at the same time."

"Stop, Blake. If Gwen's in any real danger there is no one better to protect her than Neil. If there isn't anyone out there…then at least she and Neil can hammer out the sultry come-hither looks they've been sending each other for the last year."

"I never saw any come-hither anything." The thought of his sister as a sexual person made his skin crawl.

"You weren't looking."

"That's a blessing."

"Poor Blake. If Neil knocks her up I'll have to remind you that he's the weapons expert."

"Doesn't mean I won't insist on a shotgun wedding."

"Neil's an honorable man. He's not *that* guy."

"He is if he's knocking up my little sister."

Samantha laughed so hard she could hardly talk. "Your *little* sister is older than me."

Blake growled. "Can we talk about something else now?"

Sam kept laughing. "OK, how about morning sickness. Remember how much fun that was? And diapers. Oh, joy…the fun we get to have."

Blake found his smile and kept it.

Chapter Twenty

The air was a lot cooler in the mountains than it was on the desert floor of Nevada and Utah. Neil kept an eye on the clouds. The last thing they needed was bad weather. The tent was dime store quality and meant for perfect weather conditions and not for a deluge of rain. He'd watched the weather report at the hotel, but that was several hundred miles away, and the mountains were known to have their own weather patterns.

Gwen had fallen silent after he'd revealed some of his past. He was surprised at how often she thought logically and came to some of the same conclusions he did.

He'd thought briefly about Raven having a brother…that or terrorist scum like he had been was gunning after them. Neil dismissed the idea almost immediately. Terrorists were great at taking out big targets and creating mass panic. One-on-one wasn't their style. Not enough airplay on the global platform for their taste.

As for Rick or Mickey holding a grudge…Mickey was out of reach. Probably deep inside again and halfway across the globe. Rick was the one who came to him. Weren't they both working to find the one responsible for Billy's death?

Neil knew there was the slight possibility that Rick or Mickey could harbor an issue with him. Billy didn't take the shot and Neil knew he didn't make the call. Both outcomes might make Billy or himself a target with the other guys.

Neil wanted to think longer, work through every possible angle before he gave his cards to anyone. Even Rick.

Neil told himself he hadn't called Rick the minute his plans changed because he needed to work things out alone. Neil worked solo now. No one else was on his team to depend on. No one else to get killed.

His eyes traveled beyond the spot Gwen had disappeared behind to find some privacy in the woods.

"You're not solo, Mac," he told himself. There was someone he cared about depending on him. In harm's way because of him. *I'm not solo at all.* Only this time when the mission was completed they would both walk away.

He kicked away a few rocks that would make it difficult to relax inside the tent before returning to the car to gather their things. A couple of nights camping in the middle of nowhere with Gwen. Could be worse. He thought of her the night before. He'd fantasized about her more times than he could count. Never did he picture her as responsive as she'd been. He'd made love to his share of women, some he quickly forgot, which probably made him all kinds of a bastard. There were a few he remembered with fondness. But none had left him feeling empty inside when they were gone.

Gwen would change that. He knew that from the beginning. His emotions were involved before he ever touched her. That made his mission even more dangerous. The one after them knew it and would exploit it.

The best thing for Neil to do was grasp the situation with both hands, solidify it, and deal. Once Gwen sat in the ivory tower, he could nail the mother shut and move on.

A twig behind him snapped. His body tensed.

"Setting up the tent?"

Neil sighed. Dropped his hand that reached for his weapon on impulse. He'd pulled a gun on Gwen once. Damn if he'd let it happen again. There was no one out there except them and the deer. "Yeah."

He emptied the contents of the bag onto the ground and lined up the poles for the tent.

"It's beautiful up here. Have you been before?"

"Been a few years, but yeah."

"It's so quiet. Even more than the desert."

Neil pulled the deep scent of the pines into his nose. "The highway noise travels for miles in the desert. Up here, the forest muddles the sound." He closed his eyes and listened. He moved his face away from the sun. "Listen."

He opened his eyes to find Gwen looking at him with a smile. He walked to her and turned her toward the east. "Close your eyes."

"What is it?"

"Shhh." He rested his hands on her shoulders and leaned down to her ear. "Take a few slow deep breaths and just listen."

Gwen followed his instructions and he joined her in silence. When he closed his eyes, the world of sound opened like a flood.

"Now...what do you hear?"

"Birds. Maybe a chipmunk chirping."

He heard those too. "What else?" He watched her now, the smile on her face as she listened to the sounds of the forest.

"The wind in the top of the trees...and something else." She opened her eyes and pointed east. "Over there."

"A stream if it's close, a river if it's farther away."

"How lovely. We should find it."

He rubbed the coolness from her arms. "Tomorrow. We need to set up camp before dark."

"All right."

"But first. Close your eyes again and tell me what you don't hear."

Her eyes drifted close again. Neil glanced at the ground at his feet and saw a twig.

"No cars. No distant horns or sounds of people other than us. No air traffic. Nothing mechanical."

Neil lifted his foot over the branch and waited. "Anything else?"

She hesitated and started to shake her head.

Neil snapped the twig and she jumped.

"What was that?"

She watched him now, hand to her chest.

"Just a branch. But you heard it because you removed one of your senses. Listen to how I walk, memorize it. And if anyone else approaches you, you'll know it before you see them."

Gwen turned and circled his waist with her arms. "No one would dare get close to me with you around, Neil."

"You can never be too careful out here."

She grinned, lifted on her tiptoes and kissed him briefly, and settled back to her feet. "I'll practice. Now, why don't you set up the tent while I find some firewood?"

He kept an eye on her as she foraged about, gathering wood. It didn't take him long to construct the tent and set up their sleeping gear.

"I've never camped," Gwen said from several yards away. "Not once. The closest I came was when I was twelve. I had a friend spend the night and we ended up sleeping on the lounge chairs on the patio outside my room at Albany."

He smirked. "Doesn't count."

"I suppose that's true." She dumped a few larger logs into her pile and moved away to gather more branches. "There are a few cabins on the property back home. I used to escape to them when I needed time to myself. My mother always wanted people around. There were guests at Albany continually when my father was alive and I often sought refuge in the cabins."

"Did you get along with your father?" He knew Blake didn't.

"He discounted me because of my gender. I was someone my mother needed to deal with. Not him. When Blake decided to find his own path, I mistakenly thought my father would notice that I was more than an ornament to be introduced to his friends and then set aside. Naive of me. He was an awful husband and father. If he were born a hundred and fifty years ago, he could have fit in quite well."

"Sounds like a hard man to live with."

She placed more wood on her pile and sat on a fallen log. "He was. I probably shouldn't speak ill of the dead."

Leave it to Gwen to worry about a spirit's feelings. "I won't tell." He took a log and carved into the soft earth to make a small pit for their fire.

"What about your parents? I don't think I've ever heard you talk about them."

Neil hadn't thought about his parents in a long time and it had been even longer since he spoke of them. "Mom ran off when I was a kid. My dad raised me. He was a marine. Served for twenty plus years before he died."

"When did he pass?"

"Seven years now. Lung cancer. He chain smoked himself to death."

"How awful."

Neil shrugged. "It could have been worse. Once he was diagnosed, he went quick. Count your blessings and all that."

Gwen smiled and leaned her chin on her folded hands. "What was he like?"

"He was one of the good guys. Dad didn't have a lot to say most of the time. I knew he cared for me. He had a good group of friends whose wives helped out with me when I was younger. We moved around a lot in the beginning. Settled here in Colorado when he was close to retiring." Poor bastard didn't even have a chance to enjoy his retirement. Neil gathered the smaller pieces of wood, discarding the branches he knew would cause an excessive amount of smoke, and piled them to start the fire.

"He must be the reason you joined the military."

"It's the only life I knew. Worked for him. I never thought of being something other than a marine."

"I'll bet he was proud of you."

Neil remembered the photo of him in full uniform. It sat on his dad's fireplace mantel. "Yeah. He was." He sparked a match over dry moss and urged the brush to ignite.

Gwen sighed. "He never remarried?"

"Dated a little. But none stuck." Little by little, the branches caught and Neil piled more on.

By the time the sun was low on the horizon, the fire was large enough to warm them and the food they planned on eating.

They'd pulled on their sweatshirts and sat next to the fire roasting marshmallows after they shared a meal. Gwen did the roasting and leaned against him. She asked questions about life in the military and skimmed over his MIA mother. Now there was a person Neil didn't bother thinking about. He never knew her outside what his father had told him growing up. According to his dad, they were too young to marry and she wasn't ready for kids and a life of moving around. Neil was sure there was more to it, but his father didn't go on about her, therefore Neil didn't ask.

"I never would have thought I'd be here, like this, with you," Gwen said as she swirled the stick over the fire.

"It wasn't planned."

"I can't say I'm happy about how we got here, but it's not possible for me to hate it."

She leaned her back against his chest and he traced her arm with the tips of his fingers.

He hoped she felt that way later...when the new Raven was gone.

Gwen peeled off another marshmallow, twisted toward him, and fed it to him. He opened his mouth and accepted the treat. Her seductive smile grew bigger when he licked her fingers.

"I'm beginning to believe that you're like these roasted bits of sugar. A little hard and burned on the outside and all soft and gooey on the inside."

He finished chewing and grinned. He wasn't sure he had a gooey inside. But it if made Gwen look at him with such trust, he'd let her believe it.

"You're the one made of pure sugar, Gwen."

She relaxed against him once again, this time dropping the stick. "Would you like to know a secret?" When she dropped her head against his chest, he indulged in a sniff of her hair.

"What secret?"

She laced her fingers with his as she spoke. "I always wanted to be a bad girl. You know, the kind who wears leather and drinks whiskey straight from the bottle."

He couldn't picture it. "Back of a motorcycle with a tattoo of some guy's name on your arm?"

"Not sure about the name, but perhaps something. Maybe a belly button piercing."

Now that he could picture, and the image made him hard. "We can have you pierced in Colorado Springs."

She giggled. He loved her laugh. "I'd chicken out."

"I can get you drunk and you'd wake up with it."

She laughed harder. "Count on you to find the idea appealing."

"You started it. Belly button piercings are hot." And when was the last time he'd told a woman anything like this? Never.

"What of you, Neil? Any secrets?"

"You've seen my ink."

"Yes, I have. And I'll say it is very hot, indeed." Her accent made it all so clean and proper. "Anything else you didn't have the nerve to do?"

He squeezed her hand in his and waited for her to look up at him. When she did he leaned down and placed his lips on hers. He twisted her across his lap and continued their kiss. Her taste exploded on his tongue and heated him thoroughly. When he pulled away, her hooded gaze found his.

"I've always wanted you," he confessed.

"You had to know I wanted the same. What stopped you?"

He pushed away a lock of hair from her eyes. "I'm hard inside and out, Gwen. And you're a princess who deserves a prince." Not someone like him. Someone who couldn't sleep at night because his past wouldn't let him.

She cupped his face in the palm of her hand and her smile dropped. "The princess wants the knight and not the prince. She wants someone who knows what he wants and takes risks to get it."

"There are no guarantees with me. I'm a risky gamble."

She kissed him briefly. "I've already rolled the dice, Neil. You can't talk me out of you."

"Is that what I'm doing?" He knew he was.

She nodded. "Besides, if I wanted guaranteed boredom I would have dated someone in my father's polo club."

"Motorcycles versus ponies?"

"You do drive one, right?"

Not in years but he wasn't about to ruin her fantasy. "At least now I know where you got the leather fetish."

"Oh, no. That stems from all the adult films I've watched."

"Not a proper princess after all," he said laughing.

"Certainly not." Her hand ran down his chest and moved between his legs. "Would you like to see how improper I can be?"

His smile fell and desire shot through him. "Tent. Now."

She scrambled off his lap and he kicked dirt on their fire before joining her to light hers.

Chapter Twenty-One

Everything moved slowly. Boomer, Robb, and Linden followed Billy through the dark heat. They approached each guard from behind, took them out without a gunfight, and slid their bodies to the ground. Their silent deaths robbed the terrorists of the glory they wanted and for that, Neil was grateful.

Once the guards were eliminated, Neil signaled for Boomer and Robb to move in first, with Linden close behind. Their job was to flush Raven out and give Billy a clear shot.

Somewhere in Neil's head, he felt the dream take hold. He told himself it was just a dream. A distant memory. But worry crawled up his spine as he tried to change the outcome of what came next.

Boomer and Robb hit the door first, Linden and Billy next. From behind, Mac was sandwiched between Rick and Mickey.

Raven jumped from a chair at the same time a child ran to him. They spoke rapidly to each other in a language Mac didn't understand.

There was a split-second hesitation and Raven yelled an order to the kid and another child joined the room.

That's when Mac noticed the bombs. Strapped to the children. And the kids ran toward them.

"Take the shot," Mac ordered. Raven went down, his eyes in a death stare. Billy, Rick, and Mickey ran past Mac. One of the kids grabbed Boomer. Robb pulled the kid off.

Raven, with his last act in his fucked-up life, reached for something inside his robes. Mac dived to the ground as both bombs strapped to the children went off.

"Shhh. It's OK. I'm here." Gwen's soothing voice woke him. Her lips sought his with brief kisses. "I'm here."

Her slender body snuggled around his in the sleeping bag they shared as she coaxed him awake and chased the dream away.

At least the dream spared him the image of her blowing up. Still, he felt physical pain in his chest from the memory of his lost friends.

Gwen kissed him again, tracked her hand down his hip and thigh. "Let me make it better, Neil." Her fingers wrapped around him.

She already was. The dream faded faster than the night before. As if sensing his needs, Gwen slid a condom over him and rolled on top. She wasn't looking for foreplay. And if he had to guess, she wasn't even looking for her own fulfillment. And that tore at his heart. He'd never known anyone like her.

Neil took her hips in both his hands and guided her onto him. Her tight sheath drove away his dream. All that was left was Gwen as her body opened to him. Accepting all that he was.

Their pace was slow. Gwen coaxed him with sultry unladylike moans as her body moved with his. The hours before they slept had been hot and fast passion that left them sated and exhausted. This was steam and smoke with the promise of prolonged pleasure in the end.

Gwen sat up on him, making him find an even deeper place inside her. The night air cooled their bodies, but Gwen didn't seem to notice. Neil took her breasts in his hands and pinched her nipples. "Oh, Neil. Yes."

He smiled and replaced his fingers with his lips. Gwen moved faster, until she couldn't sit up any longer.

He took advantage and kissed her, all tongue and heat. His balls drew tight and he thought of ice-cold streams in an effort to hold off for her release. The wait wasn't long. Her nails clawed into his shoulders and her breath held. Her body shuddered around his and the cold stream shot into hot lava.

He met her moan with his own and floated slowly back to earth.

Michael was on location for the next week, which gave Karen more time alone than she preferred. Tony, Michael's manager, offered to accompany her to the Tarzana house so she could gather more of her personal belongings and some of the Alliance files.

Tony was a friend as well as a manager to Michael's career. The Italian man stood at five eight and talked with his hands. En route to the Tarzana home, he talked obsessively about Michael's latest movie. "You've met the leading lady, right?"

"Sandra? Sexy little brunette?"

Tony eyed her. "Not jealous?"

Karen snorted a laugh. "Not in my DNA."

"You know he'll be kissing her for the camera."

"Nothing says intimacy quite like a crew of what, twenty or more spectators?"

Tony laughed, pulled onto her street. "You're a rare woman, Karen."

"So Michael keeps telling me."

It was early, and the street was free of the many cars the neighbors parked in front of their houses.

Still, her nerves were a little jumpy as they pulled into the driveway and pushed out of the car.

The house was quiet as she stepped inside. The alarm buzzed, and she moved to the panel to disengage it. Karen glanced at the camera pointing at the front door and waved. "Hi, Neil...or Dillon...or whoever."

Tony stepped in behind her. "Who ya talking to?"

She glanced at the ceiling. "The camera."

It was the first time Tony had been in the house. He turned in a circle, checked out the monitoring equipment outside and inside the front door. "You're serious about your security."

"I'm starting to think everyone who lives in this house finds themselves in need of it."

Tony closed the door behind him.

"Because of the neighbors?"

Karen moved to the back of the house and looked out the back window. The police had long since left but there was black powder residue on the door handle, as if they were dusting for prints. "Not just the neighbors. When Samantha lived here, someone bugged the place, digging for dirt on her husband. Eliza's story was all over the news last year."

"Witness protection program, right?"

Karen nodded and opened the refrigerator. She took the milk and a package of steaks and tossed them in the trash. *No need for the house to stink up while it's empty.* "Right. Now Gwen's run off with Neil because of the neighbors. I'm starting to think the house is cursed."

Tony smiled. "If the house was cursed then you'd fall prey."

She thought of Juan, and his comments the day before. Thought of her phobia with birds and how many of the kids at the center knew about it. Instead of voicing her concerns to Tony, a man she hardly knew, she said, "I guess."

"So what are we here to get?" Tony asked.

Karen moved into their office and turned on the computer. While it booted up she asked Tony to follow her upstairs. There, she removed her clothes from the closet by the armload. Tony made several trips to the car while she uploaded files to zip drives. Her laptop would serve her well, but many of the client files were only on the main system at the house.

As she switched off the computer, the jarring ring of the phone made her jump. She didn't recognize the number but decided to answer it anyway.

"Hello?"

"Karen?"

"Gwen? Holy cow, Gwen where are you? Are you OK?" The last thing Karen expected was a call from the missing woman.

"I'm not OK, I'm fabulous. Neil and I…oh, I can't wait to tell you everything. I don't have a lot of time right now."

There wasn't an ounce of concern in Gwen's voice. That didn't settle with Karen.

"Is Neil right there?"

"He stepped into the gas station restroom. How is everything there?"

"Confusing. Dean's running around trying to make sense of what Neil is doing. Do you have a clue?"

"The crows weren't an accident, Karen. They were planted."

"Probably. But some things have happened here since you left that makes me think the birds have more to do with me than Neil."

Gwen hesitated. "I trust him, Karen."

"You sure that's not the sex talking?"

"It's more than sex."

Well that answers that question. "Neil's time in the military made him more than a little paranoid, Gwen. You know that."

"Even if that were true, that doesn't change the fact that our neighbors are dead and someone bugged the houses."

"We haven't found the bugs." Karen talked quickly.

"They'll be found." Yet Gwen's voice wavered. "Listen, I've got to go. Didn't want you to worry."

"Where are you?"

"North. Close to the Canadian border. I'll be in touch in a few days. Tell everyone not to worry."

"Be safe."

"I have my own bodyguard." And then Gwen hung up.

Karen stared at the phone, stunned.

"Who was that?" Tony asked from the doorway.

"Gwen. She said she was on her way to Canada."

"Was she OK?"

Almost too much so.

He removed the ear fobs and tossed them into the passenger seat of his car. "Leave it to a woman to blow your cover, Mac."

He ignored the fact that he hadn't slept in days…not peacefully anyway, and turned over the engine in his car. Eventually someone would say something. Waiting had paid off. Not only did he know where Neil's general direction had turned, but he knew he was fucking his woman.

And that was useful indeed.

Before he left town he needed to plant one more bird…He'd do his best to assure that Neil's friends doubted his sanity. Not only would their tongues loosen in the bugged locations, Neil's death would appear a tragic accident, and not that of a hero trying to rescue his woman.

"We're good?" Neil asked when he returned from the bathroom.

Gwen handed him the prepaid phone and smiled. "Karen was home. I told her what you said."

"Did she question it?"

"Not at all. Sounds like they are all concerned back home. I hate to worry everyone."

Neil leaned against the car. "A little worry now's better than tragedy later."

She nodded, agreeing with him, but wasn't completely convinced.

"Where are we going next?" she asked.

"Another night of camping and then we should be able to find that bed and shower you love so much."

"You like 'em, too."

He opened the car door for her. "The chilly stream was better than caffeine."

The stream had been ice-cold. Turned her fingers blue within seconds. "I'm fond of warmer water."

Neil tucked behind the wheel and slid his sunglasses over his eyes. "Not much longer, Gwen."

"Where are we headed tomorrow?"

They were at a gas station in a small town tucked in the mountains. From the map, Gwen had seen they were close to several larger cities.

"Colorado Springs," Neil said as he pulled out of the station.

"Isn't that just down the hill?"

"It is."

"Then why not go down there now? Much as I enjoyed the tent, it isn't my favorite place to sleep with you."

"Tomorrow. Tonight we'll be more visible up here. I need our guy to think we're both up here…hiding out."

"You're setting a trap?"

"Baiting a trap. But don't worry. You'll be long gone before he shows up."

Her skin chilled. "What about you? Where will you be?"

"Waiting."

"Alone? Is that wise?"

"I'll have reinforcements. You don't have to worry about me, Gwendolyn."

"Of course I do. Who better to worry than I?"

Neil took his eyes from the road and patted her knee.

"I noticed a diner on the way here. Can I talk you into a real meal?"

He was changing the subject, but the thought of food overrode tomorrow's worry.

That evening...when his nightmares woke her, she curled around him and soothed him with her words. Unlike the previous evenings, this time he didn't wake.

Yet she lay awake, listening to the sounds of the forest and wondering if Karen was right. What if they were running from shadows and no one followed them at all?

Chapter Twenty-Two

"I expected a call before today, Mac. Where the hell are you?"

Neil wished to hell that he knew he was making the right call. "Unexpected change of plans."

"What kind of change?" Rick's cell phone sounded muffled.

"The kind that makes me hide the woman in my life and stand up and fight."

"Holy hell. He's after you? Damn it, Neil. You should have called me. Where are you?"

"Outside Fort Carson. Where are you?"

"Halfway to Dorothy's house. I stuck around an extra couple days, but when I didn't hear from you I thought something changed. Thought I'd move on ahead to see what I could about Billy. I'm turning around. Where's your girl? Hell, I didn't even know you had one."

Neil didn't either. "She's safe. Have you heard anything else about Mickey? I'm cut off from my contacts."

"Nothing new on Mickey. His dad said he's deep behind enemy lines. Not even an ETA when he'll be back."

Neil tried to judge Rick's voice. Nothing alarming stuck out. He was being paranoid about his friend. Something about this whole thing stank and Neil had yet to put his finger on what.

"Bastard bugged my surveillance, Rick. High-quality shit I've never seen before. Looked military to me."

"Who's behind this, Neil? Raven's compound was obliterated. No chance anyone ID'd us."

Neil smoothed down the goatee he'd been growing since he left California. "Has to be someone who knew about the mission. Or found out about it and wants us out."

"I don't know, Mac. Sounds too easy. This guy takes things personally."

"Yeah, well, he's gotten too personal for me. Time to reverse the stakes."

Rick laughed. "Have a plan, do you?"

"Don't I always?"

"I'll drive all night, but it's still gonna take me a day and a half to get to you."

With any luck, the new Raven was headed in the wrong direction right now. Plenty of time to bait the trap. "Just get here. Call this number when you're in town."

"Stay alert, Mac. Looking forward to meeting your woman. Anyone willing to put up with you is right by me."

"Asshole."

"Back at ya."

Neil hung up and stared at the phone. *His woman!* Yeah, the term was primal and caveman…but it felt right.

For the first time in years, he slept the night through. There was a dream in there somewhere but it hadn't woke him. There was no doubt in his mind *his woman* was the reason why he slept.

Now it was time to find the ivory tower and place her into it for safekeeping. Then maybe, when everything was washed clean of ravens and death, he could figure out where the two of them fit in the real world.

Neil dialed another number. One he never thought he'd ever use again. "Major Blayney. It's MacBain. I need your help."

An hour and a half later Neil drove through security at the base with only a flash of his ID and a smile. Driving through the gates secured by armed guards was the only thing close to the ivory tower Neil needed for Gwen.

"I've never been on a military base before," Gwen said as she peered out the window. In typical military style, there wasn't a lot of detail or soft lines and landscape. Shades of green and gray painted the surfaces of large buildings. Government-issued jeeps and Humvees drove around the base or were parked in massive lots. "Did you live here?"

"With my dad. And again prior to my last six months as a marine."

The buildings on base spread thin and the housing for the enlisted men sprouted in small neighborhoods. A few kids milled about this part of the base. Basketball hoops and bicycles were unattended in the yards.

"The houses all look the same."

"They are. Two or three bedrooms. If you're lucky you might get a second bathroom."

Gwen was perched on the edge of her seat, fascinated. "I don't think I'd care for a carbon copy life of my neighbors."

"Individuality is worked out of you in boot camp. Comes back when you find your direction. But you learn to take orders."

Gwen frowned at him. "I can't see you taking orders."

"I took my share." He gave orders better than he took them. "Everything you need is on base. There's a grocery store, drugstore...hospital, and a church. They even have a pizza parlor that delivers, burger joints. Couple of bars."

"Everything one needs."

"Everything." Neil drove past the smaller houses and up a hill surrounded by trees. It hadn't changed. Not even a downed tree.

They approached a three-story whitewashed house at the top of the hill that overlooked the base. "This is Charlie and Ruth's home," Neil said to Gwen. "Chuck offered to help us out."

"Friends of yours, I assume?"

More like a trusted colleague. "Chuck is one of only a handful of people who knew about Raven. It would be best if you didn't tell him what I've told you. The less he or anyone thinks you know the better."

"You don't trust him?" Gwen asked.

"I wouldn't bring you here if I didn't trust him. Top-secret missions aren't talked about outside of the few involved with them. I doubt Ruth knows anything about Raven. Chuck would expect that you're just as naive."

"If someone were stalking Ruth, Chuck wouldn't tell her why?"

"Ruth's a military wife. She understands there are things in her husband's life that she will know little about."

Neil parked the car in the driveway and removed the key from the ignition. "If everything goes as planned I'm going to need you to stay here for a few days," he said.

Gwen pinched her lips together. "Are you asking me or telling me?"

Her staying wasn't an option. Securing her in the ivory tower that doubled as an officer's home on a military base was the only viable way to do that. If he asked and she said no, he'd have to change his plans. If he told her and she became pissed, she might run off.

Between clenched teeth, he said, "Asking." He attempted a smile, something Gwen normally responded to.

"In that case…all right."

They stepped out of the car together and approached the steps to the porch. Gwen smoothed down her shirt and tucked a lock of hair behind her ear. "You look fine," he told her.

"I look like I've been on the run for a week and I have a strong desire to burn the clothes on my back."

Neil took her hand in his and kissed it. "It's almost over, Gwendolyn."

Her smile brightened and she leaned into him. "A hot shower will do wonders for my mood."

His too.

Neil knocked on the door and stepped back.

Ruth Blayney hadn't changed since Neil had first met her. She welcomed him with a warm smile and a tilt of her head. She knew better than to hug, since he wasn't that kind of man. In fact, most of the marines Neil knew weren't much for physical welcomes. A good shake of the hand and maybe a man-hug was the closest he came to affection. "Why if it isn't Neil MacBain. My goodness, how long has it been?"

"A few years." More like six.

"Come in." Ruth stepped out of the way and opened the door wider. "Chuck told me you were coming. I already have a guest room ready."

Inside, Neil let go of Gwen's hand and introduced her. "Ruth Blayney, this is Gwen Harrison...a friend of mine."

Ruth shook Gwen's hand. "This is a first. I don't recall you ever bringing a lovely woman to our home."

"A pleasure," Gwen said.

"Oh, are you British?"

"I am."

"Well welcome." Ruth closed the door behind them and led them out of the foyer. "Chuck is out back pretending to practice his golf swing."

"Golf?" Neil couldn't picture it.

"Preparing for retirement, he says."

"I didn't know he played golf."

Ruth grinned. "He doesn't. But the plan is to move to a warmer climate when the major hangs his hat. And a round of golf…even poorly played golf, is better than him sitting around the house all day."

It sounded like Chuck wasn't looking forward to his life off base. Not surprising since the man didn't know another life. Major Blayney could have retired years before now, but he loved what he did. Picturing him on a golf course telling the caddies to stand tall and carry his bag with pride simply didn't fit his personality. Running others' lives…that's what Chuck was good at.

Ruth led them out the back door of the home and onto a deck that wrapped around the back of the house. On the grass in the yard below, Chuck attempted to put the small ball into a hole in the ground. The ball overshot by two feet and Chuck grunted with frustration.

"Charles," Ruth called her husband. "Neil and his friend are here."

Chuck turned their way and tossed his putter to the ground. "Stupid sport."

Beside Neil, Gwen chuckled.

"Football…now that's a sport. Remember that, Neil."

"Yes, sir." Neil greeted Chuck with a strong handshake and a pat on the back. "Good to see you again." And it was, despite the circumstances. Chuck hadn't changed. He still wore his tan slacks, button-up shirt, and government-issued belt. Only a couple of inches shorter than Neil, and a good fifty pounds less, Chuck still demanded respect by the way he carried himself. With broad shoulders and only a slight peppering of his dark hair, the major didn't look over fifty. Neil knew he was much older…exactly how much was never confirmed or denied by the man.

Chuck's eyes darted from Neil to Gwen, his smile stayed firmly in place. "You must be Miss Harrison."

"Please call me Gwen."

Chuck offered a nod, but didn't shake her hand. "Welcome to our home, Gwen."

"Thank you for having us."

"Our pleasure." He dismissed her by turning his attention to his wife. "Ruth, how about you show Gwen their quarters." Leave it to the major to cut the pleasantries and get down to business.

Ruth released a heavy sigh. "The major thinks all bedrooms are quarters. I promise there's a proper bed and not a cot. C'mon, Gwen. I'm told you were on the road for a few days. I would imagine you'd like to clean up."

"That would be lovely." Gwen's blue eyes met Neil's. "Shall we get our things?"

"I'll meet you in my office in ten, Neil," Chuck said. "If you need anything, Gwen, just ask."

Gwen thanked him and Neil walked with her back outside to the car.

"Chuck has never been a warm man. Try not to take offense," Neil said as he removed their bags from the trunk.

"Ruth seems nice enough." Translation…Chuck wasn't. What Major Blayney lacked in decorum he made up for in his ability to protect and serve.

"Once you've cleaned up, Ruth can take you to the commissary…get you some new clothes."

"Isn't a commissary a supermarket?"

"They have basic clothing there, too. Or maybe Ruth has another suggestion here on base."

"Which means you don't want me leaving the base."

"Not without me."

Neil could see the situation weighing on her. Her tired eyes held acceptance and her nod said she'd comply.

With his hands full of their belongings, minus some of his arsenal he'd brought with them and their camping supplies, which he'd left set up in the mountains, Neil leaned down and kissed her briefly.

Her smile broadened as he pulled back.

"What was that for?" she asked.

"For trusting me."

"Always."

—————

Neil let himself into Chuck's home office and closed them off from the house. Chuck had already poured them drinks and suggested they sit on the couch while they talked. "Thought you could use one of these."

"More than you know." Neil let the liquid slide down his throat with a soft burn. "Nice."

"Tell me again why you think someone is trying to kill you."

Neil started from the beginning and didn't stop until he and Gwen fled California. Chuck listened with a blank expression and refilled their glasses once during the explanation.

"How did you get Blondie to come with you?"

"Told her that someone from my past was using her to get to me." Not the complete truth, but as close to it as Neil was going to tell Chuck.

"So she knows nothing about Raven?"

"She's the one who found the dead birds."

"Birds die all the time."

"Which is why she refrained from telling me about them. Ravens are found in the higher altitudes of California...not in the basin. They weren't an accident, Chuck."

"I'm not suggesting they were. Just wondering what kind of sick mind would do this."

Neil took a drink. "Been trying to figure that out for a week. I thought if anyone had information on Raven's allies it would be you."

Chuck shrugged. "There are plenty of parties seeking revenge for his death. None of which are creditable let alone have the ability to do what you're suggesting."

"This attack is personal." Gwen's image swam in his head. *Very personal.*

"These guys don't attack people, they attack nations. Who do *you* think is behind this?"

"Had to be someone with a grudge...someone who knew about Raven. I'll find out soon enough. Rick's on his way and we'll flush this bastard out."

Chuck tossed his hands in the air. "Don't incriminate yourself, soldier."

"The right to defend myself and my family is still legal in this country."

Chuck grinned. "So what you're telling me is you plan on trapping this man so you can bring him in for prosecution...right?"

Neil read through the cracks. "That's what I said."

"That's what I thought you said. What do you need from me?"

Neil set his empty glass aside and crossed his ankle over his knee. "I need to keep Gwen here. Safe. While I do what needs to be done."

"She's willing to stay?"

"Yes. For a while." For how long Neil couldn't be sure.

Chuck widened his eyes. "For a while?"

"She doesn't have all the facts and I've yet to meet a woman who takes orders like a marine. She'll stay without question for a while...a day or two, maybe three. But I need to know she's here and safe so I can wait this bastard out."

"Keep her against her will?"

Gwen wouldn't approve, which was why Neil hadn't told her this part of his plan. "If need be. For the sake of the country and all that."

Chuck stood and rubbed the back of his neck. "Do you know what you're asking me to do?"

Neil's jaw clenched. "Nothing I wouldn't do for you and Ruth."

"Ruth is my wife, Neil. I believe you introduced me to Gwen as your friend. She's not even an American. And didn't you say her brother is a duke or some such sissy-ass thing? I can see the headlines now…'Major Blayney holds British Lady hostage on an American military base because her boyfriend said so.' You're asking the impossible, Neil. Perhaps if she were your wife I could. Then at least she'd be an American by default and I'd be protecting her because her husband would be in danger if she was walking the streets of Colorado Springs."

Everything inside Neil tightened, and several life-changing blood vessels threatened to pop at the same time. Chuck was right. And even if Gwen didn't try to leave, it was only a matter of days before Blake searched for them or got a call from her. Then all their cloaked running across the country would be for nothing. Raven would eventually find Gwen and they'd be back to where they were right now.

Chuck stared at him. His face as stern as a drill sergeant.

Neil made his decision.

"There still a priest on base?"

Chuck's jaw dropped. "You're shitting me?"

"Call him. I'll be back in an hour."

Chapter Twenty-Three

As much as Gwen adored all the alone time with Neil, it was nice getting away for an hour with another woman, even a woman Gwen hardly knew. Outside the commissary was a small boutique catering to the women on base. Ruth told her that most of the women simply left base to gather whatever they needed in Colorado Springs. The small clothing store had a surprising amount of fashionable selections from which to choose. And Gwen was more than happy to spend the money Neil had given her for shopping.

"How long have you known Neil?" Ruth asked as they made their way back to the white house on the hill.

"Several years now." Most of which was while he was working for her brother…but Gwen didn't think that fact was necessary to pass on.

"I've always liked him. The kind of man I wish our daughter had been attracted to."

"You have a daughter?"

Ruth nodded with a smile. "She lives in Florida with her husband. I'm hoping to convince Charles to move there when he finally retires. I'd like to be closer to her."

"How long has she been married?"

"Couple of years now. Keep hoping for a phone call about a grandbaby. But not yet."

"Where does Charles want to retire?"

Ruth laughed. "He doesn't want to retire at all. He's fought me for years on the subject. I keep hoping that Annie will have a baby and Charles will realize there is more to life than the military."

Gwen couldn't imagine dedicating her life to something so passionately other than a family. "I'm sure he will come around." Gwen wasn't sure of anything...but it seemed the right thing to say.

"He despises Annie's husband."

"Oh...that's not good."

"Tell me about it. Andrew is a teacher. High school English. The two of them couldn't be more opposite."

"Your daughter and Andrew?"

"No. Andrew and Charles. Charles is a leader and Andrew is a follower. Or so my husband keeps telling me. Personally, I like him. He adores our daughter. But my husband thinks she should have married a military man. Between her life here and a relationship that ended abruptly with an enlisted man...Annie was ready for stability. A high school English teacher fit in her life. I think if Charles gave him a chance...moved closer so we could get to know him better, his view would change."

"Did you know Andrew before they married?"

"Not very well. We met him when they were dating but didn't think much of it. One day she said they were getting married and then the fighting started."

Parents getting involved passionately never ended well. "She rebelled," Gwen said.

"Yes. She did." Ruth sighed. "They eloped and moved south. We've visited a couple of times. Stressful ordeals those were."

"That's too bad. Life is too short to quarrel." As much as Gwen despised her father, she didn't go out of her way to fight with the man when he was alive.

"I think once I get Charles off base his attitude will change."

Ruth was old enough to know that people seldom changed, but Gwen wasn't about to remind her of that. It was obvious Ruth was ready to move on with their life, even if her husband wasn't.

"I'm sure it will work out." Gwen was sure of no such thing... but if there was one thing she had learned after living in the States for nearly a year it was that Americans were wonderful at saying things they didn't mean. To be fair, the British were, too. However, her friends in London wouldn't think of sharing such private information with a mere stranger. Ruth was in obvious need of a conversation with a woman who didn't know her husband. Perhaps Ruth knew if she spoke with people who knew him they'd offer a different opinion.

Gwen glanced at Ruth and noticed a small smile on her face. "It will."

When they arrived back at the house Gwen noticed the car she and Neil had driven there was gone.

Her heart jumped. *He left?* Maybe he moved the car?

No. The car wasn't anywhere in the drive and when they walked into the house Charles said he'd left. She panicked for a moment before he told her that Neil would be back within the hour.

Gwen decided to spend the time alone in her room. When had she become so dependent on a man? On anyone? Maybe before moving to America she'd moved through life with an escort. Since the move, however, she'd found her independence and loved it. So why did the thought of moving around now without Neil feel so wrong? It was one thing to be infatuated with the man, quite another to not see herself without him. He was a dangerous gamble that came with a warning.

Working through the drama surrounding Neil required another set of ears. Karen's or maybe Eliza's. Even Samantha would offer sound advice.

The question was how could Gwen contact one of her friends and not risk exposing any of them before Neil was prepared to deal with the bird-killing man?

———

Blake met Dean and Jim at Karen and Michael's home in Beverly Hills. Karen had called in a panic, saying something about dead birds and the need for Prozac. None of which made any sense.

Inside Michael's home, Karen sat on a sofa with her knees curled up into her chest. Beside her Michael sat and stroked her back as the both of them talked to Dean and Jim.

"I got here as soon as I could." Blake glanced at Karen and asked, "Are you OK?"

"Better now." She was pale and obviously shaken up.

"Seems our bird-guy is interested in Karen after all," Jim said.

"Someone jumped the fence here and broke into her car. She found another dead crow, this time mangled and in the front seat of her car." Dean watched Karen as he spoke. "I have a crew coming over to investigate."

"Is there anything on your surveillance cameras?" Blake asked Michael.

"I don't have surveillance cameras. Only an alarm system."

Blake couldn't imagine a man of Michael's worth and fame not having a better system. "Time to put one in."

Michael nodded.

"Guess this means we need to keep an eye on Karen and let Neil know he and Gwen can come back." Dean stood and placed an empty coffee cup on the table in front of the couch.

"Only problem with that is no one knows where Neil is," said Blake.

"I'll start a track on him…credit card use, bank account. He'll show up eventually. Or maybe Gwen will call again."

Blake would have his own people start searching. The thought of his sister running off with a paranoid retired marine made him edgy.

"Do you think we're dealing with a fan?" Michael asked Dean.

"Could be. Or maybe someone ticked at you, Karen. Any ideas who we're dealing with?"

"I don't have any real contact with the clients at Alliance and you know my co-workers."

"What about at the Boys and Girls Club?"

"Jeff is the head guy there. Happily married. Most of the volunteers are housewives. There's no one I hang out with or really know outside of the organization."

Dean paced the room. "What about the kids? A lot of kids in those places are high risk. Or maybe even mandated to go there after school."

Karen looked stunned at the question. "The kids are great." She paused. "Most seemed happy when they found out Michael and I got married."

"Most?" Dean asked.

The hair on her arms tingled. "Well yeah. There's this one boy. I think he has a crush on me. Got a little upset the last time I saw him."

Dean removed a pen from the inside of his suit pocket. "What's his name?"

"Oh, c'mon, Dean. He's just a kid. Not capable of what's been going on here."

"Do I have to remind you how many kids are sitting in juvenile hall convicted of murder?"

"Juan isn't that kid. I know him."

"Really? Where does Juan live? Who are his parents? Any priors?"

Karen glanced at Michael and back to Dean.

"I'm just going to ask him a few questions, Karen. If he's a good kid, he has nothing to worry about."

"He'll never trust me again."

"It's a risk you're going to have to take," Michael told her. "The sooner they rule him out as a suspect, the sooner they can search for whoever else is behind all this."

Karen sighed and ran a hand over her face. "Juan Martinez. He's a good kid, Dean. Last I looked it wasn't against the law to have a crush, so please don't come down hard on him."

"If he's been planting dead birds to scare you, I'm going to make him piss himself. If he isn't behind it he'll be fine."

Jim stood and joined Dean as they turned to leave the room. Blake followed them out. "You really think a kid did all this?"

Dean placed his sunglasses over his eyes as they stepped outside. "Anyone capable of killing animals can eventually kill people. And yeah, teenage kids do that shit. Most don't graduate to murder until they're old enough to get a drink in a bar, but that doesn't mean it's not unheard of."

A couple of black and white squad cars rolled down the drive and Jim walked over to greet them.

"What about the bugging of the house, tampering with the surveillance equipment?" Blake asked.

Dean shrugged. "We didn't find a bug. Yeah, there's interference in the line, but that could be anything. No guarantee the system in Tarzana was messed with either. Outside of the stolen electricity mucking up the system."

"You think this is all a bunch of shit piled up to be meaningless?" Blake asked.

Dean shoved his hands into his pants pockets and rolled back on his heels. "I think you need to open your mind to that possibility. Now might be a good time for you to consider that Neil isn't invincible and that he might just have a case of PTSD. He wouldn't be the first vet to come down with it."

Blake felt sick to his stomach. Damn it, he trusted Neil.

"Something else you might want to do."

"Yeah?"

"Search through Neil's belongings…his files. Maybe you'll find a clue as to where he is. I know I'd feel a whole lot better with him and Gwen back here. I'm sure Neil left with an armload of weapons and ammunition. If there's a war going on inside his head…that needs to be addressed before someone gets hurt."

Blake did not want to hear that.

———

There weren't many things that made Neil's palms sweat. This was one of them. A ring sat in his pocket and a lie soiled his tongue. Gwen was up in her room and a priest was on his way. All Neil needed to do was convince the woman he'd been obsessed with for longer than he cared to admit, and who he couldn't sleep without, to marry him. Then, and only then, could he move in the big, mean world to catch the bad guy and know she was safe.

Still…his palms were freaking Niagara Falls.

He'd laugh if his stomach weren't tossing like a teenager after his first beer binge.

Neil took the stairs a couple at a time and stood outside their room. He drew in a deep breath and rapped on the door.

"Come in."

He wiped his hands on his jeans and stepped inside. She sat on the edge of the bed as if she'd been resting. Her smile radiated when she realized it was him.

Might not be that bad.

"You came back."

He paused. "You thought I'd left?" He closed the door behind him and moved into the room.

"Charles said you'd return...but I-I...oh never mind. Where were you?"

"I had to get something."

She sighed. "Not going to tell me?"

"I might."

Her grin made him smile. With his smile, her worried expression softened. "I see you and Ruth went shopping." He changed the subject.

Gwen glanced at her new outfit and lifted an eyebrow. "I can't tell you how good it feels to get out of those clothes. I know I'm higher maintenance than others in the clothes department, but I dare any woman to wear three outfits for a week and not want to burn them."

She'd been a good sport throughout. "You're talking to a guy who lived in desert camo for weeks on end."

"Remind me never to join the military."

"I'll do that."

Their conversation paused and his palms dampened.

Gwen reached over and ran her fingertips over his brow. "What's going on, Neil?"

Her blue eyes met his. "W-what do you mean?"

She shook her head. "You're smiling, but your eyes aren't showing it. And you look like you're ready to pounce. What happened?"

He swallowed. "Nothing...nothing happened."

"But you need to say something."

Was he so obvious? "I-I need to leave you here tomorrow."

Her smile fell. "I know."

"But I can't." The lie soured his spirit, but he tried not to let it show.

"What do you mean?"

"We're on a military base. The only place I know where you'll be safe. Chuck can protect you…hell, the entire base can protect you…"

Gwen tilted her head. He noticed for the first time that the brown dye in her hair was starting to fade. He pushed a curl away from her eyes and attempted that smile again.

She frowned. "But?"

"You're British."

She laughed. "Last I looked my country and yours are allies."

"True. But protecting you without your country's involvement is tricky. Now if you were an American…"

"My brother has dual citizenship."

Perfect! "And he's married to an American. Blake could stay here, no questions asked."

Her brow creased.

"I need to protect you."

She shook her head. "Because of my brother?"

"W-what? No. Because I need to."

"Need to?"

Oh, damn…she was frowning. "Want to."

She smiled.

He smoothed down the stubble of the goatee with his fingers and tried again. "I want you safe, Gwendolyn. If I'm going to find the guy behind the dead birds and neighbors, I have to know you're safe. I only know one way to do that." Neil reached into his pocket and removed the small box with her ring. All she had to do was take it.

Her jaw dropped. Her eyes widened.

He opened the box and waited until her gaze moved to the square pink diamond that sat inside the black velvet box.

She sucked in a quick breath. "Neil."

"I need you to marry me, Gwen. As my wife you'll have the entire US Army, Air Force, and Marines at your side."

Her gaze moved from the ring to his. Moisture sat behind her lids. "You don't have to do this," she said.

Oh, yes he did. For more reasons than her safety. "We do. If you want out…after…" He shuddered. "I'll walk away."

A single tear fell from her eye and she looked away. "This isn't fair."

"What isn't?"

"We…we just found each other. I can be honest and say I've wanted us to be together for some time. But this…marriage? And for reasons of safety?"

Reminding her what she did for a living wouldn't bode well, so he kept his mouth quiet about Alliance.

"If something happened to me with Raven, the people here can protect you."

Her gaze snapped back to his. "Nothing will happen to you."

"There are no guarantees." He didn't even know who he was dealing with.

She stood and walked to the window in the room.

"There's always the possibility of you being pregnant." He set the ring aside and waited for her to respond.

She huffed out a breath. "We've been careful."

"Ask your brother about the success rate of condoms." He wasn't playing fair. Blake and Samantha conceived Eddie while using condoms. Neil knew damn well those condoms had been tampered with practically guaranteeing Eddie's conception. Neil moved behind her and laid a hand on her shoulder.

She moved out of his reach and turned to him. "Not the same thing, Neil, and you know it."

His hand fell. All his excuses, all his reasons fled and the truth made itself known. "I can't function if I'm worried about you. Our enemy knows that, which is why he targeted you to begin with. If you're safe I can do my job, Gwen."

Blue eyes followed his with every blink. "What are you saying, Neil?"

What was he saying? "We just found each other." He used her words. "And I want to see where that will go." He stepped closer and placed his hands on her shoulders. "Please, Gwen. Marry me."

Another tear fell from her soft blue eyes and she gave one slow nod.

Relief flooded him, and he dropped to his knees and held her. When her arms wrapped around him and stroked his head, he knew he'd found home.

Chapter Twenty-Four

They stood before the priest and Neil's friends with their heads hung in prayer. Gwen reflected on what she was doing. Skepticism ran deep in her veins about why Neil decided marriage was the best way to move forward. She felt there was something he wasn't telling her, yet his worry for her overshadowed everything and made her say yes. When he'd dropped to his knees, her heart had broken. She knew he had difficulty expressing his feelings. What man didn't? With Neil, that male trait was amplified tenfold.

Dressed in slacks and a simple button-up cotton shirt not befitting a bride she held Neil's hand and pledged herself to him. When he returned the sentiment, he placed a ring on her finger. The stunning square pink diamond sat among several smaller white diamonds in platinum. It was exactly the kind of ring she would have chosen…and Neil had managed it without one conversation. She couldn't stop the smile from spreading over her. When she looked in Neil's eyes, they sparkled.

When the priest pronounced them husband and wife, Neil took her into his arms and kissed the worry away.

After, Ruth and Chuck signed the certificate along with Neil and Gwen, finalizing their marriage.

They toasted along with the priest and accepted the congratulations of those in the room. Ruth snapped a couple of pictures with Neil's cell phone so Gwen had something to remember the day.

"If we knew you were going to get married today, we could have bought you a dress," Ruth said when she moved into the kitchen to help with the small meal they had planned.

"Neil didn't want to wait. Besides, it's a tradition in my family to marry the same person multiple times." She'd convince Neil to do this the right way…maybe with Sam and Blake in Aruba.

"Really?"

"My brother and his wife remarry every year in a different location."

Ruth sighed. "That's so romantic."

"It is."

"Charles and I are going to stay at a friend's home tonight. Give you two some privacy."

"That's not necessary."

"Don't be silly. Of course it is. We'll have a nice dinner and leave until morning."

Ruth was a very nice woman. Not the woman Gwen truly wanted to stand as a witness to her marriage. But Gwen couldn't exactly invite Eliza, Sam, or Karen to the ceremony.

"Thank you, Ruth. You've been a gem."

"My pleasure."

They sat down for dinner a short time later and Gwen realized that at this time the next day, Neil, her husband, would be off in the woods to catch a killer. And she would be left to worry about his safety.

Suddenly she wasn't very hungry.

"Where are you?"

He dropped his speed on the freeway and kept the phone close to his ear. "On the tail of our guy, sir."

"Are you headed here?"

"Why would I be? He's north."

"You'd like to believe that, wouldn't you, grunt. I told you he was the smart one. You're going in the wrong direction. He's here and setting up to catch you. Stop fucking around with the birds and get your ass here before you're on my list of prey. Got that, soldier?"

"Yes, sir! On my way, sir. What about the girl? Do I need her to get to him?"

"Leave her to me."

And then the call was disconnected.

———

Once their hosts left, Neil and Gwen sat outside on the back patio and watched the sun set. The mix of emotions rolled in and out of Gwen's mind and was making her crazy. What happened when Neil walked away tomorrow? How would she manage to stay in this home with strangers? How long could she last without contacting her brother, her friends? What if Neil wanted this marriage to be temporary?

"What is my princess thinking about?" Neil interrupted her thoughts with his question.

"This isn't how I pictured my wedding day."

Neil moved closer to her and sat back down. He picked up her hand that held his ring. "I can top that," he said. "I've never *pictured* a wedding day for me."

"Well…women think of these things from the time they are old enough to understand fairy tales. I even have a wedding dress picked out."

"What does it look like?"

"My wedding gown?"

He nodded.

"It's white, of course, with a jeweled waist...slim fitting. Strapless. The train fans out below the waist." She'd not only picked out the dress months ago, she knew who sold the dress in Los Angeles who could help her at a moment's notice to pick it up. "It's beautiful."

"And what would I wear?"

She liked this game suddenly. "At first I thought black. Traditional. But I think gray is better. But this is silly. We're already married."

"Doesn't mean we can't do it again."

Funny, she didn't think she'd ever get him to marry her the first time. "In Aruba...with my brother and Samantha?"

He stroked her cheek with the backs of his knuckles. "Your hair will be back to its normal color by then."

"A trip to the salon can fix that."

"I'll look forward to it. That is if you still want me after this is over."

"Oh, Neil. How can you worry about that?" The question was never if she wanted him but if he wanted her.

"I'm not a prince."

"I already told you that isn't what I want."

"You might...later."

Gwen leaned forward and touched her lips to his. He softened and drew her close.

She was scared, down to the core of her being. When he was close all her worries were washed away.

"You know what we need?" she asked when she drew away.

"What?"

"I noticed a large bathtub upstairs. I know my back could use a good scrub."

He smiled and lifted her to her feet.

Twenty minutes later, she pulled him into the bathroom and removed the borrowed bathrobe from her shoulders. When he reached for her before they made it into the warm water, she batted his hand away and laughed. "It's your wedding night, soldier. Do you really think I'd deny you?"

He grinned, and let her pull him into the water. He sighed as he sat back. His huge frame filled the space and left little room for her, but she didn't mind. She'd added bubble bath to the water and regretted it once half of his amazing body disappeared in the white foam.

"When was the last time you took a bath in a tub?" she asked.

"I couldn't tell you."

"Life's little pleasures. Here," she said as she moved in the water until his back was in front of her, "let me do you, first."

Like the first time they'd made love, she traced the ink over his shoulder and back, but this time she did it with soap and hot water. The small space of the tub and the hot water surrounding their bodies added to their intimacy.

Something else filled the mix of desire. When Gwen ran her soapy hands over his broad back and shoulders, she realized what it was. It was the comfortable hum of knowing she could be herself with this man and not fear him running away.

"Have I told you how much I love this tattoo?"

"You mentioned it."

She smoothed her hands over his shoulders and eased some of the tension from his neck. "How often do you have to work out to make these as large as they are?" She squeezed his shoulders as she spoke and moved to his back and waist.

"Four, five nights a week."

"You must be going through withdrawal running across the country the way you are."

"Our personal exercise routine has its rewards."

She laughed, once again surprised by the humor behind his stoic exterior. The front of his chest held a slight amount of hair and tickled her fingers as she scrubbed him. "We haven't exactly slept."

She let her hand drift lower and he clasped it in his, stopping her from touching him intimately. "I've slept more with you than I have in years."

On some level, Gwen knew that. Her hand stalled and she allowed him to shift them inside the tub until she rested between his legs and his hands traveled her shoulders and back. At first, his touch was innocent enough. When he cupped her breasts in his soapy hands, she went lax in his arms and let her head fall into his shoulder.

As he touched her, she felt him harden. "This is going to be a short bath, I'm afraid."

"Depends on how you look at it."

His hands moved below her breasts and to her stomach. She twitched under his fingers, wanting them...

"Have I told you how beautiful you are?"

She swallowed. "I'd have remembered if you had."

He kissed the side of her neck and dropped his hands lower, sliding between her hip and thigh.

"You're beautiful, Gwen. Much more than a man like me deserves."

His confession broke her heart. She opened her eyes and looked up at him. "You deserve everything."

"I don't deserve you."

She twisted in his lap. "Well it's too late to back out now."

His lips found hers in a slow sizzling kiss. She moved closer and the water sloshed out of the tub to the floor below. It didn't matter. The only thing that did was getting closer to the man who held her. To let him know how much he deserved her. How worthy he was of her and so much more.

She opened for him, accepting his tongue, his touch. Slow wet hands moved over her body, down her hip and bum. With little effort, he picked her up and had her straddling him. His lips left her and moved over her neck and shoulder. The water lapped at her waist and the bubbles dripped off her breasts.

Slow teasing hands moved between her legs and played. He knew exactly where to touch to render her mind to nothing. The thought of leaving the tub to find protection filtered in. She scooted closer, grasped his cock in her hand. "I've not been with another man in years," she managed. "The doctor's given me a clean—" Neil slipped a finger deep inside. "Oh, do that again."

He did and she squirmed.

"I don't want to think of another man touching you," he said in her ear.

"No one has…not like this." He pressed against her nub with the perfect amount of pressure. "It's wise to ask about our sexual health before marriage." She rolled her thumb over the tip of his penis and took pleasure in his moan.

"I would have told you if there were any issues before we made love the first time," he said.

Of course he would have. She stroked him hard and he lost his pressure on her. When his hand fell away, she slid up his body and positioned herself over him.

He grasped her hips and held her motionless as his gaze found hers. Gwen smiled and leaned forward to take his lips. Her knees bumped the side of the tub as he lowered her onto him. Between the warmth of the water and the thickness of her husband, Gwen couldn't remember ever feeling so full. Neil moved within her, guiding her hips with his strong hands in a way she couldn't inside the tub.

Water splashed from the tub but neither of them bothered with the mess. It was the only time Gwen had made love to anyone without protection and she was going to savor every moment. It was the first time she made love to her husband and not just a man she'd grown to care for…and she'd do everything she could to fulfill his needs.

His strong fingers gripped her hips to move her faster. She squeezed him tight inside of her. "I'll lose control if you do that," he told her.

She did it again.

He growled and slid a hand between them, found the center of her pleasure and forced a moan from her. The angle of the tub made it hard to get closer but Neil worked her into an explosive orgasm within seconds. He followed her into bliss, spilling himself deep inside her womb.

A cramp in her leg had her wiggling off him much sooner than she'd have liked. "Bathtubs aren't ideal for making love," he said as he rubbed her hip to ease the pain.

"They're great for cleanup."

He laughed and looked at the floor. "And mopping."

She sighed. "I suppose we should clean this up before retiring. Wouldn't want our hosts to think the worst of us."

Neil helped her from the tub and covered her with a towel. When he left the room to find something to mop up the mess, Gwen glanced at her appearance in the mirror.

I've fallen in love.

Chapter Twenty-Five

How was he going to leave her? *You're in deep, Mac! Real deep.*

They'd made love so many times the night before, and in so many positions, he didn't think she'd be walking come morning… but she was. They'd thrown all caution out the window with the lack of condom use and he couldn't bring himself to care. The thought of her carrying his child made him feel like a god. And that was new.

He'd all but bullied her into marriage, lied to get his way. At some point he'd come clean…after.

Early in the morning, he'd called Rick to see how close he was. He'd made great time and was on his way up the mountain to scout out camp. Rick also made a phone call to Neil's landline in California to get the attention of the dirtbag who stalked them. He and Rick had to think of every scenario. Raven could have access to a plane, or even a commercial flight, which would bring him there within hours. Or Raven might have to drive. It was hard to judge. Neil didn't know if they'd wait out the guy for a few hours or a few days. In that time, he couldn't risk contacting Gwen. If anything, Neil wanted Raven to think he and Gwen were hiding out together. The lure of a vulnerable woman was what this man went after, and Neil would exploit it to his fullest.

That beautiful woman had fluffed the pillows on the bed for the third time in ten minutes and was doing a poor job of hiding her anxiety.

"You'll be safe here."

"It's not my safety I'm concerned about."

"You don't have to worry about me."

"Too late." She attempted a smile. "I'd feel better if I knew what you were planning on doing." Gwen picked up one of the pillows and pulled it into her lap as she sat on the edge of the bed.

"We're going to bait him, bring him to justice." The answer was simple, the execution…not so much.

"Sounds easy. How do you know he'll find you up there?"

"I won't be hard to find."

"Won't he catch on to that? He might think it's a trap and not show up at all."

That was always a possibility. "I doubt that will happen. The longer this guy is hidden, the more people will be watching for him. Now with you out of harm's way he has no choice but to come after me."

"Unless he gives up."

"I could gauge that better if I knew exactly why he was coming after me. But I don't. I doubt he'll walk away, Gwen."

Neil moved to her side and removed his wallet from his back pocket. From it, he took a still photo of him and his regiment before their last mission.

She took the photograph from his fingers and pointed him out. "That's you."

Several years younger with less of the world's weight on his shoulders. "That's Rick," he said as he pointed to the man standing beside him. "We call him Smiley. He's the one coming up with me to find this guy."

Gwen pointed to the next man. "Who's this?"

"That was Billy. The one they say committed suicide."

"He looks so young."

"He was." Now he was dead. "That's Mickey…the only other one alive."

"Do you know where he is?"

"Top secret, and I don't have a clue. This was Boomer and Robb." There hadn't been enough of them left to bring back to bury, but he didn't tell Gwen that. "Linden almost made it out alive. They were great guys. I failed them once and can't do it again."

Gwen placed a hand on his arm. "I'm sure they don't blame you."

Someone from the mission blamed him…all of them. "I led the operation, Gwen. I was responsible for their deaths."

She straightened her shoulders and gave him a stern look. "Is that right? Did you squeeze the trigger? Did you toss them out of a plane without a parachute?"

"No."

"Then I'll hear no more of your fault for their unfortunate deaths. If your military found blame, they would have held you prisoner, and that obviously hasn't happened. It's time for you to forgive yourself for what happened, Neil. Once you've done that you can move on with your life. If not, then you'll have one sleepless night after the next until you're jumping at every noise."

She described his existence up until then…up until her. "How come you're so smart?" he asked. He captured her hand and kissed the back of it.

"School of Princess. It's in the curriculum." She laughed.

He kissed her softly the way one would when they said good-bye. "You'll be all right here. Stay on base," he told her. "And don't leave the house without an escort."

"When do you think you'll return?"

"A few days at most." And because he had to give her something should he not return, he added. "If I'm not back in a week... Chuck will contact Blake."

The smile she wore fell. "You'll be back."

Or die trying.

———

Blake stood beside his best friend Carter and watched through the mirrored glass while Dean and Jim interrogated the poor teen with a crush on Karen. Not ten minutes into the questioning, Blake knew they were looking in the wrong place.

"He's not our man."

Carter shook his head. "I agree."

Juan finally caught on to the problem in the next room and started to get upset. "Is someone trying to hurt Miss Jones? Is that what you think I'd do?"

"We don't know, Juan. Why don't you tell us?" Jim asked.

"She's like our mom."

"A mom?" Dean asked.

"OK, maybe not a mom. More like a hot aunt, but she's like family. If someone's trying to hurt her you should be out there protecting her instead of talking to me."

Blake turned away from the mirror. "We're one step ahead of you, kid."

Carter shook his head. "Waste of time. Maybe we'll get lucky and catch this guy on a monitor once they're up and running."

"What a cluster. Wish to hell Neil was here." Then he would have one less thing to worry about.

Dean walked out of the interrogation room and into theirs. "It's not him."

"We figured."

"Are you ready to go through Neil's things?"

Blake hated invading his privacy like that, but what choice did he leave? He ran a hand through his hair.

"Gotta be clues somewhere as to where he is," Carter said.

Blake pushed out of the room. "Let's get this over with."

Dean walked them out of the station. "I'll be along in an hour. I have a couple of leads I want to follow up on first."

On the way back to Malibu, Blake gave Carter some good news. "Samantha's pregnant."

Carter swiveled in his seat and removed his sunglasses. "No shit."

"We've been talking about it for a while." Blake pulled onto the freeway and merged into the crowded California interstate.

"Sounds like you've done more than talk about it."

Blake smiled, remembering the not talking nights with his wife. "Morning sickness is kicking her ass. I wanna get all this shit wrapped up and get back to her, Carter. It's the only reason I'm going ahead with searching Neil's personal space."

"I get it. Neil's a private guy. But when you run off and think a murderer's on your tail there's no telling what's going on. Neil wouldn't expect you to sit back and do nothing."

"He'd expect me to trust him."

Carter placed his sunglasses back over his eyes. "If anything was panning out to suspect foul play toward Gwen or Neil then it would be a hell of a lot easier to trust the man."

Back at his estate, Blake and Carter let themselves into Neil's home. The house was a guest quarters that mimicked the main house in style and structure. The sparsely furnished inside space suited the needs of a bachelor. One room was dedicated to monitoring the main house and Gwen and Karen's place in Tarzana. The other was a bedroom with the bare minimum of furniture. Although the small kitchen had everything it needed to feed a family, the only things that looked used were the refrigerator and the microwave.

There was a leather couch and a recliner along with a flat screen television hung on the wall of the living room.

"Where do we begin?"

"I'll start in his office," Blake told Carter. "You look in his bedroom."

Carter headed around the corner and into Neil's room. "What are we looking for exactly?"

"Anything personal. Pictures. Addresses to a friend, family."

"Aren't his parents dead?"

Blake sat in Neil's chair and opened the top drawer of his desk. "Yeah...but I remember him talking about a grandmother." The drawer held the usual suspects. Pens, notepads, old bills, and receipts for miscellaneous items.

"If Neil thought someone was after him, I don't think he'd lead whoever that is to his family."

"True, but the grandmother might know where Neil would go to keep Gwen safe and capture the bad guy."

"You think that's what he's done?"

"He sure as hell wouldn't run forever." The next drawer held files of equipment purchase dates and software updates. There were employee files in print, which Blake wondered about. Why print out any of these things? Why not keep them on a computer hard drive?

As his mind moved in that direction, he turned on the computer monitors and waited for them to power up. The wall of monitors lit the room with images throughout the Malibu house and Tarzana. Blake clicked on the main screen and shifted between images. Each one that he highlighted opened the audio of the room it was in. Inside the Malibu house, Mary was in the kitchen humming.

The phone on Neil's desk rang, and Blake reached to pick it up. "Hello?"

"It's Dillon, Mr. Harrison. I noticed someone on Neil's channel watching. Is he back?"

"No. It's just me."

"Oh. Any word yet?"

"None. Nothing from your end?"

"Nothing. Sorry to disturb you, Mr. Harrison."

Before Dillon hung up, Blake stopped him. "Wait, Dillon. Before Neil left…was there anything going on that struck you as odd? Something unlike him?"

"He…he was a little more edgy. Not sure that isn't his normal, though. He always worked long days and didn't ask me to take over much while you and Mrs. Harrison were away."

None of that sounded out of character for Neil. "Any luck on finding the bugs he talked about?"

"I wish I did. There was definite interference at the Tarzana house. It didn't feel right to me."

"Like it was planted."

"I wish I could say that for certain. It just wasn't right."

Everything felt odd. "Thank you, Dillon."

"No problem."

Blake hung up the phone and continued to search the desk. There wasn't anything personal there. Just piles of work-related invoices and bills.

Carter walked into the room with a picture in his hand. "Found this."

It was an 8½ by 10 photograph of what looked like Neil and some of his marine friends.

"Neil looks thicker. I didn't think that was possible."

Carter laughed. "You ever see this before?"

"No. He doesn't share that part of his past. Except that one time in the bar."

"You think these are the guys that died?"

Blake took the photograph and looked at each face. His gaze popped over to Neil's and another one that looked familiar but he couldn't place. "Could be. Not all of them died. Just a few." *But which ones?* "Have you thought of calling in a favor and finding out what the Raven thing is all about?"

Carter leaned against the desk. "There are plenty of secret missions done every year overseas. The military doesn't take it kindly to have their top-secret missions blabbed about to just anyone. Although I'm the governor, I'm one of those 'just anyones' at this point. If we've exhausted all our resources, and haven't heard from Neil or Gwen, then I'll make the call. I don't want to stir up more trouble and have Neil on the tail end of a court martial because he's overly paranoid. We owe him that much."

Blake agreed.

"Knock, knock?" Dean let himself into Neil's house.

"We're in here."

Dean fanned himself. "Damn tired of the heat," he said. "You guys find anything yet?"

Blake handed the picture to Dean and shrugged. "A picture and a bunch of bills."

"I keep forgetting how big Neil is," Dean said.

"Not a lot riles him."

Dean dropped the picture on the desk. "Well, we got a break."

Blake sat taller. "What?"

"Looks like Neil broke down and used a credit card."

"Where?"

"Colorado Springs."

"I thought Karen said something about Canada," Carter said in obvious confusion.

"Well unless they flew to Colorado, in which case we would have known about before now, they weren't anywhere near the border." Dean's smug smile didn't sit well with Blake.

"What are you *not* saying?"

"Wanna guess what Neil used his credit card on?"

"Hotel?" Carter asked.

"Car rental?" Blake suggested.

Dean shook his head.

"Ammunition?"

Dean smiled and stared at Blake. "A very large, very expensive, diamond ring."

The blood in Blake's head dropped once again. "What?"

Chapter Twenty-Six

Before Neil left the base he confiscated, stocked, purchased, or otherwise pilfered anything he and Rick would need to catch Raven and hold out while waiting for him. The marines taught him everything he needed to know about surviving on his own and capturing a criminal. The only difference was not knowing with whom he was dealing.

Maybe Rick could shed light on that. Between the two of them, they'd work it out.

Still, as Neil made his way up the mountain, he kept an eye on his rearview mirror and worried about what he'd left behind. Chuck would take care of her. Gwen was safe. His wife was safe.

The smile on his face spread. *His wife.*

He made it to his camp long before the sky darkened. He parked his car far from the campsite to set up his second base, and to map out his fallback location. A knoll overlooked his planned spot of execution, the perfect watch point for either him or Rick.

Neil sat there now with a pair of binoculars and scouted. Within an hour, he noticed a figure working his way slowly toward camp. In less than a minute, Neil knew it was Rick. He waited until Rick walked the perimeter of the camp and doubled back to his car. As Rick returned to the site, Neil worked his way down the hill, keeping himself hidden.

Neil moved behind his friend and didn't make a sound.

"I was wondering when you'd join me. Thought you'd stay up there all night," Rick said without turning around.

Rick had always been good at detecting the enemy, or in this case a friend sneaking up from behind.

"How did you see me?" Neil moved in front of his colleague and extended his hand.

"I showed up an hour before you did. Moved from the knoll to the fallback by the creek and waited."

Neil laughed. Rick had executed the same moves he had.

"Good to see you."

Neil agreed. They spoke for a few minutes about the drive, the weather…any damn thing but why they were there.

"We have work to do if we're going to get this guy," Neil finally said.

"Any idea who we're dealing with yet?"

Neil shook his head, frustrated. "Wish I did. Think he's military."

"And knows about Raven."

"Or maybe he was told about Raven."

Neil didn't like that scenario. "Which suggests a second party is on to this."

"They're either a party to it by calling the shots from somewhere else, or we have two guys on our tail," Rick said and nodded toward the tent. "We setting up here for the night?"

"Part of it anyway. No use getting comfortable."

"Don't think comfortable is possible until we catch this guy."

Neil set his pack aside and shrugged off his coat.

"You really think there are two people involved here?"

"I think we need to consider the possibility. It would have taken some work to make the drop on Billy. Even if a woman was involved. Not a lot shook him."

"We need to get inside this guy's head if we're going to win this," Rick concluded.

"I survived the Middle East. I'm not dying in my backyard." Not when he suddenly had so much to live for.

"What about your girl?"

"She's safe." And for reasons he couldn't, or didn't want to identify, he didn't elaborate as to where she was to Rick.

"I still can't get over the fact you have one." Rick's signature smile spread on his lips.

"Me either."

Rick snorted and swatted Neil on the back. "I don't know about you, but I can't sleep without a woman at my side."

Neil hesitated. "I know the feeling."

"It's gotten better. But the memories never really leave me. I think it hit us all like that, which is why we all left."

"Mickey stayed in," Neil reminded him.

"Mickey was just a kid. Wasn't it his first time out?"

"Second. With special ops anyway. He'd done a tour in Afghanistan before meeting up with us."

Rick rolled out his pack and laid it on the fabric covering the dirt. He bundled the bulk of the material under his head and he stretched out. "Mickey was moldable. Just what the major wanted on his team. He took his purple heart, shoved it in a box, and moved to the next mission."

He'd forgotten about Mickey's injury. Damn unfortunate that was.

Neil took a space by the burned-out campfire he'd shared with Gwen only a couple of nights before. "We were moldable, too."

"Until we saw our guys get blown to bits. Tends to shake the mold."

"And for what? Didn't stop the war...didn't even calm the fighting for a day." For that, Neil left. He and his team were given base assignments for a short time and then were allowed to disappear.

Unheard of. "Ever wonder why Major Blayney let us all go?"

"I didn't question it. Figured he knew we weren't functioning the way we needed to. He was like family to most of us." To Neil anyway.

"I wonder if he knows who could be behind this? He knows those above him that called the order."

Neil already knew Chuck didn't have a clue. "You think the higher brass is behind offing us now?"

"Never know."

"Why would they bother leaving a token? Why go after women to get to us then?"

Rick shook his head. "You're right. It's personal. Someone's need to get back at us for surviving."

"If I believed in ghosts, I'd think Boomer, Robb, or Linden was behind this."

Neil ran his fingers over the hair on his face. "That's the problem with us. We have a hard time believing in anything we can't see. Rules out ghosts." Yet the ghosts of his past were catching up to them...to all of them.

"So what's the plan?" Rick asked.

"First we see if Raven takes the bait and comes after us here."

Rick glanced around. "A sharpshooter would make quick work of us right here."

Neil agreed. "But our guy needs to make it look like an accident. A bullet to the head isn't how this will play out. If we end up dead, or disappear, questions will be asked. If there's someone calling this execution, they aren't going to want that. It's not like we're on enemy soil, or that we're even on the inside any longer. We can't be classified as collateral damage."

"So if Raven doesn't show up here? Or if he does and he's not alone?"

"We'll spot him first. I've already set up sensors on the road leading up here. We'll know anytime something bigger than a dog rolls by. If he doesn't show up here then we'll fall back and search him out."

Rick's brow rose. "Snagged some of our old toys, did you?"

"Old and new."

"I brought some toys, too." And he did. Rick removed a set of night vision goggles, multiple weapons, explosives with fuses, and even diversionary tools…smoke bombs, flash bombs.

Neil removed two wireless headsets and switched the channels to line them up. "Here," he said, handing one to Rick. "So I can whisper in your ear."

Rick blew him a kiss. "I never knew you cared."

This felt good. More like the hunter than the hunted. Now all they needed was their prey.

———

"We need to find you a pastime," Ruth told Gwen after her first dinner without Neil in the house. "Waiting for your husband to return to base is difficult in the best of situations."

"What I need is an occupation." If she were home, she'd plan a proper wedding for her and Neil. Maybe work with Eliza and Samantha on a double vow ceremony. Anything to keep her mind off the fact that Neil was chasing a murderer.

"I can always use help in my flower garden. Perhaps tomorrow—"

"Oh, yes…please. Anything."

Ruth patted her hand. "I've some bulbs we can plant, and there are always weeds to pull."

"Physical work is better than mental at this point."

"We have a collection of movies to choose from, most are war-related documentaries the major watches repeatedly."

"I doubt those would ease my mind."

"I have a small library."

Gwen's eyes lit up.

In the den, hidden behind a closed bookshelf, Ruth encouraged Gwen to pick whatever she wanted to read during her stay.

"I read everything from mysteries to romance. There has to be something of interest in here for you."

There had to be over three hundred books. "You've quite a collection."

"I've packed away boxes. I'm hoping to have a small library in our next home. Charles likes things tidy and he doesn't see books on a shelf as neat. If we had a library designed for books, he couldn't complain."

The more Gwen heard Ruth talk, the more controlling her husband seemed.

"A proper library is a fine addition to any home. Not everyone watches television, after all."

"I completely agree."

Gwen pulled a couple of books from the shelf and glanced at the covers before turning them over to read the descriptions on the back. One was definitely a romance, which she did enjoy, but reading of someone else's love while hers wasn't near wasn't something she wanted to do. She placed the purple covered book back on the shelf and decided on what looked like a medical mystery. She removed a couple more titles from the shelf and noticed something hiding behind the books.

It was a framed photograph of a young couple. They were smiling and looked to be standing on the porch of the Blayneys' home.

"Oh, where did you find that?" Ruth asked as she came up behind her.

"Behind the books."

Ruth took the picture from her fingers and sighed. "This is our daughter…and an old boyfriend. I thought I'd thrown this away."

Gwen glanced at the photo again. She could see the resemblance between Ruth and her daughter. The man had a military haircut but instead of wearing a uniform, he had on a pair of jeans and a T-shirt.

"They look happy," Gwen said.

"They were. Charles and I thought they would marry eventually."

"What happened?"

Ruth blinked a couple of times. "He'd changed after returning from overseas. Annie broke it off with him. Charles was unbearably upset for months. He tried to change Annie's mind, but she wouldn't have it."

"What did you think of the breakup?"

"I wanted my baby happy. I understood why she wanted something else for her life other than a moody military man. They aren't always the easiest men to live with." Ruth glanced over and covered her mouth. "Oh…I'm sorry. I'm sure Neil is nothing like that."

Gwen grinned. "Of course he is. It's something I find endearing and vulnerable about him. I'm not offended."

"Well, Annie wanted something different." Ruth replaced the picture on the shelf and tucked books in front of it. "Perhaps Charles is keeping this. I'll just pretend I didn't see it."

What else did Ruth pretend not to see?

Dead birds weren't going to keep her away from the kids any longer. Besides, if she didn't explain why the police were poking into their private lives, she would lose all the ground she'd gained with them.

Karen ignored her virtual shadow that Michael and Dean insisted on. He drove her around like a child during the day and left only if Michael was home in the evenings. Otherwise, he or one of his colleagues slept in the guest room.

The man wasn't as big as Neil, but he had the same sunny disposition. Complete with a scowl and a hooded gaze that followed her everywhere. What Gwen found appealing about having a man follow her around all the time, Karen would never understand.

Although Karen knew it wasn't the man's occupation that attracted Gwen, but the man himself. She sure as hell hoped the sex was spectacular for her friend. Maybe when they forced their heads out of the sheets they'd realize no one was following them and come home. Karen couldn't wait for a heart-to-heart with her prim and proper friend.

"Try not to freak the kids out," Karen told her bodyguard.

He looked around them and followed her into the club.

Her gaze roamed the room, searching for Juan. When her search came up empty, she tried to hide her disappointment.

"Miss Jones!" Amy ran up and threw her arms around her.

Karen hugged her back and smiled. She loved these kids. Missed them.

"How are you, hon?"

"I aced my algebra test."

Karen slapped Amy's palm in the air. "Good news."

A couple of the other kids joined them, hugging and telling her how much they missed her. She dropped her purse at her math table and looked at the work spread out for the kids. Each one was at a different level but it appeared that they had all moved ahead in their studies while she'd been away.

"Are you back for good?"

"I am." Unless birdman arrived again. But she'd keep that to herself.

"There was a cop in here the other day asking us about you."

Karen shrugged. "Yeah, he's a friend of mine. Sorry about that."

"Is everything OK?" Steve, who'd been quiet the whole time asked.

"Seems like someone out there is trying to scare me."

The girls lost their smiles and the boys listened closer.

"Is that why they took Juan in to talk to him?" Steve asked. His voice angry.

Teenage gossip traveled fast. "The police talked to a lot of people. I'm sorry they had to come here."

"You're here all the time. Maybe they thought one of us saw something." Amy was like a middle child, always trying to see reason and come between the extremes in a family.

"So who's the goon at the door?"

Karen swiveled away from Steve's scornful face. He and Juan were friends, and it was obvious he wasn't happy about the police questioning him.

"He's my bodyguard."

"Seriously?"

"I don't think I'll have him for long. Just till they catch the guy following me."

"Wow, Miss Jones. Aren't you scared?"

"I was at first, Amy. Now I'm just pissed. You know? Like how dare someone try and get under my skin."

Steve kept looking at the bodyguard and then back at her. "You don't need a bodyguard here," Steve said. "We can take care of you."

Karen smiled. "Maybe you can convince Juan to come back."

Steve shrugged. "Maybe."

It was all Karen could ask for.

Chapter Twenty-Seven

Gwen stretched her back and ignored the ache the gardening was creating. At least if she were tired that night, she'd manage some sleep. Tossing around and dreaming of her husband, of where he was and what he was doing, wasn't leaving her time to rest.

To make matters worse, shortly after she and Ruth stepped on the path of restoring her flower garden, a call came in on behalf of Annie, asking for Ruth to fly to Florida. Something about her being sick, or so Charles had said.

Now it was only she and Charles in the house.

Gwen didn't like the arrangement in the least. The man watched her, but never made eye contact. She shifted her gaze to the house and noticed him in the window watching. He dropped the curtains but didn't move away.

He's only helping out Neil.

Neil…who'd been gone for nearly twenty-four hours. Twenty-four long and lonely hours.

You can do this.

Over her shoulder, he still watched.

You can do this! It's only a few days.

She shoved her hands back in the dirt and yanked on a stubborn weed.

"Well at least it isn't raining," Rick said in his ear from three hundred yards away.

Neil watched the trees swaying in the wind that had kicked up from nowhere. "Careful what you say." It wasn't uncommon for the late summer storms to knock out a couple of inches of rain before blowing to the east. They were prepared for anything. That's how the marines rolled.

Inside the tent, where neither of them planned on sleeping, was a decoy that only someone with heat-sensitive goggles would be able to see. Hot rocks from the campfire were placed inside a thermal bag that radiated heat and made anyone with the right equipment believe that someone slept inside. The knoll Neil was perched on backed up to a cliff a good three hundred feet above. There was no way anyone would scale it to get to him. Essentially, he was boxed in the canyon with only two ways in. Rick scouted on the northeast side while Neil watched for any activity on the southeast.

"Ever get the feeling we're waiting around for nothing?"

"You think Billy wasted himself?"

"Hell no," Rick's harsh whisper rang in Neil's ear.

"Raven will come."

"He's going to know we're waiting for him."

Neil moved his goggles to where Rick sat, and scouted all around him. Nothing. "He'll know *I'm* waiting for him. For all we know you're next on his list."

"Still convinced he's not coming in guns blazing?"

"Not unless his motivation has changed. Only way his motivation will have changed is if he thinks we've ID'd him."

The wind blew around the giant pine above him and made it creak.

Damn wind.

The dark sky didn't even sport a sliver of a moon. It wasn't too long ago he was looking up into the stars and sharing his childhood dreams with Gwen. He hated leaving her behind. He'd hate having her here more.

"Think you could nod off for an hour?" Rick asked.

"I might."

"I'll pull back, and watch your back."

Neil tucked back into the rock while Rick moved into position. An hour of sleep here and hour there was all any of them ever managed while in the field. The night before, Neil didn't even get that. Between his worry and need over Gwen and internal debate that Rick might know more than he was telling, Neil didn't chance sleep. Yet it became increasingly apparent that Rick was as much a target as he was. If Rick was behind any of this, he'd have made a move on him long before now. He needed to trust and God knew he needed to sleep.

They ducked under the wind created by the blades of the helicopter. Billy and Rick hoisted Linden's dead weight to the men on board the chopper. On board they pulled Mickey, who was limping but carrying himself, in with them.

Mac twisted toward the fireball they'd just left. His ears rang from the blast that took out his men. His back and head took a blow with his fall but he was otherwise OK. Alive.

Rick pulled him into the chopper and they were instantly airborne.

Mouths were moving but Neil couldn't hear what they said. Only ringing and the hum of the chopper. His chest ached and he coughed for what felt like an hour.

Billy knelt on the floor beside Linden while the two men Neil didn't know cut away Linden's clothes and exposed the blast wound in his gut and thigh. Blood was everywhere.

Neil grabbed the army blanket someone had draped over him and shoved it in Linden's side.

"Don't you fucking die."

But the color in Linden's face had gone stone white and before they could apply a field dressing his eyes lost focus and he took his last breath.

The chopper listed, and Neil had to hold on or risk falling.

The silence in his ears made his eyes focus.

Billy hung his head beside Linden. Rick's expression was equal parts rage and remorse. Mickey was doubled over.

Neil managed to get to Mickey's side and met the man's eyes. Neil lifted his hands in question and Mickey shook his head.

That's when Neil saw the shard of wood sticking from Mickey's groin. The bleeding was minimal, and they knew to keep the object in place until medical could see where it landed. He shook his head toward Mickey as if to remind him not to tug out the wood. Mickey was known to act against reason on occasion. Didn't seem he had the desire to do so now.

Neil slumped on the side of the chopper and hacked up a lung.

———

Blake had his secretary arrange his ride to the airport in the morning. He was headed to Colorado himself to trace Neil's steps. Everything had been too quiet for his taste and not hearing from his bodyguard or his sister weighed on him.

He no longer worried that someone was listening in on his conversations. There weren't any bugs detected and no one had left any dead birds lying around in days. Carter had flown back to Sacramento with the promise to make the phone calls to DC if need be.

Blake just hoped that Neil and Gwen had come to their senses and weren't running around with guns cocked and loaded.

He pulled off his tie and reached for the phone, intending to give Sam her nightly call.

The phone rang under his fingers, and made him jump.

Get a grip, Blake.

"Hello?" he answered when he didn't recognize the number on the caller ID.

"Mr. Harrison?"

Blake tossed his tie to the side of the bed and sat. "This is."

"I'm sorry to call you so late, Mr. Harrison. Even more sorry for why I'm calling."

Blake stopped midway through toeing off his shoes.

"Who is this?"

"Oh, I'm sorry. This is Bernard, the manager over here at First Class Services."

"The car service?"

"Right. Right. That's us."

Blake's anxiety dropped and his shoes fell to the floor one at a time. "What can I do for you, Bernard?" And why was he calling him now?

"We received the order for your car request in the morning."

"Is there a problem with tomorrow?"

"No, not at all, sir. We'll have a car ready for you."

Blake pinched one button after the other on his shirt and then moved to the cuff links. "Then why are you calling?"

Bernard was breathing a little fast, obviously worked up over something. Blake wanted to tell him that whatever his worries were, they had nothing on his. Instead, he just waited while the man started to apologize.

"I'm sorry. We here at First Class Services are so very sorry."

"Sorry for what?"

"I checked to see who your driver was earlier in the week. We try to keep them consistent whenever possible. As you know, we take great pride in the privacy of our customers. And you are a very valued customer—"

Blake rolled his eyes. "Bernard, can you please cut the crap and tell me why you've called? I have a busy day tomorrow." And at this rate, he'd still be on the phone with the poor sap.

"Sorry. Right. You see, the driver who picked you up. We don't know who he is."

"What do you mean you don't know who he is?"

"We received the request and a car went out earlier in the week…but none of our men were behind the wheel."

Blake stopped undressing. "Well someone sure as hell picked me up."

"Right. But it wasn't our man."

"He said he was from your service."

"I guarantee you, Mr. Harrison. He wasn't. We have security tape of the yard where we keep our cars. A man in our uniform is seen leaving the yard with a car and then returns a couple hours later."

"If he wasn't one of your men, then who was he?"

"We don't know. Your privacy is paramount to us. We have the police coming here now to view the tapes. I'm sure they'll want to talk to you. For that I'm very sorry."

"How the hell did this happen?" More deals were made in the backs of limousines than boardrooms.

"I'd suggest you consider who you were talking with and what about on the way home. Perhaps there was someone in need of the information you relayed on that short trip?"

He and Dean had to talk in the car because Neil suggested the house was bugged.

"Oh, damn."

"We're gravely sorry."

"Yeah, yeah…I'll be there with Detective Brown in an hour. I want to see those tapes."

"Of course, sir. Anything we can do."

Blake shoved his feet back in his shoes and made a call to Dean.

Forty-five minutes later, they were sitting in the offices of First Class Services with a nervous Bernard and a half dozen uniformed officers.

Blake listened to the story of how a complete stranger made his way onto the property, managed to get the keys to a company car, and then proceeded to leave said parking lot to pick him up at the airport without being detected.

"It had been an exceptionally busy weekend. Several of our drivers were still out from the night before. It's not unheard of for us to move drivers around from one lot to another." Bernard rambled on about the company and how it was run. According to the sister service in Orange County and the one in San Diego, none of their drivers had been given the green light to take assignments in the LA area on the date in question, therefore ruling out a driver on their staff.

An officer took Bernard's statement while another manager cued up the video of the man in question. The distance from the camera to the cars was anywhere from a hundred feet to three hundred feet. The man's face never turned directly toward the camera, making Blake think the man knew the camera was there. He wore the driver suit and even opted for a hat. Not all drivers wore them, but some did, which was why Blake didn't think much of it when he'd seen the man.

"Can you get in closer?"

As the image moved up, the quality of the picture dissipated. As Blake remembered, the man had a short haircut and nothing growing on his face or chin. Caucasian about six feet tall, medium build.

He looked familiar. But then he should. Blake had spoken briefly with the man and had given him a generous tip.

"We can enhance the image at the station, try and match him with those in the database." Dean stepped away from the monitor and glanced around the room. "Someone here must have spoken with the man."

Bernard shifted from foot to foot. "I've questioned my drivers. None of them have said they noticed him."

"What about dispatch?"

"We're not like a taxi service. We have a computerized system that lets our drivers know when one of their clients needs a ride. Like I explained to Mr. Harrison, we try to keep the same drivers with the same clients to better meet their needs. Mr. Harrison only uses us on occasion so we didn't have a request in for any one person."

"Then how do you pick which driver goes on the run?"

Bernard moved his stiff collar away from his neck. Blake almost felt sorry for the man.

"We rotate between who needs a run, and who best knows the area and protocols. Taking a car on the tarmac to pick up clients right from the airport requires a different level of security than someone taking a celebrity to a red carpet event. Lots of things are factored in."

"Show me how your drivers check a car in and out," Dean said.

Bernard moved to the monitor as the uniformed officer who'd been searching the video feed got up and moved. He opened up what looked like a home page for the service and clicked on an icon with a car graphic. A list of last names and locations sat neatly in a row. Beside them was a column for the driver to place their name.

"This first set of names are our regulars. Notice the color coordination of the drivers and the regulars. This next set of names are one timers. Special occasions, proms...beside the names are symbols. A martini glass for a known party where the driver is going to keep our passengers from driving while intoxicated. I try and use my male drivers, unless it's a bachelorette party..." Bernard got a little carried away in his explanation of his system, obviously proud of what he did. "Here is the airport symbol. If a driver is free to take the ride and sees this, he knows the ride is only open to him if he has the clearance."

"Let's see the date Mr. Harrison arrived."

Bernard clicked around on the calendar and brought up the date. Blake leaned forward and saw his name, location, time, and airport symbol. He was happy to see an absence of a martini glass. His mirth about that died when he saw the name of the driver. "Mac."

Blake's hand went down hard on the side of the computer desk. "Sonofabitch."

"Don't jump to conclusions," Dean told him.

"Who needs to jump?"

Dean grabbed his arm and pulled him from the room. "We don't know anything for certain."

"What the...we know Mac wasn't behind the wheel. We know a stranger listened in on our conversation we had in a car to avoid being heard in my home. We know whoever this guy was he had the ability to hack into this system and take off with a car, then return the damn thing without question. We know Neil believes someone of intelligence and ability is gunning for him and my sister. I don't have to jump in the water to know I'm going to get wet, Dean." And if Neil had managed to keep this ass from knowing where he was, Blake and Dean had blown that by openly talking about their findings in his house over the last couple of days. Which explains the extra dead bird in Karen's car. The tight tongues made this ass plant another dead bird and throw them off track. Make them think Neil wasn't sane.

"We've been conned and Neil isn't crazy." Neil was in danger and Blake had probably led his enemy right to him.

Chapter Twenty-Eight

Dinner the night before had been a strained affair. It didn't help that the wind had kicked up and the threat of rain had Gwen wondering where Neil was. Gwen took the pathetic path of pleading a headache and retired to her room early to avoid conversation with her host.

She couldn't place what about Charles bothered her most. The quiet plotting that seemed to happen behind his gaze, or the smile that reminded her of a clown at a circus. Neither were redeeming qualities in a person. *I'm sure he makes a great drill sergeant.*

Gwen moved quietly through the house, purposely leaving her room once the breakfast hour had passed. The house was quiet to the point she wondered if she were alone. In the kitchen, she placed a cup of water into the microwave to heat for tea. With the exception of a few clouds, the sky was clear.

"Be safe, Neil," she whispered to herself.

When the microwave chimed, Gwen turned to grab her cup.

Charles stood directly behind her, his lip turned up slightly. She screamed and stepped back into the counter, bruising her hip.

"Bloody hell," she gasped.

"I didn't mean to startle you." His coy smile fell and an expression of concern replaced it.

The hell you didn't. "I didn't hear you come in." She rubbed her hip and willed her pulse to calm.

"Wanted to make sure you had everything you needed." Charles moved a few paces away. The next county would have been better. The man wore the exact same clothes he'd worn since Neil had left. They were pressed and clean, but the exact style of military issue. Charles didn't leave the house, or even have a visitor. For a man of his rank, Gwen expected a little more of a revolving door.

"Your wife directed me to where things were in the kitchen."

Charles moved behind the counter and pulled out a tall stool.

Oh, great...company. Gwen found the tea and slowly removed the bag from the paper packaging. It became apparent that Charles wasn't going to open the conversation.

"Have you heard from Ruth?"

"She arrived in Florida."

Gwen dipped the tea bag, and waited for a more elaborate answer. "How is your daughter?"

"Happy her mother is with her." Gwen reminded herself that Neil used to give her such short and precise answers. Their time alone changed that.

"No one quite replaces our mum when we're ill."

The corner of Charles's lip turned up again. "One of the things women are good for."

Smiling when your back teeth are grinding is impossible. "Are there many women in the service under your command?"

His smile fell. "A few."

"You don't approve." She could see it in his face.

"Women belong in a home fixing *tea* and not in the wild removing targets."

Gwen crossed the room, made sure she had a way out without walking by him.

"Allowing women in must have been difficult for you to accept."

He shrugged. "I'm a soldier. I do what I'm told."

"As a major, don't you do most of the telling?" She blew over her tea.

Charles's hand rested on the counter and the index finger on his right hand started a slow, intermittent tap. "There are always people above you."

She thought of the picture Neil had shown her of his troop, or whatever it was they called themselves. *Friends.* "True. And those under you don't always survive their missions. That must be difficult." She couldn't imagine sending troops into battle and learning that some weren't coming home. The entire concept of war boggled her mind. Didn't every human want the same things? A happy and healthy family, food, a home? A world in which their children could grow to the best of their abilities and have families of their own? Truly, what more was there to need? Why fight? It made no sense to her.

"There's always collateral damage." His finger tapped a little harder. "A leader can't dwell on death. Not here."

If Gwen were to guess, she'd say that Charles didn't dwell. In fact, he probably erased the name of the lost and penciled in the next. Cold.

She'd rather have her Neil, who did think about the men who'd followed him into battle.

It came to her then, that if a man returned from war unaffected she wouldn't want to know him.

Gwen stared at a tree out the kitchen window, and noticed it bending in the wind. The desire to leave the major's presence turned her thoughts to the outside garden. If not for the muscles in her back that had screamed since she woke, she'd make her excuses and find a flower bed.

"I would never make a proper soldier, I'm afraid. I have difficulty squishing a bug."

"Let Neil stomp the life out of the insects."

She allowed a passing grin. *No, Neil set the bugs outside the door to fend for themselves.*

"Would you mind if I searched your library again? Seems the book I chose isn't helping me pass the time." Actually, she'd noticed a few photo albums Ruth had pointed out and thought it would be helpful to look through them. Perhaps Charles wasn't always so jaded.

"Help yourself."

"Thank you." She made as graceful an exit as she could. She was hungry, but not enough to stay in the man's presence.

Instead of having his pilot fly him to Colorado, and potentially hand deliver Neil's enemy to his side, Blake placed a call to Carter from his office in hopes of keeping some of what he had to say private. Once Blake brought his best friend up to date, he started pulling the hard favors.

"Do you have any contacts at the Pentagon? Anyone who can search out where Neil trained and who with? The men on his team? Anything?" Desperation seeped into his bones. More than the lack of control over everything unfolding, Blake hated the unknown. Where was Neil and where had he stashed his sister to keep her safe? He didn't even want to consider the diamond ring that was purchased and the meaning behind it.

"My contacts there are shallow at best," Carter informed him. "But we both know someone who might be able to get the information we want."

Blake squeezed his eyes shut. "Your uncle?"

"Right."

Senator Maxwell Hammond had been in the political game from the time he was in high school. Blake didn't trust the man. Not that he was a *known* dirty politician, but Blake believed Max had no problem getting his feet in the mud to get his way. Oh, they washed up before he donned his shoes, but there was always a little dirt left behind. Being indebted to the man was not something Blake would choose.

What choice did he really have?

"You sure you're ready to pull that card?"

"We need to know who birdman is. Need to find Neil and Gwen. The whole thing is smelling up our life. We've given Neil the quiet time he requested and we've not heard anything for what… three, four days? Anything could have happened."

"What are we asking Max to search for?"

"Neil directed us to contact the president and use code name Raven. This has something to do with his time in the service. I know Neil spent time on a Colorado base, but there's a bunch of them, several in Colorado Springs. We need to start there. Did he stash Gwen with one of his buddies? Did he solicit one of his old friends to help? Did he need something to catch this guy that he can only get from a military warehouse?"

"You've given this a lot of thought."

"It's all I've thought about. That and how much I miss my wife and son."

"Do you have the picture from Neil's room?"

Blake opened his desk drawer and removed Neil's file. "Yeah."

"Scan it in and send it to me. Maybe someone will recognize him…or someone else in the picture."

While they talked, Blake placed the picture in his scanner and made the copy. "Makes me wish I'd had deeper conversations with the man."

"Deeper with Neil is what exactly? Two sentences in a row?"

Blake grinned. "Best damn security agent I've ever had."

"Well be prepared, Your Grace…Neil just might elevate to 'best damn brother-in-law' you've ever had."

"Thanks for reminding me, Governor. Gwen could do worse." Now that he knew Neil wasn't nuts, it helped ease the concerns about her shacking up with the man.

"OK, I got the e-mail. I'll get on the phone and see what Max can do. Let me know if you hear anything."

"You'll be the second to know behind Dean."

They said their good-byes and hung up.

Blake stared at the photograph, memorizing the faces. They were all big men, as he would expect of marines. One guy had a huge smile on his lips and another held a rifle in each hand with ammunition belts strapped over his shoulders. Two of them had a freshness behind their eyes that reminded Blake of Kansas farm boys. One had his hair so short his ears stood out. Or maybe his ears were just large.

His cell phone in his pocket rang. He checked the ID before he answered. It was Dean.

"Hear anything?"

"From Neil? No. I'm at your place with Neil's security team. Ken Sands called in a specialist who deals with some of the higher-tech bugs seen in political circles."

Blake's skin started to crawl.

"Guess what we found?"

"Neil's bug."

"Seriously high-tech shit, too. We're talking classified, spy on the president stuff. Sands sent a team over to Tarzana to check the system there. Homicide was just about to wrap up the naked hot tubbers as an accident. I'm going to have them call in the military police and look again."

Blake looked at the photo in his hands. "Any ID on the driver?"

"Not yet. Wish I had a set of prints. All military personnel are fingerprinted, blood typed, and photographed when they go in. The picture we have cleaned up a little, but it's not great."

"Send me a copy. I'll turn Neil's place upside down and compare it to any he might have."

"You're thinking this guy knows Neil?"

"Or someone gave him a detailed description."

Dean cussed under his breath. "This reeks."

"Tell me about it."

Raven tucked his car off the road and slept for four hours straight. Didn't even bother calling in to let his boss know he was in town. There was no way he was going to take Mac on a couple hours of sleep. If anything, he'd wait until Mac was exhausted and he was rested.

He stepped out of the car and into the cool, moist air of the Colorado Rockies. A few feet away was a tall pine. He pissed on it before wiping his hands on his pants. *Gotta love the great outdoors.* A nice cabin in the woods away from everyone and everything would be perfect for him and his girl. He could hunt, and she could take care of their home. Once he took care of his little leftover problems, everything would fall back into place.

His left leg stiffened in the cold, reminding him of the pain he'd suffered. All because Mac didn't call the shot in time.

Damn Billy for not stepping over Mac to do the right thing. Billy saw it coming, and weaseled out because of a kid. A stupid fucking kid that would have grown up hating all of them anyway.

That's all right. Billy got his. And he got Billy's girl right before he filled her with C-4 and blew the fuck out of her. That was sweet.

Raven couldn't tell his boss that part. Wouldn't be wise to make the boss think he liked blowing people up. When he came home, he had talked to so many shrinks that he knew exactly what questions they'd ask. More importantly, what answers they wanted to hear.

Raven made his way back to the car and tossed a handful of sour candy into his mouth.

After turning on his phone, he called in to see where his assignment had landed.

Chapter Twenty-Nine

"What if he doesn't come?"

Rick posed the question Neil didn't want to think about. They were going on their third day. He'd taken one of the bugged hand receivers from Blake's home and was using it as a homing beacon for Raven. All the man had to do was check out the frequency.

But every hour that passed without the man making an appearance made him crazy. Worse, he didn't have any contact with Gwen to know how she was holding up in his absence. If Raven were watching, he could be waiting for them to give up and go home. Thus leading him to Gwen. And that couldn't happen.

Both he and Rick circled their camp, changing positions often. If Raven was out there, they weren't going to give him time to settle into any one spot.

"I've been thinking," Rick said in his ear. "Raven wants to kill us, right?"

"Ultimately."

"But he wants it to look like an accident…like with Billy."

Neil peered through his binoculars, noticed a flock of birds taking flight from a faraway pine. He kept his gaze on the activity at the base of the tree, wondering what disturbed them.

"No one will think I offed myself."

"Double for me. So that leaves what? A hunting accident? Traffic accident?"

"We're not driving." A deer stood under the tree, his nose lifted in the air. Neil moved his gaze in the opposite direction of the animal.

"Where did you park your car?" Neil asked.

"Oh, damn...you don't think he'll blow it up?"

"Wouldn't you?"

Rick cussed. "Knew I should have just parked it here."

"But then he'll know for sure there are two of us. This way there might be some doubt."

"Not going to help my car. I just got a Cat Back system in her. Sweet ride. Fuck. Maybe I should go check on her."

Neil chuckled. "Sure...walk into his trap. Good thinking."

Rick mumbled another series of curses. "It's not like I have a bank load of money to replace her when this is done. Insurance doesn't cover everything."

"Haven't you been working?"

"Here and there. Nothing steady. Being in the marines is a hard life to follow with a paper-pushing job. Ya know?"

He did. "Let's get through this first. I can always use another set of eyes."

"Private security?"

"Might sound boring, but it seems the people I work with always have someone after them."

"Maybe."

"No pressure. Job's yours if you want it." Having Rick on his team would be like having a brother on his side.

"Might not have a choice if this fucktard blows up my ride. Damn it, I should have thought of that."

Neil took a few steps out of his hiding spot and looked around. Nothing.

"I'm going toward camp. Start a fire and see what the smoke attracts."

"Copy that."

Neil zigzagged through the trees until he reached camp.

He'd already oiled up leaves to make more smoke than fire. He lit them, and piled green wood on top. Once assured that the smoke wouldn't die out the minute he stepped away, Neil back-tracked.

"Remind me never to camp with you."

"Bite me."

"Errr, cowboy…didn't think you cared," Rick teased.

Neil couldn't help but laugh. Before his laugh faded a large crash sounded north of their perimeter.

"What the fuck?"

Neil's skin prickled. "Stay down."

Everything calmed. "It's a diversion."

Exactly what Neil thought. "Where's your car?"

"Ah, fuck!"

Yeah, that's what Neil thought, too.

On the bright side, it was game on.

The photo albums could have been any home in America. Backyard picnics and holiday affairs and several pictures of Ruth, Charles, and their daughter Annie vacationing in national parks. Some of the early pictures indicated that Charles used to smile. At some point, the pictures became snapshots of their life void of any emotion.

What Gwen didn't find was any pictures of Annie and the man Ruth described as her husband. Even though Charles didn't approve of the union, there had to be some kind of relationship. Even a strained relationship would have found its way around a Christmas dinner table.

Finally, Gwen gave up on the photo albums sitting out for her to search through and she decided to see if there were any other pictures tucked into the shelves of Ruth's books. She started with the photo she knew was there. The couple looked happy enough. The man kept a possessive arm around Annie and she smiled for the camera. Recognition tickled the back of Gwen's mind, which made her itch in a strange way.

She removed books from the shelves, looked behind them, and then replaced them. She did this one shelf at a time until she came upon another photograph. Annie was younger, but she sat in a pub with a man in uniform. Not the same man, Gwen noted. She replaced the photographs and kept looking.

She was about to give up her search when she noticed several books pushed out away from the rest on the shelf. Sure enough, behind them was another picture. This one wasn't in a frame, or cared for with any honor. Gwen unfolded the picture and instantly recognized it.

The same picture sat in Neil's wallet only this one was a larger copy. It was easier to see the faces of the men who were deployed on that ill-fated mission.

She scanned the faces knowing something significant was in there. Otherwise why would it be hidden among the books and not framed and on a mantel?

Neil attempted a smile and just seeing a picture of him warmed her a little. Her eyes traveled back to one particular face several times before she realized what it was she saw.

She found the hidden picture Ruth had told her about a few days before and removed it. Sure enough, the man in that picture was one of Neil's men. Did Neil know that Annie dated one of his men?

Gwen took the pictures to the desk in the room, and eyed the door. She considered closing it, but thought that might look suspicious. Instead, she closed her eyes and listened to the sounds of the house. The central air-conditioning unit kicked on with a hum. In the kitchen was the faint sound of the refrigerator. Beyond that was the sound of a television. Probably something Charles was watching.

She opened her eyes again and peered at the photographs.

Ruth had said Annie had given up on the man because he'd changed after returning from overseas. It's possible the mission Ruth spoke of was the one that affected Neil so profoundly.

If Gwen remembered correctly Charles was extremely unhappy with the breakup...wanted his daughter to give up her husband Andrew and find a military man.

Gwen's head started to ache. "How upset were you?" she whispered to herself. She hated damning the man who'd only been kind to her. Creepy, but kind.

On the desk next to her was a phone. So close it practically called out her name. A call to Eliza, just to say she was alive...and maybe she could find out a thing or two about Major Blayney. And wasn't she safe here if indeed Charles was her protector? And if he wasn't...then she wasn't safe at all.

Gwen tapped her finger on the desk, inched her hand toward the receiver, and then pulled it back. She jumped up from the desk and returned the pictures. Her feet nearly made it to the door of the room when she abruptly turned and grasped the phone.

There wasn't a dial tone.

She clicked the on button several times.

Nothing.

Her palms started to sweat.

———

"I have a meeting in thirty minutes but I think you need to hear this now."

Blake held his breath as Carter spoke. "Well don't keep me waiting, counselor."

"The picture of Neil's troop came up with a few unusual hits. Not one of the men in the picture is still in the service. Look at the thing, Blake…all those guys were young. Most men go in for life."

"I know Neil said he lost some of his men in battle."

"Right. Three died in a classified 'training accident.' Could be anything."

Blake expected that. While Carter talked to him, he brought up the photograph on his cell phone and scanned the images with his eyes. "OK. What else?"

"One of the men in the picture recently committed suicide."

"Suicide?"

"Yeah. Apparently his wife left him and he jumped off a cliff."

"A cliff jumper? Why would a man with military experience pick anything other than a gun to kill himself?"

Carter sighed. "My thoughts, too. The last thing to know is that every man received discharge papers within the same month."

"Dishonorable?"

"No. Just let go."

"Does that happen?"

"Not often. If at all."

"Who gave the order for discharge? Maybe the brass knows something."

"Max is looking into it."

Blake picked up the picture of the driver. He looked at the picture on his phone again. "Oh, shit."

"What?"

"This guy…the one who stole the car…he's in the picture with Neil."

"What? You sure?" Carter asked.

"Yeah…second guy on the right. Big ears. How did I not see this before now? I need a name. This is our guy. And Neil won't realize his old friend is behind this."

"Get Dean on the horn. See if he can track the guy. We have to get to Neil."

"Colorado is a big state. They could be anywhere by now."

"You said yourself Neil won't run forever. He'd find a safe place and fight."

"I'm going to Colorado Springs. There are nearly a dozen bases there. One of them is going to know something about Neil."

"I wish I had a better idea."

"This is giving me more gray hair than my son, Carter. We need to catch a break," Blake said.

"We know more today than yesterday. We're getting somewhere."

"Too damn slow for my taste."

"Hang in there. Call me if you find out anything."

They hung up and Blake called his pilot. Then he called Dean.

———

Gwen calmed her nerves the best she could before she returned to the room where Charles was watching TV. The news program spotlighted two beautiful people who told the fate of the world. Their plastic smiles looked as fake as hers felt. *You can do this!*

"Did you find a book?" Charles asked.

"Ah…yes," she lied. "A couple."

He glanced toward her, but didn't catch her eyes.

"I noticed a pizza parlor on base and thought it would be nice to have for an early supper. I was going to call and have it delivered but it seems the phone isn't working."

Charles twisted his head in a slow and methodical matter. "Pizza?"

She gave a coy smile. "Yes."

"I think Ruth has the frozen kind in the freezer."

"Uhm, I suppose that will work. Is there a problem with the phone line?"

He turned his attention back to the TV. "The phone is fine."

"There's no dial tone."

"I believe Neil asked you to avoid calling anyone while he's away."

Her skin itched. "I can't imagine anyone could get to me here."

Charles focused on the news and for a moment, she didn't think he was going to say any more on the subject.

"Women don't know how to take orders," he said.

"I believe Neil was requesting me to stay quiet for a time. It's been nearly three days. I'm starting to worry."

"A woman's job is to worry. Glad to know you have that down." His fingers started to tap the edge of the chair.

A proper British cut sat on her tongue but she bit it back. This man wasn't right in the head. His view on women proved he was the wrong man to protect her. He'd find her useless at some point, or maybe not worthy of Neil and let whoever might want to harm her have free rein.

She backed off. "I am terribly worried. I suppose I'll help your wife with her garden."

He nodded toward the TV. "Looks like rain."

"A little rain doesn't stop the British from much." She tried to smile.

"I thought you wanted pizza."

Lost my appetite. "It's early." She turned from the room and felt his eyes on her as she walked away.

Chapter Thirty

It would be suicide to check on the noise. They'd set traps throughout their camp and circled around to them to see if any were tripped. None were. He knew Raven was using psychological bullshit to make them sloppy. The cat and mouse game could go on for a while.

"Anything?" Neil asked.

"Too fucking quiet."

"Going up." Neil let Rick know he was moving to his perch. Each time he moved through the forest, he used a different path. Five yards from his destination, he noticed a patch of black feathers. He stopped and turned. He donned his heat-sensitive goggles and scanned the area. At ground level, he didn't see anything with a body temperature. With the air temperature dropping, it was easy to see a heat print of wherever he'd been. And if he could see the imprint, there was a strong possibility that his enemy could, too.

Which meant he had to keep moving.

"Keep moving."

"I am."

Neil scoped out his lookout, didn't see anything out of place, and moved in. He scanned the forest floor for more feathers and found only leaves and twigs. Once he secured his back against the cliff, he scanned the area below. A heat signature was due east. "Is that you?"

The arm of the heat moved away from the bright middle color and waved. The area was too fucking large. Trees were everywhere. The kind he could hide behind…the kind Raven could hide behind.

A high-pitched alarm went off in his earpiece. "Trip sensor," he said aloud for Rick's sake. He turned on his cell and mapped which sensor he'd placed was tripped. "South." Where the road passed through. They had to be careful. Didn't want a civilian to stumble upon this little war and get hurt.

"You hold. I'll look," Rick said.

The clouds overhead started to darken, destroying the light they had. From the smell in the air, Neil guessed they'd all be wet in a matter of minutes. The thought no sooner left his mind when a clap of thunder reached his ears.

"Great," he heard Rick mumble.

Neil watched Rick's movements, and then he saw additional movement. "On your right, two hundred yards." The heat signature was weak, but whoever was responsible for it wasn't strolling through the woods on a walk, nor were they walking with purpose.

Rick stopped and ducked. His silhouette nearly disappearing from Neil's range.

Raven moved north…slowly.

Neil walked along the face of the cliff until he had to move to ground level to intercept.

"I see him," Rick said.

"Taking position in front of him." They spoke just above a whisper.

Neil managed a few more yards before he heard Rick say, "He stopped."

He peered through his goggles and noticed a blurring of heat behind several trees. Only he couldn't tell if it was Rick or Raven.

"Are you on the move?"

"Yes."

So the blurring image was Rick. Neil looked north. His target came into range. Then he vanished.

"Sonofabitch."

"What?"

"He disappeared."

"I still have visual," Rick said.

Neil removed the heat goggles and replaced them with binoculars. There, in the trees was his target ducking behind a tree. He was camouflaged so well, Neil hardly noticed him. Camouflage didn't reduce the heat of the human body, which meant their man had some sort of cloak.

Moving slowly, Neil positioned himself so Raven was between them. "He's watching you," Neil told Rick.

"I feel him."

Neil removed the AK from his back and cocked it.

Another clap of thunder filled the air; behind it, large droplets of rain followed. Neil used the noise of nature to hide his movements. He managed to get closer.

They all paused.

Raven moved east with the next flash of lightning. Not the direction Neil wanted.

Neil crouched on the ground and removed a detonator from his field jacket. "Stay alert. I'm bringing him back."

With a press of a button, a smoke bomb went off in Raven's path.

Their target shifted his body and broke through the northeast flank. Neil rushed to get ahead of him. Behind him, he heard Rick moving.

When Raven neared another diversion, Neil let the bomb go off.

The area started to fill with smoke despite the heavy rain that started to fall.

Neil lost sight of Raven.

"Where is he?" Rick asked.

"Don't know."

Neil scanned the area, but on ground level, he couldn't see jack. It was times like this he wished he were built like a squirrel so he could scurry up a tree and look.

He swiveled around, in case Raven managed to dart by without him seeing. He was about to give up when he noticed a blur fifty yards west.

Right in the face of the cliff. *Perfect!*

"We've boxed him in."

———

Gwen bundled into the sweatshirt she owned and used the extra material to hide the fact that she had on a couple of layers of clothing. There was no possible way Neil knew how off his friend was. She'd find a way off his property and manage a phone call at one of the stores on base. Between her brother and Carter…she'd be safe.

Safer than she was here.

She managed to maneuver through the house, placing a couple of snack bars in her pockets in case it proved difficult to wait for her brother. Every squeak in the house made her pause. The television had been turned off and the silence made her shiver.

In the backyard, she found the spot she'd abandoned the day before and pretended to pull weeds and turn the soil. Within fifteen minutes, her back ached from the previous day's labor, not that it would stop her from acting as if she were settling into the job.

She didn't need to look to know Charles watched. He wasn't obvious this time by standing in a window, but she felt his eyes on her nonetheless. Once she'd accumulated a pile of weeds, she gathered them in her gloved hands and acted as though she were searching for a trash can. The side of the house was bare of cans, which she knew from the day before. There was however, a gate, leading to the front yard. She dropped the contents of her hands and eased the gate open. With her path clear, she walked swiftly, avoiding a run. The rock crushed beneath her feet and the sound of soft rain was all that accompanied her.

She smiled, despite the cold.

At the end of the drive, she turned toward the main road and rounded the corner. She peered over her shoulder and didn't see if he followed her.

Gwen released a nervous laugh and turned toward the road.

Charles stood a few feet away. His clothes wet. "Going somewhere?"

It took every effort not to scream. Not that there was anyone near enough to hear her. And what would she say anyway? "A short walk." She ignored the fact her hands were still covered with dirty gloves.

His humorless face strode to her. "Alone?"

"This weather reminds me of home," she told him. "There's no need for you to come along."

His eyes narrowed.

"You aren't dressed for a walk. I won't be long." She moved to step around him.

He blocked her path. "No. You won't." He reached out and grasped her arm, turning her back to the house.

"Excuse me?" She tugged away from him but his vise grip wouldn't allow her to move. His fingers dug into her flesh beneath the layers of fabric she wore, and pain shot down her arm.

Charles said nothing as he marched her up his drive and back into the house.

"Release me," she insisted once they were inside and he'd closed the door behind him.

He twisted the lock and chained the dead bolt, all the while holding her to the point of bruising her skin.

"Mr. Blayney, I don't take kindly to violence. Release me at once." Between the cold and wet of outside and the growing concern of what the man holding her was going to do, Gwen began to tremble.

Instead of acting on her demand, Charles shoved her ahead of him down the hall and to a door in the back of the kitchen. Through the pantry was another passage, one she'd hardly noticed before. Behind that was a set of stairs descending to a basement.

Gwen dug her heels into the floor and braced her hands on a doorframe.

"What are you doing?"

"What I was told to do should you attempt to escape."

"What?" *Told to do?* What was he talking about?

Charles peeled her fingers off the doorframe. "Keeping you against your will for the sake of our great country."

"That's preposterous. I'm not a threat to your country." Although she might consider bodily harm to the man holding her.

"I don't know about that. Snooping around my home, finding classified information…"

What information? She'd only found pictures.

"And since you're practically a US citizen I'm within my rights to hold you against your will."

Her thoughts turned to Neil. Did he know Major Blayney would hold her like this? The expression on her face must have shown her question.

Charles released a sadistic laugh. "You don't think he married you because he wanted to, do you?"

Her heart dropped. "Of course he did."

"You go on believing that."

Without further words, he shoved her down the stairs and into the lower quarters of the house. Like any basement, it was dark, damp, and smelled of mold. The walls were finished but the dark pegboard was less than comforting. An old sofa sat center room and boxes were stacked along the back wall. There were only a couple of lights above her head and not one window to be seen.

"You can't leave me down here."

"You've proven you can't be left to your own recognizance."

Charles shoved her down and twisted her arms behind her. Dirt from the couch drifted to her nose and made her cough.

"Stop." She struggled under his grasp but didn't manage any leverage. She felt the steel on her wrist before she realized what Charles was doing. "This isn't necessary. Clearly you can overpower me."

"Neil will not approve of what you're doing." She pleaded, using everything she could. "Your wife might come home and find me here."

"My wife is in Florida searching for retirement houses she'll never live in. Once she realized no one was dying I needed to give her a reason to stay. You don't think her leaving was an accident, do you?"

The metal around her wrists clicked into place, but Charles kept his knee in her back, rendering her immobile.

"Why are you doing this?"

"I have my reasons."

Reasons that had nothing to do with keeping her safe. She kept her head and lay still. She needed to think and plan her escape.

He left her facedown and handcuffed on the smelly sofa.

As she remembered the other precaution she'd done for her own safety, Charles delivered all the evidence she needed to understand his ultimate intent. "Don't worry, *Lady Harrison*. As soon as

I have word that Neil has been taken care of, I'll take care of you quickly. Only need to keep you around if your husband outsmarts my man. Leverage. A man always needs leverage."

She gasped, and Charles shoved something between her teeth to keep her from screaming.

"He worked under the command of Major Charles Blayney. The major still lives on base at Fort Carson with his wife. Word is he keeps putting off his retirement."

Blake listened to Carter on a phone at twenty-three thousand feet. They were flying over Utah, trying to avoid a storm that was covering the Rockies and delaying air traffic due to lightning strikes. Twice his pilot told him they might have to divert south to Santa Fe or north to Cheyenne.

"You think Neil is there?"

"Could be. I'm trying to get you clearance so you can talk to the man. Looks like he was the one who called the discharge of Neil's troop."

"So he'll know who our killer is?"

"Killer?"

"Dean called before I left. Homicide ruled on the neighbors after he called in a military expert."

"Know something, Blake? All this is starting to sound like a damn conspiracy. Military-grade bugs, wired Jacuzzis that fry those inside...dead birds left as a diversion. I keep coming back to why? Max can't find a damn thing about an Operation Raven. Brings me to the question of who knew about Raven? Who wants the soldiers that were involved with Raven dead?"

"You think someone is going after all of them?"

"The suicide reported about Neil's friend had a tidbit in the police report about a dead raven under the body. I have a call in to the local sheriff in Tennessee, suggesting he reopen the case."

"Anyone ever find the man's wife?"

"No. The mom filed a missing persons report but nothing has come of it."

The turbulence in the air dropped the plane a few feet, and kept Blake in his leather seat. "Major Blayney should know about Raven...right?"

"Should. But I doubt he'd say anything to you."

"It's a start. Hell, it's the only lead we have."

"Call me when you land."

Blake hung up, more worried than ever.

Chapter Thirty-One

Rick moved in from the south, Neil took the north.

The rain fell in steady sheets, adding to the misery of the situation. Their advance on their enemy moved too quickly. So much so, Neil questioned it.

"Hold back," he instructed Rick.

"Feels too easy."

"Right." He loved the fact that he and Rick had always read the other's thoughts.

"There's no way out for him. Not without going through one of us."

Neil looked behind him for the thousandth time. "Think he's working with someone else?"

"Haven't seen anyone else."

Neither had Neil. Pivoting, he checked behind him.

Nothing.

The rain around him hit the forest floor with a force that made a constant sound against everything around him. Having spent a large portion of his life in California, he enjoyed the rain when it came...just not today.

"Assume someone else is out here."

"Good plan," Rick murmured.

Or Raven had a trick up his ass. They encroached on the cliff with caution.

Neil's fingers cooled with the dropping temperatures. He lowered his weapon to the ground and stopped long enough to look behind him. His eyes landed on something purple on the ground. He shifted toward the object, noticed something like it in a yellow color. Peering closer he noticed candy. He turned away, thinking at first that someone had left it on the path long before now.

He hesitated.

Candy? Who did he know that ate the stuff...the small bits easily tucked into a pocket?

The chopper was ten miles from their destination.

Someone had covered Linden's body with an army green blanket, covering his face. Rick held on to one of the straps in the wall and stared blankly out the open door. Billy hung his head in his hands.

Mickey reached into his pocket, removed his ever-ready candy, and popped a few pieces into his mouth. Even through the pain of his injury he managed to live up to his name. Mickey Mouse...land of big ears and kid candy.

Neil dropped back. His insides curled onto him.

Mickey.

Why?

"Rick...stop."

A few moments passed. "What?"

"Drop back."

"He's right there."

Neil swallowed. "I know who it is."

I know who it fucking is.

Gwen rolled onto her back, her hands behind her.

The door at the top of the stairs closed with a resounding click. She knew if she made it up the stairs without falling, she'd find the door locked.

The cloth in her mouth cut into her cheeks and dried her mouth out instantly. A dry mouth was the least of her worries.

Her heart beat so fast and hard in her chest it threatened to explode. Charles was directing their enemy. All her reservations about the man were spot-on. Not that being right was doing her any good now.

Gwen twisted her hands in the cuffs a few times even though intellectually she knew getting them off without a key was futile. Didn't stop her from trying. As the adrenaline started to wane, fear took its place. The dingy basement didn't bother her as much as it could, but the realization that there was only one way out did. When she felt her eyes start to fill with moisture, she struggled against the handcuffs again, and felt the metal bite into her skin. With the pain, her tears dried up. She would not pity herself and fall further victim to her captor. He'd love nothing more than to return to the basement and find her helpless and crying.

She wouldn't give him the satisfaction. All his talk about what women were good for, and what they weren't, told her how much he underestimated her gender.

He'd left the light on, giving her the ability to see what might be hiding in the corners of the room that might aid her. She stood and moved around the room. Above her head were pipes and wiring running the length of the room. There was a water heater in one corner and what looked to be a fuse box close by. Sadly, she'd never had a need to open an electrical box in her life and could only identify it because of some of the television shows she'd watched in the past. With her hands behind her back, she couldn't reach the thing anyway.

There were boxes piled on one wall about three deep. Several were labeled Christmas, and a few more had the name Annie scribbled on top. Gwen kicked at a box that wasn't labeled. When the box hardly moved, she pushed her knee into it.

Heavy.

With a little effort, she twisted her hands to the box and used her fingertips to pry open the cardboard.

Books. Looks like I found Ruth's library.

She couldn't imagine books doing her a lot of good. Perhaps if her hands were free she could throw them at Charles, but that wasn't an option in her current state.

Gwen turned toward the boxes with Annie's name on them. Inside one box was what looked like a gallery of children's artwork. The kind a child would bring home from primary school and litter the refrigerator with. Gwen easily pushed one box off of the other and opened another one. This one held items from an earlier time. Plush toys, a baby blanket. Nothing useful.

The Christmas boxes held the typical suspects. Lights, ornaments, knickknacks that needed to be dusted throughout the month of December and then put away again. The thought of the holiday brought a chill down her spine. If she didn't find a way out of this basement, she might never see another Christmas.

What about Neil? He was out there thinking she was safe… and the man he chose to protect her wanted him dead. The back of her throat tightened.

He can take care of himself.

She had to believe that.

Gwen backed away from the boxes and leaned against the arm of the dirty couch.

Think, Gwen. What can I use here?

The boxes represented the women in Charles's life. His wife's books, which he apparently didn't care for. And his daughter's childhood. A daughter whom he wasn't happy with at the current time. It seemed he'd packed up his daughter and tucked her away. Out of sight, out of mind. Much like Gwen's own father had done. Yet Gwen knew her father loved her in his own way.

But did Charles always think about Annie in such a sour way? If he saw the items in the boxes, would they evoke a compassionate memory? A memorable and pleasant holiday? The man had already made it clear he planned on killing her. Provoking him to hasten his desire wasn't smart...but maybe reminding him of what he'd lose if caught would make him think twice.

If she made him hesitate...

Gwen leaned on the edge of the couch and lifted her right leg to her hands behind her back. She assured herself that she could reach what she secured to her ankle before she'd left the house.

Removing the revolver now, however, wasn't necessary. She could reach it, which gave her some comfort. Not that she knew how she would fire the thing at him from behind her back, but she damn well would if she had to.

Neil met up with Rick, seeing him face-to-face for the first time in three days.

His friend's questioning eyes met his. It killed Neil to put his thoughts to words. "It's Mickey."

Rick's face went stark white. "What the—"

Neil opened his palm and displayed the bits of candy he'd found on the path. "Know anyone else who eats this stuff like it's crack?"

Rick grabbed at the candy, stared at it, and then threw it to the ground in disgust. "Fuck. Why? Why would he do this?"

"I don't know. But if we find out we stand a chance of getting him out of here alive...so he can get help."

"The fucker killed Billy. I don't give a crap if he has a lunch date with the devil."

Neil grabbed Rick's arm as he turned away. "It's Mickey, Rick. C'mon. Of all of us, he's the one who lost the most. The man doesn't even have his balls anymore." The groin injury left the man impotent. A fact Neil forgot until the moment he knew Mickey was the one gunning for them.

"You think he blames us for that?"

Neil let Rick go when his friend stopped pulling away. "I don't know. Maybe. I know he was dating someone before Operation Raven and when he returned she let him go."

"We were all on the same mission. None of us is to blame."

"Logic doesn't play into a sick mind. Explains all the class A military bugs and toys he's using. Stuff that's come about since we were in."

Rick turned in a circle, and then glared at the face of the cliff. "I checked on him. Heard he was deep undercover."

"Who told you that?"

"The major."

Neil's skin chilled. "The major?"

"I called him…you know, hey, how ya doing…by the way do you have any idea where Mickey ended up? I didn't want to alarm the guy. He said he'd get back to me. Called a couple days later and said Mickey's file indicated an assignment."

Neil took a breath. "What made you think he was deep under-cover?"

Rick shook his head. "I found Mickey's dad's number. The old man said his son was on a secret mission. Dads do that. Brag about their kids. I added the information together."

"Only we're his secret mission."

"Wouldn't his superiors realize he was AWOL?"

"Blayney doesn't know," Neil said.

"How can you be sure?"

Neil clenched his teeth. "I left Gwen with him."

Rick stilled and stared. "For her protection?"

"Right. Who better than the US Marines to protect my wife?"

"Your wife?"

"Married her right before I met up with you."

"Damn, Neil. Why didn't you tell me? That's huge."

Yeah, well, now wasn't the time for pats on the back and the sharing of beer. "Chuck implied that he'd have a better chance of keeping her safe if she were my wife. In case she started to get anxious and wanted to leave. I didn't want Raven…Mickey finding her and using her against me like Billy and his wife."

Rick narrowed his eyes. "So you married her *only* to keep her safe?"

Neil shook his head. He loved her. Oh, how he loved her. "Would have married her anyway."

"Chuck suggested marriage?"

"No. I suggested marriage, Chuck expedited the priest and stood as witness."

Neil peered toward the cliff, wondering if Mickey watched them as he kept hidden behind the cropping of trees.

"Something doesn't feel right," Rick said. "If that's Mickey up there then someone knows he's AWOL. Unless there is a price on our heads."

It didn't feel right to Neil either. "We need to find out who Mickey is working with. The guy was good, but I never thought he'd win a prize for intelligence." Mickey was the youngest one on their team. What he lacked in leadership ability, he made up for with raw power and enthusiasm. Always popping his sugar fix and pushing the team to move faster. Neil remembered when he'd heard about the extent of Mickey's injury, that the man would survive mentally so long as he had an outlet for his energy. The marines always needed men like him.

He'd be OK.

Only he wasn't.

"We need to draw him out. Get him talking."

"Suggestions?" Rick asked.

"We get close and start talking. Make him put our faces in his head instead of a target. If he's working for someone, something will come out. If he's alone…well, we'll deal with that later."

Rick nodded. "I'll take the south."

"Be safe."

Rick winked, and disappeared into the brush.

Chapter Thirty-Two

Moving around the room kept her warm. She managed to remove a few strands of colored lights and plugged them into the sole outlet in the room. One set started to blink, adding a twinkle to the dismal room. The irony of the image would have worked up a manic laugh if her mouth weren't as dry as cotton.

Every once in a while she heard Charles roaming the floor above her and she'd stop. No need for him to come into the room until she had everything where she wanted it.

She realized that the only weapon she had to take Charles off guard was a psychological one. Strewing as much of the room as she could with Annie's childhood memories along with their household Christmas items was bound to provoke some memories with the man. Something other than the hate that lived inside his soul. If the kid paintings and baby blanket did nothing for him, at least there would be some evidence that she'd been down there against her will. She'd dropped one of the bulbs and nicked her fingers, causing them to bleed. She purposely touched as many of Annie's things as she could with her bloody hand, and went on to touch the walls, the rail on the stairs, and the underside of the stairs. The idea came from the book she'd attempted to read to pass the time earlier in the week. Crazy how life sometimes imitated art.

If he focused on the mess in the room, maybe she could manage to shoot her way out of there. It was all the hope she had. It wasn't as if she could talk him out of what he was doing with her mouth gagged.

Using her fingers, and her feet, she tipped over boxes and spread first grade art around the room...all the while Christmas lights twinkled in a heap on the floor.

———

Neil shook the droplets of rain from his head. The thunder and lightning had stopped, leaving liquid sunshine. He wasn't sure what was more wrong...the fact that he and Rick were now hunting someone they once called friend, a man Neil would have defended to the death, a man he once felt sorry for, or that like the clouds overhead, something larger surrounded him. Something close enough to smell, but not taste.

His heat goggles picked Mickey up close to where Neil had his fallback position. The strong desire to finish this quickly so he could retrieve Gwen and assure himself that she was well ate at him.

"I'm in position," Rick told him in his ear.

Neil scurried from one tree to another, keeping his cover. "We still don't know what his plan is."

"Keep hidden." He didn't have to be told twice.

With his back to a tree, and several bushes at his feet, Neil scouted their enemy. "Ready. I'll do the talking. Keep him guessing where you are. See if you can get in tighter."

"Copy that."

Neil drew in a deep breath and blew it out between cold lips. He positioned his binoculars to see if his words had any impact. "Why are you doing this?" he yelled above the sound of the rain.

There wasn't any movement...nothing.

"We were friends."

The brush in his view moved.

"Damn it, Mickey...talk to me. We were all brothers."

That worked. "I don't have brothers."

Hearing his voice again hit his solar plexus. For a moment there he could have been wrong. But not anymore. "Once a marine, always a marine."

"I'm the only marine left. You left. You all fucking left."

Neil tracked the moving brush. "He's coming toward you," Neil told Rick.

"I see him," Rick said.

"Our tour was finished, Mickey." The major granted them leave until their time was served. It was as if the man knew any more would have twisted their minds. Twisted them like Mickey's.

"It's all I had."

"Why blow it now? You gotta know this isn't going to work. Someone is going to find you AWOL."

Mickey's laugh met Neil's ears. It sounded like nails on a chalkboard.

"AWOL? You think I deserted my country? And *he* says you're the smart one. You're fucking stupid, Mac."

Neil pulled back and shifted to a tree five yards to the north. "Who's he?"

"I think it's much more entertaining for you to figure that out on your own. You won't live long after. Those last moments will make all your hope fade. Just like mine did."

"What's he talking about?" Rick whispered in his ear.

"Don't know." But it made him itch like he'd rolled in a hill of army ants.

"Your life still has hope, Mickey."

"What do you know? Ever watch the light in a woman's eye die? Ever feel the light in your own fade when she walks away?"

Neil pushed the image of Gwen away. He didn't need Mickey playing him now. Now he knew that Mickey had planned on using Gwen to get to him. Best not fall into Mickey's trap now. "There's other women out there," Neil said.

"Not when your cock isn't good for anything other than taking a piss." Mickey's anger was palpable.

Neil cringed. "There's more to life than sex." Lord knew he didn't know what he'd do if he couldn't perform anymore. But killing his friends wouldn't be the answer.

"Says the man who's been fucking the little blonde number." Mickey laughed again. "How's Lady Gwen anyway?"

Neil bit his tongue until he tasted blood. He pulled his AK off his back and pushed in closer.

"This has nothing to do with her."

Mickey laughed, and shifted his position straight toward him. He moved with methodical ease, keeping himself hidden.

"You'd like to think that, wouldn't you?"

"He's playing you, Neil. Don't fall for it." Rick's words registered, but they didn't manage to calm him.

Beyond Mickey, Rick moved closer to the cliff, and closed in.

"Gwen's safe. You can't get to her."

Mickey laughed again. "I don't have to get to her, Mac. That's the beauty of this. The man at *my* back is better than Rick."

Neil froze, his nose flared as his vision went red.

"Bastard," Rick murmured as he drew in tighter.

"Stay the fuck back, Smiley."

"Or what?" Rick finally spoke.

"Or I press this button and put in the order for Lady Gwen's unfortunate accident."

Neil's hands started to shake.

"He's bluffing," Rick whispered.

Neil shook the rain from his head and forced his head to clear. *Major Blayney?*

No.

"You never were a good liar, Mickey," Rick said.

"Is that so?"

Neil closed his eyes, the pain in his head intense. *Blonde? Blondie? Who'd said that recently?*

"Know who I was banging before Operation Raven? The operation that Mac and Billy fucked up?"

Hearing that aloud hurt, even though Neil knew it was bullshit.

"Why do I care who you were with?"

Neil regrouped and opened his eyes again. Mickey stood two hundred yards away, Rick less than a hundred from him.

"The name Annie mean anything to you?"

Annie?

Blondie…Chuck's question came back to Neil. *"How did you get Blondie to come with you?"*

"Told her that someone from my past was using her to get to me."

It came back to him now. The lack of surprise on Chuck's face, the ease with which he accepted everything. His eagerness to expedite his departure. And damn it, Gwen's hair was brown when they arrived at Fort Carson. *Fucking brown, not blonde.*

"He's not bluffing," Neil told Rick.

"How do you know?"

"Chuck's daughter is Annie. The major is calling the orders for our death. And he has my wife."

"Oh, no," Rick said.

They needed to finish this…

"Figured it out, didn't you, Mac?"

"Hurt her, and you're a dead man."

"I'm half dead already."

Let's see if I can help you with the other half. Neil dropped to the ground and moved closer.

"Back up, Mac. My finger is inching on this switch. Let's let Blayney know he's clear to take your woman out." Mickey waved something in the air. Neil couldn't tell what it was from his angle.

"What's he got in his hand?" he asked Rick.

"Hard to say. Looks radio controlled. Could be a signaling device. Could be a detonator."

"What do you want, Mickey?" Time to change tactics. Let Mickey think he had their attention.

"Now that's what I'm talking about. How about you and your sidekick here move on up to your perch. You know, the one you've been sitting on for three days looking for me from."

"And then?"

"And then I call the boss and ask him what he wants me to do."

Neil backed up a few yards and moved slowly in the direction Mickey wanted him to go.

"Feels like a trap." Rick stated the obvious.

"Probably booby-trapped our fallback. Stay wide."

"Why does Blayney want us dead?" Neil yelled.

"Keep moving, Mac. I don't see your ass on that ledge yet."

Neil stopped, looked over his head. If Mickey had been scouting them for three days, he probably could have come in closer sooner. Yet no shots had yet been fired. "Still think he needs to make this look like an accident?" Neil asked Rick.

"More than ever."

"Move soldier." Mickey's voice rose above the rain hitting the leaves on the trees.

"Tell me why, Mickey."

"How should I know? Wants you gone...wants Annie's husband gone. Makes room for me."

Neil cringed. Blayney was playing Mickey, too. Probably planning on killing him as soon as he and Rick were out of the picture.

"You stupid fuck," Rick yelled. "Think Blayney's gonna hand over his daughter to a gullible prick like you?"

Rick's words struck a chord. Mickey pivoted and fired off a couple of rounds in Rick's direction. The air around them exploded, the noise raising every testosterone charged cell in Neil's body.

Neil took cover, cocked his weapon.

"I never liked you, Smiley."

"Lousy shot, too." Rick laughed.

"Call your dog off, Mac. Getting rid of you isn't an option. Your woman, however…Blayney might let her go. If she thinks you died by accident."

Neil's mind raced…Would the major kill her? Neil didn't think Chuck was capable of being behind this. There had to be something going on that Mickey had no idea about.

One thing was certain to Neil. Keeping Gwen alive would be Chuck's only insurance should Mickey fail. And Mickey was going down.

"Draw him out," Neil told Rick. "I'm moving in."

Chapter Thirty-Three

The lightning let up long enough for Blake to touch down in Colorado Springs. His pilot dealt with airport security and arranged for the jet to refuel. Blake informed his pilot that they might need to leave at a moment's notice.

"I'm on the ground," he told Carter as he searched the arrival lobby for the driver he requested to meet him.

"I've arranged clearance for you at Fort Carson. It's up to you now."

Blake waved at a driver with his last name on a large white card.

"Any idea if Major Blayney's on base?"

"I didn't get that information. The guards at the base will ask you what your business is. Tell them you need to speak with Blayney."

"And if he's not home?"

"Chances are they won't let you in."

Blake covered the receiver on his phone to speak to his driver. "I'm on my way to Fort Carson. You know where that is?"

"Yes, sir."

Blake nodded and returned his attention to Carter while he followed the driver out of the airport.

"Then what?"

"I don't know…hit a local bar, ask around. Neil was stationed there for a while. Someone was bound to have seen him. Maybe know where he'd be holding out."

"Needle in a haystack."

The driver opened the back door to the town car and Blake slid into the seat.

"Thanks, Carter. We'll find them." They had to.

"Good luck."

He'd need it.

The base wasn't twenty minutes from the airport. Two guards in slickers stood at a closed gate, military rifles in their hands. Another man sat in a booth and watched as they approached.

The driver rolled down both his window and Blake's. The guard moved toward them without a smile. "How can I help you?"

"I'm here to see Major Blayney." Best to act as if the major was expecting him, he mused. Blake removed a business card and handed it to the soldier. "Governor Carter Billings arranged security clearance."

"Wait here, sir."

Blake sat back and watched the men. The soldier inside the booth picked up the phone and started talking. His eyes narrowed during his conversation and one of the other guards walked around the car while he wrote down the license number.

Blake drummed his fingers on the seat beside him.

The man from the booth stepped out and approached the car. The expression on his face unreadable.

"I'm sorry, Mr. Harrison. Major Blayney isn't seeing anyone today."

Blake's jaw clenched. "It's a matter of life and death. Can you call him back and tell him this is regarding Neil MacBain?" This was not happening. To be so close and not be let in the door was unacceptable.

The guards glanced at each other but their resolve didn't change.

"I'm sorry. There's nothing I can do for you today. You might try setting an appointment with Major Blayney's secretary."

Blake considered pushing out of the car and decided that would appear as aggressive as he felt. He didn't need to spend a night in jail and delay his quest even more.

Through clenched teeth he asked, "Is there a number I can call?"

The guard returned to the booth, came back with a number.

"One more thing…who is Major Blayney's superior?"

"On base? No one."

Great!

"You really think Annie will take you back?" Rick taunted Mickey as he weaved through the trees, closer to the edge of the cliff.

"Annie loved me."

"Not gonna go over well if you kill her husband."

Neil inched closer.

"She won't know it's me." Mickey twisted around. Neil ducked out of sight.

"Blayney must be seriously twisted to sic you after him. What makes you think Blayney will keep you around after we're gone?"

Mickey was turning around now, having lost visual on Neil.

"Where'd ya go, Mac? I'm telling you…one press of the button and Blayney takes her out right now."

As much as it killed him, Neil said nothing and kept moving closer.

"Blayney doesn't take orders from you, Mickey. You should know that by now." Rick kept talking.

"I've been proving myself to Blayney for years. Worked plenty of 'loose end missions.'"

And we're the loose ends. The rain aided in Neil's advance. Mickey was facing north and Neil had managed to get behind him on the south. Twenty yards away, Neil set off another smoke bomb, causing Mickey to fire his weapon to the north.

Rick spoke in his ear. "He's nervous."

Neil set off his last bomb in an attempt to fill the area with smoke.

He heard Mickey swear under his breath as he darted to the east, directly into Neil's path.

Neil waited until the last possible moment and aimed his weapon. "Drop it."

Mickey swung toward him, weapon raised.

Neil aimed for his shoulder, fired off a round. Two more sounded in the rain soaked forest.

Mickey jerked back, lost his grip on his gun. Adrenaline took over and Neil leapt onto the man and took him to the ground. His arm went back, connected with Mickey's face once, twice. Blood gushed from Mickey's arm, too much for a flesh wound.

Neil disarmed him and rolled him onto his back. Neil flexed his neck tasting his rage and wanting the man dead. "You took out Billy."

Mickey's mouth twisted into a sick smile. "Blew up his woman, too."

Neil let his fist fly again.

"I should kill you right here."

Mickey coughed. A gurgling sound filled his chest. Neil looked down, noticed Mickey's field jacket pooling with blood.

What the fuck? Neil's aim wasn't that bad.

"You never had the balls," Mickey managed between his cough. Blood escaped his lips.

Realizing his enemy was incapacitated, Neil tossed his gun aside and ripped open Mickey's shirt. Blood was everywhere.

"Is he down?" Neil heard Rick in his ear.

"Yeah." From the looks of the hole in his chest, Rick had taken aim from behind. Mickey was dying.

Mickey stared beyond Neil, his eyes glossed over. "She would have taken me back. My Annie."

Neil didn't have the heart to destroy Mickey's last thoughts.

"Where's Gwen?"

Mickey met his eyes, huffed out a breath, and stopped breathing.

Neil squeezed his eyes shut. "You stupid fuck." He pushed away from Mickey's body and peered through the rain to see where Rick was.

"Rick?"

"I'm here." His friend's voice didn't sound normal.

"Where?"

"Base of the cliff. Our target down?"

Neil glanced at a man he once called his friend. He thought of the picture of all of them...in happier times. "Yeah. He's down."

"Good."

"Where are you?" Neil didn't see him anywhere.

"Caught a bullet. I'm OK."

Neil ran through the brush, ignoring the branches as they slapped against his legs, his waist. He found Rick against a tree, his right thigh in his hand. "How bad is it?"

"Not my gut."

"How bad, Rick?" Neil knew there were major arteries in the thigh that could end a man's life just as easily as a shot to the chest.

Rick attempted his signature smile. His second set of dimples didn't kick in. "Could be better."

"Ah, hell."

"I'm OK. You gotta go get your girl. Before Chuck realizes what happened here."

Neil looked over at his car and then back to Rick. "I can't leave you."

"You better fucking leave me. I'm fine, Neil. Go. I have a phone, I'll call for help when you leave. Besides, I think this hillside is set up to go off. Mickey was trying too hard to get us up there."

Neil glanced at the cliff above him. Large boulders protruded from the sides of the rock. Large enough to crush those below. Getting Rick to safety, disarming bombs...police questions, all of this would take time. Precious time.

"Go," Rick told him again. "I'll avoid your name until I hear from you. Don't want to tip Blayney off."

Neil attempted to look at Rick's wound to see for himself if his friend was all right.

Rick shoved him away. "Go. Get the hell out of here."

He stood, and shoved his hand into his pocket. "If something happens, call Blake. Tell him everything."

"Go get Gwen and tell Blake yourself."

Neil shoved the card into Rick's hands anyway. "Go, Lieutenant."

He nodded once, dropped his hand on his friend's shoulder. "Don't fucking die." Tears swam behind his lids.

"Get the hell out of here."

Neil didn't have to be told again.

———

Blake sat in the back of the town car a few miles from base. The rain slowed to a drizzle reflecting on his sour mood. He couldn't remember the last time someone blew off a call from him.

He made a call to the major's secretary and ended up talking to an answering machine. He left an urgent message, with shameless name-dropping littering the recording. Not that it mattered. Blake would call out the queen and the president if it would do him any good in locating his sister and Neil.

Minutes ticked by as impatience crawled up Blake's spine. Carter was due to call anytime, hopefully to tell him that Max arranged his audience with the major.

When the phone rang, he didn't bother to look at who the call was from before answering it.

"Carter?"

"Blake?"

Not Carter. "Neil?" His arms prickled and his mind went numb. "Neil?"

"Listen, Blake. I don't have much time."

"Where are you? Where's Gwen?"

Neil didn't answer his question. "I need you to write this down. Are you listening?"

The intensity of Neil's voice was unlike anything Blake could remember hearing in the past. "I'm listening."

"I need you to call a Major Blayney at Fort Carson in Colorado Springs. Keep him on the phone."

"Neil?"

"I need him distracted...you getting this?" Neil was rushed, not listening.

"I'm three miles off base, Neil."

"You're what?"

"Off base. Carter located your last commanding officer. He won't take my call. I came here looking for you."

Neil sighed. "Write down this number." Neil rambled off nine digits. "His personal number. Call him. Keep him on the phone. I don't care what you do...keep him on the phone."

Blake's stomach turned on itself. "Where's Gwen?"

Neil hesitated. "Call him."

Blake's body grew cold.

Charles paced the floor above her head, his footsteps heavy and fast at times, slower at others. So slow in fact that she wondered if someone else was in the house. When the phone rang, she heard only one voice upstairs and it wasn't someone new.

Gwen leaned against the wall of the basement surrounded by Annie's art and the Blayney household Christmas lights.

She had no idea of the time, or what was happening above. To aid in her discomfort Charles cut the basement lights. He would have plunged her into darkness if not for the lights she'd managed to plug in herself. The laugh, as they say, was on him. Even the occasional squeak of a house mouse didn't do much other than comfort her. She was alive, alert.

Surely Neil would realize something wasn't right eventually. Behind her back, she twisted the beautiful ring he'd placed on her finger. The way he'd opened his soul to her was fresh in her memory. He had to be alive.

He had to be.

She banished the thought of anything bad befalling him and waited for Charles to make his next move.

The hours waned on, forcing her eyelids to close for short periods of time. Equal parts of her wanted something to happen, and for nothing to occur. The longer she sat in the basement the bigger the chance of something awful happening to Neil.

And that threat was a larger psychological torture than being locked in a basement with a madman as her jailer.

Her eyes were closed when she heard a lock click at the top of the stairs. The lights above her head blinked on, making her wince away from the sudden glow.

"What the?" Charles flew down the stairs faster than she could reach for the gun hidden on her leg. She managed to scramble to her feet, her eyes wide as he made a quick assessment of her basement decorations.

"What have you done?"

"Maaa miii elfff aa hoom," she attempted to say under the gag in her mouth.

Charles was on her in seconds, the back of his hand slammed against her face and knocked her to the floor. Pain awakened her brain.

Charles stood over her, ran a hand calmly down his neck, stretching it. The only evidence of his anger of a moment ago was in the way he flared his nose as he drew in a breath.

He lifted her from the floor with one hand, and slammed her against the wall.

Stars flew in her head.

"Enjoy yourself?"

Gwen attempted to move her head away from his stare. He didn't allow it. She gave in and stared him down. Every ounce of hatred filled her gaze. She'd spit at him if she could find an ounce of moisture in her mouth.

He grasped her chin in his fingers and squeezed. "Your brother came."

Her heart kicked in her chest.

"What does he know?"

She mumbled behind the gag. Charles placed a finger between the material and her cheek and forced it from her lips.

"What?"

The ability to move her jaw together felt like heaven, regardless of the fact that the devil held her against the wall. Her dry tongue touched the roof of her mouth as she attempted to find moisture.

"What does he know?"

"I don't know."

He slapped her again. Moisture in her mouth came by way of a split lip.

Tears sprang to her eyes with the pain, but she refused to let them fall.

"What does he know?"

"I haven't spoken with him."

Charles moved closer. She wasn't sure but she thought she smelled tobacco on his breath. "He knows you're here."

What could she say...she had no idea how Blake had found her. "Where is he?"

Charles let his hand slip to her throat, reminding her how easily he could snap it if he chose.

"On his way here."

Hope sprang in her chest.

"You make one noise, one squeak down here and I'll kill him. You got that?"

She nodded. He'd be so close. Maybe he'd sense something?

"One noise."

Charles wrapped her mouth again, taking less care in securing the rag. He shoved her to the floor and left the room.

He left the lights on.

Chapter Thirty-Four

Neil knew his way around base better than any marine there. As day turned to night, traversing known passages into the base became easier. Not much had changed since he was a kid there with his father. Teenagers always wanted to know a way off base. Who knew he'd be sneaking back in so many years later.

One singular thought kept his feet moving.

Gwen.

Getting to her, keeping her safe. The sick thought that maybe something had already happened tried to inch into his brain, but he refused to hear it.

She's fine, he told himself.

Perfectly fine.

It took twenty minutes to cross the base and meet the bottom of the hill where Blayney's house perched. He paused for a moment and looked up at the dark windows.

Was he even there? Was Gwen?

Neil banked on the chance that without word from Mickey, Chuck would think the worst of his grunt. Logic told Neil that Chuck would use Gwen as a hostage at that point. Unless he gave up.

Neil had yet to meet a marine who gave up.

Chuck wouldn't be the first.

A light flickered inside the house, evidence that someone was inside.

Neil circled around the back, hopped the fence, and ducked under the dark kitchen window. He took a small mirror from his field jacket and angled it on the floor to see inside the house from the back door.

The kitchen was empty. A light from the hall was on.

Neil held his breath and waited for the phone to ring. He told Blake to give him forty minutes to get into position. He had five minutes to wait.

Five minutes of absolute terror that he was waiting five minutes too long to help his wife.

The image of Chuck harming her made his fist clutch and his back teeth grind together. Sitting immobile for five lousy minutes left him shaking. When the phone finally rang, Neil nearly missed the sound.

The second ring grabbed his attention and sprang him into action.

The back lock to the sliding glass door was easily breached. The major wasn't hypervigilant about his safety.

Stupid man.

Neil eased the door open enough to hear the one-sided conversation.

"Mr. Harrison? Yes…I was told you were here." Chuck's voice was on edge. Something Neil recognized but Blake wouldn't. Neil closed the back door quietly behind him and locked it. He ducked behind the island before he made it to the back hall.

"No," Neil heard Chuck say.

Neil moved up the stairs every time Chuck spoke.

"How did you get my number?"

Neil hesitated.

"Oh, I see. Yes…they were here."

Neil moved up the stairs and to the room he and Gwen shared. Inside the room was dark. A part of him expected to see her there.

She wasn't.

He moved quietly about the space, looking for evidence that she had been there.

Nothing…the room was bare of anything personal.

Gwen was gone.

The house had gone quiet. He didn't hear the major…didn't hear any other person in the home. Neil tiptoed from the guest room and glanced into the master bedroom. It too was dark. From what Neil could tell Ruth was gone, too.

Downstairs a door shut, and then quiet resumed. Neil lent his ear to the hall desperate to hear anything.

A loud thump brought him to a stand and soon after he heard a door slam.

Halfway down the stairs, he heard Chuck's voice. "Yes. I'm expecting a guest."

Neil waited, dropped down three more stairs. "Mr. Harrison. Right. In twenty minutes. No. He won't be here long."

Neil froze. Blake was on his way?

Neil retreated down the back stairwell to regroup. Blake needed to stay away. The last thing Neil needed was a civilian fucking things up. Not when Neil had no idea where Gwen was.

Neil removed his M9 and positioned it in front of his chest before he inched his way into the room with Chuck.

Chuck stood in front of his desk in his office. A cigarette smoked in a nearby ashtray. Neil didn't remember the major smoking before.

Could this man…the one who'd been there early in his military career, be responsible for so much pain? For Mickey's death? For Billy's?

With his back to him, Chuck stared out the window. "You going to use that weapon, soldier?"

Neil kept his gun steady. His jaw stiffened, his mind remembered better times.

He shook his head.

"Where's Gwen?"

Chuck picked up his cigarette, sucked it down, blew it through his teeth. "Not sure why I quit. There's nothing quite like balancing life and death through such a simple device." He stared at the tip of his cigarette and sucked in another lungful of nicotine.

Neil's trigger twitched. "Where is she?"

Chuck glanced to the floor over his shoulder. "Drop the gun, Mac."

"Where's my wife?"

Chuck laughed. The sound grated on Neil's raw nerves.

The major turned, removed the cigarette from his lips, and blew the smoke over his head as if he had nothing to care for in the world.

It pissed Neil off.

"Where is she?"

"Drop the weapon."

Neil glared. "Why should I?'

"You want to see her again? Drop the gun." The arrogant bastard sucked on his cigarette again. He knew damn well Neil wouldn't squeeze the trigger without knowing where Gwen was. His enemy knew his weakness and was using it against him.

Neil purposely took two strides closer before uncocking his weapon and tossing it to the floor well out of Chuck's reach.

Chuck witnessed the weapon skitter across the floor with a smile.

"And the others?"

Neil swallowed. No use pretending not to know what the man in front of him taught him. Neil lifted his right leg, removed the smaller revolver, and tossed it to the floor.

Chuck witnessed the disarming as if bored. He made a small rolling motion with his fingers and Neil removed a third gun from the small of his back. Other than his cell phone and a knife, he didn't have anything left.

Major Blayney moved slowly to his desk.

Neil was too far away to rush the man, so he waited until his next move.

From behind the major's back the man produced a service weapon. No surprise.

Instinctively, Neil moved to the side. *No need to give the man a broad target.*

"Step back, Mac."

Two steps later Neil held his ground. "Where is she?"

Chuck's eyes lingered beyond Neil for a moment, in the direction of the kitchen.

He waved his gun. "In the back."

"I've been in the kitchen. She's not there."

Chuck smiled. "You didn't look very hard, soldier." Chuck waved the gun again.

Neil followed the barrel of the gun and took several steps back. The island in the kitchen met his back and Chuck moved around him to the pantry and opened the door. He nodded inside.

"Go."

Neil thought of the small space and considered himself trapped if he moved inside.

"Fuck you."

"Gwen's in there."

Neil hesitated. He didn't hear her…didn't see her. "You're full of shit."

"Gwen's inside, Mac. Why would I lie to you now?"

Neil cringed. His mind brought to the surface nightmares of Gwen's torn body. Could Chuck have killed her and left her lifeless in the pantry? There was only one way to find out. And if she were gone...what was left for him? Could he survive her death? Was life worth living without her light?

He moved into the pantry and noticed a door.

"Open it."

Neil's stomach was in his throat as he reached for the knob on the door. The slow twist was met with little resistance. The lack of a lock made him think the worst. Chuck would have locked a live person inside...right?

Unable to stop himself, Neil swung open the door and encountered a rickety set of wooden stairs descending into a basement. Lights flashed from below.

"Go."

Neil placed a foot on the step, a second one...then he heard it. The muffled voice. A high-pitched voice.

He leapt down the stairs and saw her.

Alive.

Never in his life did he feel like crying with joy. He did now. He rushed to her side, placing himself between her and Chuck. He reached for the gag in her mouth, noticed the red marks on her face and the bruise forming on her cheek.

Her eyes met his and tears sprang in them.

"I'm sorry," he said softly. This was all his fault. She wouldn't be here had he not put his faith in Chuck.

"You're here," she choked between cracked lips.

"Isn't that nice? The newlyweds reunited."

Neil twisted to the man he once called his friend. "Why, Chuck? Why sacrifice us?"

Chuck narrowed his gaze. "You were supposed to take Raven out quietly. Not blow up his whole fucking family. *That* was imperative to the mission."

"We weren't responsible for the bombs."

"You knew what he was capable of. Take out the single target and come home. Then Washington would have been happy. They didn't need to know who called the order. Didn't need to know."

Neil squinted his gaze. "Washington didn't know about Operation Raven? You called it on your own?"

"Suits don't know how to run a war. Take out the leaders and the fucks willing to kill their own kids for their cause...that's what had to happen."

Neil was starting to see the picture now. "You're about to retire. No one would have known..."

"There's an exit interview process. They'd already called Billy in to ask about me. Any of you could have uttered something and destroyed forty years of dedicated service. I couldn't risk it."

The irony was, Neil wouldn't have said a thing. Neither would Rick...or Billy.

"Mickey's dead," Neil told him. Hoping to see some sort of recognizable emotion cross Chuck's face.

Chuck shrugged. "Collateral damage," he said. "Now back up."

Neil bumped into Gwen, keeping her behind them. For the first time since walking into the basement, Neil noticed *the* twinkling lights and adolescent art and keepsakes all over the floor. Looked as if Gwen had been busy. Smart move, too. Chuck's eyes shifted around the room and his gun arm started to waver.

"We've known each other a long time, Chuck. You knew my dad." Gwen pressed up against his back. Her body trembled.

He reached one arm behind him and held the side of her body.

Chuck narrowed his eyes. "I've known lots of dead soldiers. What's one more?"

Gwen twisted around behind him. He gripped her arm to keep her from moving in front of him. His fingers landed on something hard in her hand. It took a second to realize what she held.

Relief swept up his back. He wanted to praise her foresight right then but didn't. Neil took the weapon and kept his hand behind his back. "So you kill me, kill Gwen. Then what? You don't think I'd come here without telling someone, do you?"

"He said Blake was on his way here," Gwen said. "Said he'd kill him if I made any noise."

Chuck blinked, his eyes traveling between the lights and Neil's face. "Blake knows I'm here. And he won't arrive without backup." Neil inched forward. "It's over, Chuck. There's no way out of this for you."

His eyes focused on the barrel of the gun pointed at them, Neil held his breath and flinched with every movement Chuck made.

The tip of the barrel tilted to the floor. Neil jumped on Chuck's show of retreat and swung Gwen's gun in front of his chest. "Drop it." Neil's voice was deadly. He didn't want to kill the major. He would. But he didn't want to. "Do the right thing, Chuck. Drop it."

Chuck's eyes landed on the weapon Gwen had brought into the basement and he huffed out a laugh. His displaced humor was a testament to his mental state. Chuck's gun hung to his side.

"You always were the smart one. Should have had Mickey take you out first." Then, with no preamble and no warning, Major Chuck Blayney lifted the barrel of his weapon to his own head and squeezed the trigger.

Chapter Thirty-Five

Gwen felt the major's intent as he lifted the weapon and she closed her eyes. Her scream echoed along with the blast from the gun. Her entire body shook as the room grew silent.

Neil's arms gathered around her. She stumbled into him, buried her face in his shoulder.

"It's over," he cooed in her ear. "I've got you."

Her knees went out from under her. Neil lifted and cradled her into his arms. He kept her as stable as a mother with a child, even with her hands handcuffed behind her back. She squeezed her eyes shut, refusing to open them until Neil had taken her up the stairs and set her gently down on a sofa.

He started to move away and she huddled closer. "Don't go. Don't go."

"I won't," he whispered. "I'm right here."

She blinked her eyes open. "Is he?"

"Yes."

Her stomach rolled.

Neil reached around the sofa and pulled a blanket over her shoulders. His eyes met hers with such concern she wanted to weep. "He started acting strange after you left. Then Ruth went to Florida and he got worse. I tried to leave." She shook, unable to control her body.

Neil rubbed his hands along her arms. "I didn't know. I thought you'd be safe."

Gwen attempted a smile. "I know. It's not your fault."

"He could have killed you."

She tried to move her hands to comfort him, remembered the cuffs. "Can you get these off?"

He nodded, and looked behind her back. "You're bleeding," he said.

"Just a scrape. I'll live."

His fingers tugged at the cuffs and then he patted his pockets. "Do you know where he put the key?"

She shook her head.

Neil moved in front of her and laid a hand to her cheek. "The MPs will have a key. I need to call this in."

When he did, the house would be swarming with military personnel. Her brother. "Make the call."

He stood to walk away.

"Neil," she said, stopping him. "Thank you for coming back to me."

He reached down to her again, and brought his soft lips to her dry ones. He wiped a tear she didn't realize fell from her cheek and picked up the house phone.

In less than two minutes, the house was filled with military police. Someone unlocked her hands, which she was sure would never feel normal again, and offered her a glass of water. The liquid trickled like fire down her throat.

A female sergeant sat at her side as Gwen answered questions. The MPs kept Neil away, probably asking him the same thing and making sure their stories didn't vary. All the while Gwen kept saying to herself that it was over. All of it was over and they were both alive and whole.

A uniformed soldier approached her. "Miss Harrison?"

"It's Mrs. MacBain," she corrected the man.

"Seems your brother is outside and raising all kinds of hell. We have more questions and can't release you yet. He wants to see you for a few minutes."

"Of course."

Someone helped her to her feet. When she made it to the door, she shook off the set of hands helping her. "I'll be fine. He won't leave if he thinks I'm hurt."

Blake stood beside a military jeep, a cell phone in his hand and a guard by his other. He noticed her and pushed around the guard.

"I'm OK."

He squeezed the air from her lungs. "You scared me to death, Gwendolyn."

"I *was* scared to death."

Blake pulled away and peered in the dark at her face. Good thing the light was bad. She knew how bad she felt and could only imagine how she looked. "Is Neil in there?"

"Yes. Talking with the authorities."

Blake shook his head. "He should have kept you safe."

"He did. I'm alive."

Her brother didn't seem convinced. "I need to get you home. Everyone is worried about you."

"Tell them I'm fine. We're both fine." Rain started to fall and Gwen pushed a strand of hair from her eyes.

Blake caught site of her ring and grasped her hand.

"What's this?"

"It's called a wedding ring, Blake. Neil and I are married."

Her brother narrowed his eyes and stared beyond her at the house.

"Listen," she said as she placed her hand on her brother's shoulder. "Let one of these men know where you're staying and we'll be along as soon as we can." She ran her hands along her shoulders, warding off the chill. "I would rather not stand in the rain. I've been cold enough for one lifetime."

Blake shrugged out of his coat and laid it over her shoulders.

"Mrs. MacBain. We have more questions for you."

Gwen turned toward the sergeant and offered a wan smile. "I'll be right there."

She kissed her brother's cheek. "Go tell Samantha that we're OK. She doesn't need to worry."

It was nearly dawn when Sergeant Piper told her she could leave. "That's all we need from you for now, Mrs. MacBain."

Gwen rubbed her tired eyes and watched dawn break through the bay window of the Blayney home.

"Where's Neil?" She'd not seen him in hours. The coroner had arrived only a few minutes ago and she wanted nothing to do with witnessing Charles's body come up those stairs.

"He's in a debriefing."

"He's not here?"

The sergeant shook her head. "Left a while ago with an MP escort."

"Is he under arrest?" She couldn't imagine he left on his own without saying good-bye. Not after all they'd been through.

The woman in front of her wouldn't meet her eyes. Gwen stood up and shoved her hands on her hips. "What is he charged with?"

"I didn't say he was under arrest."

"You didn't say he wasn't. Who is your commanding officer?" Gwen believed that was what they called the boss around here.

The sergeant nodded to the kitchen. "One of them is currently laying in a pool of his own blood, and the second-in-command is Major Gilmor who isn't available to you right now. Until we can determine exactly what transpired, Mr. MacBain will need to stay with us."

"This is preposterous. Neil did nothing wrong. I told you what Charles Blayney did to me. What he said to me. You can't believe that Neil and I are lying."

"No one is accusing you of lying, Mrs. MacBain. We just need to keep Lieutenant MacBain a while longer."

"He's retired," Gwen corrected her.

"He'll contact you when he's released."

"That's not good enough. I demand to see my husband before I leave here." She crossed her arms over her chest to emphasize her point. Did the woman in front of her not understand how little control she'd had in her life over the past several weeks? Gwen was tired of being told what she could and could not do. Perhaps it was time to remind these people who they were dealing with.

"That isn't going to happen."

"Is that so?"

The sergeant smiled. Her hair was tied back so severely in her bun it had to create pain deep in her scalp. Funny, under the army colors and minimal amount of makeup, Sergeant Piper was probably a beautiful woman. She severely underestimated Gwen...and that would be a mistake.

"Can I use the phone to call my brother?"

Sergeant Piper gave a tired smile as if saying *finally*.

Gwen dialed her brother's cell phone number and waited for him to pick up.

"Blake?"

"Gwen? Are you here at the hotel?"

"Not yet." She turned so Sergeant Piper heard every word. "Listen I need you to call a press conference. I'll be talking about Operation Raven and the series of murders that were—"

Sergeant Piper grabbed for the phone in Gwen's hand and gave her a deadly stare.

"That's confidential information. You can't—"

Gwen held the phone in front of her so Blake could hear what she said. "I'm a British national, Sergeant Piper. My husband may think I'm an automatic citizen of the United States because of our marriage, but I'm quite aware I need to go through the process and apply like anyone else." Actually, the facts hadn't come to her until after several hours alone in the Blayney basement. She remembered a conversation with Blake years before about becoming a US citizen. Marriage to an American might speed the process up, but it didn't give instant approval from the government. "All I'm asking for is a few minutes with my husband and I'll keep my tongue in my mouth. If not…my brother, the Duke of Albany, and our many friends…governors, senators." She thought of her list of clients. "High powered attorneys, diplomats, law enforcement of all kinds, even actors who know how to play the media like a piano will spin this story so far and wide your precious marines will have to declare a state of emergency just to avoid the scandal. If you'd like to circumvent an international incident, I suggest you let me talk to Neil. In private."

Sergeant Piper scowled and stared at the phone in Gwen's hand.

"I'll see what I can do."

Gwen smiled and lifted the phone to her ear. "If I don't call back in thirty minutes, you know what to do."

"I've got your back, Gwen."

—————

It wasn't like he had a choice when the military police ordered him into the back of a van and drove him to an interrogation room.

"There was no such thing as Operation Raven." Colonel Montgomery flew in from the Pentagon as soon as the call went out about Major Blayney's suicide. The man moved to intimidate. His bulk alone rivaled Neil's, and that said something for top brass. Most left the bodybuilding to the grunts. This man obviously didn't want to be outrun by his men. On any other day, Neil would have admired that.

Not one salt or pepper hair was out of place as he stared Neil down.

Neil sat forward against the table and prepared to reveal all the details he'd kept to himself until that point. "You might want to make sure the person recording this is secure, Colonel. I'd hate for a leak this late in the game."

Montgomery left the room. He heard shouted orders and when Montgomery returned he arrived with another man and a recording device. Once the assistant was ready, Neil began.

"It had been over a year since the war began…after the towers went down. Blayney rounded me up and had me handpick my team. Each of us had worked together on one mission or another. He was readying us for the mission of our career. Sent us on three trials together. Operation Wrecking Ball, Operation Tidal Wave, and Operation Storm. Like all special ops, we went in, did our jobs, and got out." Neil hoped to hell now that the other operations were legit. There's no way to know how long Blayney had played them. "When it came to Operation Raven we were ready. We understood it was big. Something Washington would order at any time. We had one objective, remove Raven." Neil gave Colonel Montgomery the name of their target and went on. "Cause as little collateral damage as possible and get out."

Montgomery listened.

"Only things didn't go smoothly. The choppers dropped us on target, and we moved in position. Raven was on his compound but so was his family. When we penetrated, Raven did the unthinkable. He demanded his children run toward us. We didn't know the kids were wearing bombs. Boomer and Robb died on scene. Linden made it onto the chopper and died shortly after. Their deaths were labeled as 'training accidents.' Within six months, we were all removed or left our positions. Signed off by Major Blayney. Except for Mickey…or so we were told. Mickey stayed in." Neil went on to explain about Billy, about Rick, about how Mickey was played by Blayney to kill them all off to hide the truth about the mission.

Neil talked for hours. Ending with the last night of his life.

Montgomery listened, his face unreadable.

Once he was finished Montgomery asked questions. "Who were the pilots?"

"I'd never seen them before. We flew overseas in a cargo belly, jumped immediately into a chopper, and rappelled to our target. The pilots who picked us up never removed their headgear. I don't know who they were."

Montgomery swiveled away from him and dismissed his assistant. Neil witnessed the man pace the room. As much as Neil hated the position he was in at that moment, he pitied the colonel.

"You do realize the position this puts me in, Lieutenant?"

"Retired, sir."

Montgomery tilted his head. "Not from where I'm standing. Until we have the details you're officially reinstated."

Neil sat taller. "And if I refuse?"

Montgomery stared him down. "That wouldn't be wise."

Noise from outside the room brought Neil to his feet.

"You were told to take her to a hotel. Not here!"

Neil heard the voice of an angel. "I didn't give her a choice, soldier. Not why don't you be a dear and tell me where my husband is."

Before Neil could prepare the colonel for what walked through the door, Gwen was there. He couldn't help but smile as she stormed the room. "There you are." She threw herself into his arms and life fell into balance. "They tried to make me leave without you."

"Gwen Harrison, I presume?" the colonel asked.

Gwen turned around and offered her hand. "Gwendolyn MacBain," she corrected. Damn if Neil didn't love the sound of his name attached to hers.

"Mrs. MacBain, you have five minutes before you need to call your brother back." A nervous looking sergeant who'd walked into the room with her was waving a cell phone in her hand. She noticed the colonel and immediately saluted her superior.

Gwen shooed the woman off. "I'll not call anyone until I know I'm leaving with my husband."

Neil pushed Gwen away so he could see her eyes. He ignored the bruise on her cheek that brought a wave of rage over him. She was tougher than she looked. "He's calling a press conference in what...four minutes, Piper?"

The other woman nodded, still standing with her right hand to her forehead. "I tried to stop her. I was told she could leave."

"Press conference?" Montgomery asked, returning the sergeant's salute and putting her at ease.

"That's right," Gwen began. "You know...the one where I tell the world that a major in the US military took me hostage after using a military man to search me out to kill my husband. And how now the same military was holding my husband prisoner."

Neil lifted a hand to Gwen's mouth and kept her from saying more. "Is Blake awaiting your call?"

Gwen gave an innocent smile. "Four minutes...give or take a couple. Right Piper?"

"Colonel, sir. What she said is true. I don't know her family, but if half of what she says is true, sir...we might want to...It doesn't look good, sir."

Montgomery twisted around to glare at Neil and Gwen. "Lieutenant?"

Neil couldn't help the self-satisfied smile that fell on his lips. "Lady Gwen and I know quite an influential list of people. Do you know of a Governor Carter Billings? His uncle Senator Maxwell Hammond?"

Gwen sat her tiny ass on his lap and linked her arm around his shoulders.

"Colonel? That's a high rank...right?" Gwen asked all innocent. Neil knew she wasn't that dense.

"It is." He kissed her cheek.

"You'll forgive me for being less than impressed, Colonel. But your Major Blayney had held me against my will for the better part of two days. He handcuffed me, gagged me, and didn't provide me with food or water, not to mention his threat to kill me." She touched her cheek. "I simply want the right person prosecuted here and not the one who rescued me."

Montgomery stared at both of them. "How can I be assured you won't go to the media?"

Gwen glanced to her lap. "I rather liked Charles's wife, Ruth. She doesn't need to know how awful her husband really was. I want my husband and me to go home."

Neil met Montgomery's eyes. "We won't go to the media. Gwen's family, on the other hand, will think nothing of it."

"I don't like being blackmailed," Montgomery said.

Neil felt the muscles in his neck tighten. "I don't like being held hostage."

Everyone was silent for a moment.

Sergeant Piper spoke up. "One minute."

Gwen kicked her leg in Neil's lap as if she were a schoolgirl on a bench awaiting a city bus. Reminded him of her wearing cheap high heels and skintight shorts outside of a No-Tell Motel.

Good Times.

Neil knew they had the colonel over the fence. He also knew the US military didn't take kindly to threats.

"Call your brother. You can both go."

Gwen smiled and took the phone from Piper's outreached hand. She dialed a number and waited. "It's busy."

Everyone tensed.

"Just kidding."

Neil wanted to laugh. The pain in his stomach from holding it back felt dire.

"Hi, Blake. No, we'll be there in fifteen. Both of us. Yes… please and a hot bath. I'd kill for a warm tub and food. Love you."

Gwen jumped off Neil's lap and handed Piper's phone back. "A pleasure to meet you, Colonel," she said as she walked by him. "Oh, and by the way. Buried in the Blayney library you'll find pictures of Charles's daughter and the man I believe Neil told you was Mickey. There was another picture of Neil's team…and another man. I'm not sure how it will help with your investigation but I thought you should know."

Neil walked by the colonel and extended his hand.

"She's quite a handful," Montgomery said.

Neil glanced at his wife. "Yes…yes, she is."

"We'll be in touch, Lieutenant."

"Sir."

Neil took Gwen's hand and walked out of the room.

———

A driver took them to Blake's hotel. Outside the world started to wake. The rain from the day before was gone, the blue skies were littered with fluffy white clouds.

Gwen clasped Neil's hand and refused to let go.

"Do you realize who you just told off?"

She giggled. "No."

"You have balls, woman."

"Oh, I assure you I don't. I'm simply tired and hungry and I don't feel particularly safe without you by my side. I'm sure in ten or twenty years that will fade." She waited for his response to her statement. He could always come back to her and suggest they dissolve their marriage now that the threat was gone. That wasn't what she wanted.

Not by any measure.

"Or it might last thirty or forty."

She bit her bottom lip and scooted closer. "So we're going to do this? This married thing?"

He lifted her hand that carried the ring he'd placed on it. "On one condition."

She scooted closer...her heart filled with love. "What's that, Lieutenant?"

"We get married the right way. In Aruba with that dress you're dreaming of. With witnesses we want to remember."

Tears sprang to her eyes. She was desperately tired and so very happy. "I love you, Neil MacBain."

He dropped his lips to hers in a crushing kiss. Her head swam as all her emotion rose up into one meeting of lips. She couldn't imagine how awful she appeared, how she tasted. But Neil kissed her as if she were the finest nectar and she didn't have the heart to pull away.

"I love you," he said as he moved away.

Everything inside her shifted into position and clicked into harmony.

Epilogue

Neil left her an hour after dropping her off at Blake's hotel to search out his friend Rick. She hated to say good-bye after such a short time, but understood Neil's need to find his colleague. To assure himself that he was OK.

He'd called from the hospital the next morning saying Rick was undergoing surgery. When Gwen suggested she come there to be by his side, he encouraged her to return with Blake to California. He wasn't going to leave his last remaining team member until he knew he was well and that wouldn't be for several days.

"This is something he needs to do on his own," Blake had told her. "He lost everyone else."

"He has me."

Blake patted her on the back. "He's a lucky man. Give him this, Gwen. Let him do it alone and be there when he comes home."

They spoke daily for a week and a half. All the while, she planned a wedding on a beach in Aruba. Apparently Samantha was in the throes of morning sickness and wanted nothing to do with saying "I do again" with the threat of her breakfast coming up. Karen, Eliza, and Sam were more than happy to help Gwen plan a proper ceremony for her and Neil. That was if he ever left the hospital.

The day before their planned ceremony, she woke in a hotel room alone. She'd not seen her husband since that morning in Colorado Springs. The warm breeze of the tropical climate caressed her skin as she opened her blinds to take in the day. Blake had assured her that Neil would be there when she walked down the aisle, but a tiny part of her worried that everything she felt was only a dream. A dream destined to end.

Karen was the first to greet her. "Oh, my God. You're still in a bathrobe. Holy cow, woman. You only have three hours to get ready."

Gwen laughed. "Is Neil here?"

"He'll be here."

Which meant he wasn't. "Are you sure?"

"C'mon, Gwen. Have faith. And get in the shower. The stylist will be here in an hour."

The next three hours flew by. Her hair was swept up around her face and her golden locks were left to drape on her shoulders. Carefree. Just the way she pictured her wedding attire. When Eliza zipped up the back of her dress Gwen felt like a proper bride. Samantha stepped behind her and pressed the colorful bouquet into her hands. "You're stunning."

Gwen smiled.

"And we're not wearing god-awful yellow concoctions in the Texas sun," Eliza said.

"Oh will I ever live that down?"

Sam and Eliza both said no at the same time.

The bridesmaids wore gray silk. Each of them lovely.

"Thank you all for being here."

"Oh, hon. We're so happy this is working out for you." Eliza hugged her first. And as much as Samantha tried to smile, her stomach simply wasn't cooperating.

"Now will one of you kindly go out and make certain I'm a bride who isn't walking to an empty altar."

Karen laughed and left the room. "I'll go check."

"He said he was coming. He'll be here."

"But none of you have seen him."

"Blake would kill him," Sam said.

"Neil would be hard to take down," Eliza murmured. "Just sayin'."

Karen popped back into the room less than five minutes later. Behind her was a man Gwen had never seen in person before, but she knew who he was.

Neil's friend Rick walked into the room, doing his best to disguise his limp.

"Holy…Go, Neil. He said you were beautiful, but…well, men say those things all the time."

Gwen giggled. "You must be Rick."

"You sure you want that old guy down there? I'm a couple years younger," he teased.

Rick was cute…tall. Those dimples would play a number on the right woman.

"I'm taken."

"Can't blame a man for trying." Rick stepped forward. "Rick. A pleasure."

"I'm so happy you're well."

"Me too. Those nurses weren't even cute. Isn't there a cute test for nurses?" Rick smiled at the women in the room.

Eliza was laughing. "'Fraid not."

"Should be. Anyway. Neil wanted me to come up and give you this." Rick handed her a note. "And, ah, he needed me to get your ring."

Gwen smiled and removed the pink diamond from her hand. "I get it back."

"That's the plan. See you down there."

Gwen sucked in her lips and tore open the envelope.

The cardstock bore the semblance of a ballerina. Tears instantly sprang to her eyes. *He remembered.*

To my Princess in the ivory tower.
I'm not very good with words. In fact, most people think I have a third grade vocabulary. But I promise to always find the right words to make you feel safe and loved.
Before you, I was lost. With you, I'm whole.
Now please come down and marry me in front of our family and friends so they know you're mine.
I love you,
Neil

"Oh damn…she's crying. Quick someone get a tissue."

"Is it bad?" Karen rushed to her side, glanced at the note in her trembling hand. "Oh…Oh!"

The note was passed around the women. "Who knew?" Sam whispered.

"Go, Neil," Eliza chuckled.

Gwen dried up her tears and smiled. "All this and the man's hung like a bear."

"Ahh!" Karen screamed with laughter.

Eliza's jaw dropped and Samantha held her stomach. "Oh Lord. We skipped your bachelorette party."

Karen waved them off. "It's OK. We can make up for it at my divorce party. Michael and I are already planning it."

"So soon?"

"No…still over a year off. But he's a planner. Loves a good party."

Gwen rolled her eyes. "C'mon. Let's not talk of separation when I have a man who's waiting for me."

The warm waters of the Caribbean lapped up on the shore. The wedding party preceded her down the aisle and the gentle music of a local ensemble changed as she rounded the corner and walked toward her future.

He stood there, wearing a gray suit, just as she pictured. His broad shoulders stood tall, his gaze never left hers. Rick stood beside him, and then Blake and Carter. Perfect.

He looked nervous. Like he had anything to worry about. She was his already. Even without the vows, without the rings. She'd been his for months even if he didn't know it.

She made it to the minister and smiled.

"You're beautiful," Neil whispered.

She chewed her lower lip.

Then, as if he couldn't stop himself, he kissed her.

Someone beside Neil cleared their throat. "Ah, Mac…we're not at that part yet."

Gwen giggled, turned toward the minister, and pledged her life to her husband…again.

Acknowledgments

A big shout out to Elaine McDonald from Elaine McDonald Photography. What started out as a online fan/friendship turned professional. Beautiful covers start with spectacular pictures, and this one was no exception. Thank you.

Chad and Caitlin Kutz for allowing me to use their wedding photo for Neil and Gwen's story. Thank you!

To my own cheerleading squad at RT and RWA conference who stand beside me with the same shocked look on our faces. TJ McKay for making sure I stay grounded.

Caridad Pinero for your never-ending support. Jennifer Probst, HP Mallory, Katharine Ashe, and Megan Mulry for laughing at the same jokes and comparing notes.

For the random fans who just make going to conference such a joy.

Robin, drink wine and be happy. Felicia, who has a Chicago accent!

Sheryl, who takes more pictures of her food than she eats. And Bernie, the happy reader! Love you guys.

For everyone at Dystel & Goderich Literary Management and the entire Montlake team.

For Sandra Stixrude, always!

And finally, Crystal Posey, to whom I dedicated this book. You're proof that not everyone you meet online is a flake or out to mess with you in a bad way. I can't express enough how much I appreciate everything you do. To your family who supports your work and shares you with me.
Love you!

Catherine

About the Author

Photo by Lindsey Meyer, 2012

New York Times bestselling author Catherine Bybee was raised in Washington State, but after graduating high school, she moved to Southern California in hopes of becoming a movie star. After growing bored with waiting tables, she returned to school and became a registered nurse, spending most of her career in urban emergency rooms. She now writes full-time and has penned the novels *Not Quite Dating*, *Married by Monday*, and *Wife by Wednesday*. Bybee lives with her husband and two teenage sons in Southern California.